First edition May 2021
© Cherry Publishing
71-75 Shelton Street, Covent Garden,
London WC2H 9JQ, UK
ISBN 9781801161183

Saying Yes

Ella Sparkle

Stormy Love
Book 1

Cherry Publishing

Subscribe to our Newsletter and receive a free ebook!

You'll also receive the latest updates on all of our upcoming publications!

You can subscribe according to the country you're from:

You are from...

US:
https://mailchi.mp/b78947827e5e/get-your-free-ebook

UK:
https://mailchi.mp/cherry-publishing/get-your-free-uk-copy

Chapter 1
Jenna

You know in Charlie Brown cartoons when the teachers are talking and it just sounds like "wah wah wah wah?"

That was all I could hear. It was like my brain had already shut down trying to protect itself from the words that it somehow knew were coming at it.

I shook my head and tried to focus on what the woman sitting across from me was saying. I think it was something about the history of the law firm and what being a partner involves. All things I had thoroughly researched before applying, so luckily I would be safe if she tried to quiz me, even if I hadn't been paying attention. I'd never had a quiz that I didn't pass. That's where my planning and preparedness always paid off.

"Jenna, are you listening to me?" Cynthia clasped her hands together and leaned forward on her desk.

"Yes, Cynthia. I'm sorry, you were saying?" She totally knew I hadn't been listening. You don't get a reputation like Cynthia's unless you're able to read people instantly and know exactly what they're thinking, before they even knew it themselves.

Cynthia raised a perfectly arched eyebrow at me, conveying that she knew the truth, that I'd let my mind wander while she was speaking, that I wasn't as sharply focused on our conversation as I should have been. She cleared her throat before starting again. "I was saying that as a partner in this law firm, one of my responsibilities is to ensure that the people we bring on permanently are not only the best and the brightest, but that they will be a good fit for the firm and the clients that we work with."

I sat up a little straighter in my chair and tried to use my most professional voice. "I understand completely. That is exactly why I want to work here. This firm has an excellent reputation. I am hoping that after I start law school, I can move up from my current position as an assistant into an intern. My plan would be to move into an associate position once I have my law degree, and one day I hope to make partner in this firm and be sitting right where you are, Cynthia." I tried to give Cynthia a confident smile but, based on the cold look she gave me in return, she was not impressed in the least.

"Well, Jenna, that is certainly ambitious. It sounds like you have the next several years of your life planned out." Cynthia looked directly at me with an unreadable expression. Damn, this woman had a good poker face.

"Yes, I do. I have always had a plan and when I make a plan, I stick to it." I said the last part as confidently as I could while maintaining eye contact with Cynthia. It was only then that I noticed she had moved her hands to the arms of her black leather chair and leaned back away from her desk a bit. Cynthia took a big deep breath in while maintaining eye contact with me the whole time. It was almost like she was a cobra getting into a strike position after she had zoomed in on her prey. A late forties blonde cobra, with a perfectly styled bob and a very expensive designer suit.

2

I had seen that look on her before. It was usually right before she tore into the opposing attorney or a witness on the stand, and they were left feeling less than two inches tall by the time she was done. Cynthia was known as a vicious, but brilliant, attorney.

Suddenly, I realized it was after five o'clock on a Friday afternoon and she and I were very likely the only people left in the building. I felt my entire body tense up in an utter panic as my realization took hold. That look was for me, once again, she was the cobra. This time though, I was the prey, and she was going to strike me down where I sat.

I tried to remain calm on the outside, but inside alarm bells were ringing as I braced for what was next. I could feel beads of perspiration popping up on my forehead. I clenched my teeth together, as I tried to maintain some type of confident-looking smile. In reality, I probably had the same fearful look in my eyes as a small furry animal when it realizes that the cobra is about to pounce and eat it for lunch.

"Jenna, I am going to get right to the point. You have been an assistant here for a few months, and frankly, this is just not working."

"What do you mean 'this is just not working?'" My voice came out squeaky and laced with shock. I tried to take some deep breaths in through my nose to steady my mind and stop my heart from racing, as I fought the rising sense of panic that started to crush my chest.

Cynthia looked at me and sighed. The only thing I could see on her face was a look of absolute annoyance. Her voice was clipped and sharp as she said, "Jenna, don't make this harder than it needs to be. Your employment with this firm has come to an end. I have some paperwork from HR here for you to sign and a box for you to gather your personal effects in on your way out."

My mind raced as it tried to absorb what it had just heard. "This can't be happening! This is where I want to work! Tell me what I have done wrong and I will fix it. This is where I planned my career to be!"

Cynthia drummed her perfectly manicured fingernails on her mahogany desk as she continued to look at me like I was an inconvenience, taking up too much of her time. "We have determined that you are not a good fit for our firm and the vision that we have moving forward. There is nothing to be fixed. This is just not working and it is time to move on." Her voice was completely devoid of any emotion as she broke eye contact to shuffle the stack of papers sitting in front of her. It was her way of showing that she was done, and I was dismissed.

I could feel the hot sting of tears behind my eyes. I bit the inside of my cheek as I tried to hold them back. I wasn't going to cry in front of Cynthia. I wasn't going to show her anything that could be considered a weakness... and crying in the office was on Cynthia's top ten list of 'Despicable Signs of Weakness.'

As hard as I tried not to cry, her words made it exceedingly difficult; *this is just not working and it is time to move on.'*

That was the exact same phrase Brett had used six months earlier when he broke my heart into pieces. I had planned on us having the perfect life together: successful careers, a big house, white picket fence, and two brilliant, well-rounded children. He'd clearly had a different plan in mind.

"Now, there are just a few final things to finish up here and then you can pack your personal belongings and be on your way." Cynthia pushed the stack of papers and pen across her desk to me.

I was in shock. The rest of what Cynthia had to say went back to the "wah wah wah wah" Charlie Brown teacher's voice playing on a loop in my mind. I could feel myself going through the motions of signing the HR forms and turning over my office keys and ID badge, but nothing was making sense.

The next thing I realized, I was standing by the front doors clutching my purse and a cardboard box filled with a few framed photographs and my coffee mug.

"Well, that seems to be everything. Good luck to you, Jenna," Cynthia said briskly, showing me to the door.

I mumbled something back and walked through the door. I stood in stunned silence on the front steps for a few minutes before the tears started to slide down my cheeks. Once they started, I couldn't stop them and within seconds I was full-on ugly crying on the front steps of the law firm, where I had planned on building a long and illustrious career.

Everything in my life was falling apart.

Chapter 2
Jenna

Hot tears continued to run down my face as I tried to wrap my mind around what had just happened. I don't know how long I stood on the steps, clutching the stupid cardboard box like my life depended on it before my phone rang, snapping me out of my fog.

I looked down and saw that it was my best friend, Cassie, calling. I took a few deep breaths before wiping my tears and nose on the sleeve of my sweater and answered the phone. "Hello?" I said, trying to make myself sound as normal as possible.

"Hey, girl! Happy Friday! You're not still at the office, are you? Get your sweet ass out of there and come have some drinks with me!" Cassie's bubbly voice burst through my phone.

"Hey, Cass. Thank you for the invitation, but I don't think I'm really in the mood tonight." I wedged my phone between my ear and my shoulder while I tried to balance the cardboard box, my phone, and my purse. I still had to somehow walk across the parking lot to my car with all of my stuff.

"Jenna, don't make me do it. Do not make me play the best friend card because you know I will. We are two brilliant and beautiful twenty-three-year-olds and we are not going to waste away in sweats in front of the TV on a Friday night. Now get your bodacious booty shaking and meet me at High Five. The first round is on me and you sound like you could use it."

"Cass, you are not only my best friend, but you are my only friend. I'm sorry, but I just can't go out tonight." I took a deep breath as I stood by my car, the only car left in the whole parking lot, trying to balance my phone and the stupid box while I dug through my purse for my car keys.

"My best-friend-spidey-sense is telling me this is about more than just not wanting to go out. Spill it, Jenna Morgan. What's really going on?"

I had been best friends with Cassie since the first day of fifth grade. I was the quiet girl with brown hair in braids sitting in the back row by myself and Cassie was the new kid. Cassie burst into the classroom, with her bright red hair, like she already owned the place on her first day in a new school. I remember she scanned the classroom before she walked down the aisle and confidently sat at the desk next to me. She leaned over to me and said; "You and I are going to be friends." Even back then, Cassie was outgoing, a little wild, made friends easily, and totally lived in the moment. I was the exact opposite of all of those things, but somehow ever since that first day of fifth grade, our friendship had always just worked.

I knew from past experience that Cassie was not going to let it go until I told her what had happened, so I decided just to rip the band-aid off and do it. "I got fired today."

Cassie didn't even pause for a second. "You what? Did I just hear you right? What the fuck happened Jen? And whose ass do I need to kick?"

The last question pulled the corners of my mouth up into an almost smile. I knew for a fact that Cassie would totally kick someone's ass for me without thinking twice. Someone once told me that there are two types of friends in this world;

7

the kind that you could call at two o'clock in the morning, say 'hey I need to move a sofa' and they would show up right away, no questions asked; the other kind would just hang up on you. Cassie belonged to the first group. In fact, she would show up, no questions asked, plus she would bring a truck, a bottle of tequila, and a couple of random hot guys to actually lift the sofa, then take everyone out to breakfast after it was done. She was that kind of friend.

I sighed and dropped the box on the pavement as I momentarily stopped looking for my keys. I squeezed my eyes shut trying to ward off the impending headache. "According to Cynthia, it 'just was not working and it was time to move on.'"

Cassie gasped. "No freaking way! Did she really say that or are you still hung up on that bastard Brett's lame-ass reason for stomping on your heart?"

"Nope. Those were her exact words." Since I was no longer holding the box, I resumed digging through my purse for my keys. I swear it had never been so much trouble to find them before.

"Ouch! Babe, I am so sorry. That is beyond terrible. Forget the first round, your whole night of drinks are on me. Come on out and have some fun. End this shit day on a good note!"

I finally located my keys and unlocked my car door. I threw the cardboard box into the passenger seat as I slid into the driver's seat, thankful that I was finally going to be able to get out of there and go home. "Thanks, but I really just want to go home, Cass. Maybe another time."

I knew Cassie was trying to cheer me up, but the last thing I wanted to do was go to a crowded bar and pretend to have fun. I didn't want to do that on a good day, so there was absolutely no way that I wanted to do it after getting fired.

Cassie sighed and suddenly her voice was filled with concern. "Jen, you have not been down to do anything fun for months. I worry about you. You cannot just hide out in your apartment. You're only twenty-three! You've got to live!"

"I am *fine,* really." I stuck the key in the ignition and leaned my head back on the headrest. I knew there was no way Cassie would let my answer slide.

"Don't try and feed me that shit, Jenna Morgan! I can tell by your voice that you are *not* fine. Plus, I know that working there was part of your plan, *and* I know how much your plan means to you. It's *me* you are talking to. You don't have to pretend."

"I know, Cass. But right now, I just want to head home and call it a day. I'll talk to you tomorrow." I closed my eyes again as the massive headache started to take over.

Cassie was quiet for a few minutes. "Okay. You are my favorite."

I smiled. Cassie had a hard time telling people she loved them. Instead, she sometimes made up something else that in reality, had the same meaning as saying 'I love you.' It was one of many complex pieces that made Cassie, Cassie.

"I love you too, Cass." I hung up the phone and with another deep breath, I started my car and headed home, ready to end the day.

***

9

A little over an hour later, I was back home in my apartment where I'd traded my pencil skirt and heels for some flannel pajama pants and an oversized sweatshirt. My long brown hair was thrown up in a messy bun and my face was thoroughly scrubbed of what little makeup I had worn during the day. I was just making myself comfortable on the sofa, ready to pull up Netflix when there was a loud knock, followed by shouting, at my door.

"I know you are in there, so don't try and ignore me!"

I sighed and leaned my head back on the sofa. I loved Cass, but sometimes her loud and outgoing personality clashed with my quiet and introverted ways. I wasn't sure why she was at my apartment, but I did know I was not in the mood for another discussion about going out.

Cassie banged on the door again. "If you do not open this door in the next thirty seconds, I am going to tell the building superintendent that you accidentally locked yourself in the bathroom while you were taking a shit and he needs to come let me in to save you. You know he likes me and will totally do it! I am also not above going all Mardi Gras and flashing a little boob - if needed - for him to let me in."

I had no doubt that Cassie would actually do either of those. Plus, it was true, my building super, like every other human being on earth loved Cassie. With a sigh, I got up and opened the door.

"Surprise!" Cassie shouted as the door opened. She was standing in front of my door holding a bottle of wine in each hand. "You won't come out for drinks, so I brought the drinks to you. Now, let me in and grab some wine glasses. We need to have a conversation and I have a feeling it is going to take a whole lot of alcohol before we are done."

Chapter 3
Jenna

Cassie and I each sat down on the sofa with a glass of wine. I had no idea what she wanted to talk about. I was already feeling defeated about being fired. To add injury to insult, Cynthia telling me that 'this was just not working and it was time to move on' had opened up the still-raw wounds left on my heart by Brett. I wasn't sure how much more I could take in one day.

Cassie took a big drink of wine before she set her glass on the coffee table and turned to face me. "You know you are my favorite and there is nothing I would not do for you. Not only are you my best friend, but you are the sister I never had."

I took a sip of wine and felt myself starting to let my guard down a bit. Cass was here to try and cheer me up. I gave her a small smile. "Thank you, Cassie. The feeling's mutual."

I set my wine glass down on the coffee table as Cassie cleared her throat. "That is why I feel it is my duty to tell you that it is time to get off your ass and make some big fucking changes in your life. Like, now. Otherwise, the next thing you know you're going to be living alone in a house full of cats, sitting around in your bathrobe, watching Forensic Files reruns on Netflix every night, wondering where it all went wrong."

It was like a record scratching sharply inside my head. What did she just say? That was not at all what I had expected. I grabbed my glass and took a big gulp of wine, not even knowing what to say or how to react to that statement. Cassie just sat patiently, not taking her eyes off of me. She had a look of genuine concern on her face. I took another drink and a deep breath before I responded. "That is a very specific scenario you have just laid out." I ventured, not really knowing what to say to the vision she'd drawn of my potentially bleak future.

"Don't try to deflect from the issue at hand. I am being serious, Jenna."

"I don't think that there is anything wrong with my life," I said quickly, feeling a bit defensive. "It's just fine."

Cassie looked at me like I had lost my mind. "That's a big part of the issue. Fine is not good enough for you. You are so amazing, Jenna. You deserve nothing but the best. You are the whole package... smart, beautiful, kind, hardworking, and incredibly loyal. I know that what happened with Brett really did a number on you, but..."

"I don't want to talk about Brett," I quickly interrupted Cassie. I didn't even like hearing his name. "I am over that."

Cassie sighed. "No you're not, honey, and that is part of the problem. You two were together almost all of college and I know you were planning on a future with him that included a big poufy white dress and a walk down the aisle. What he did to you was terrible, and one of the worst possible break-ups that someone could have happen to them."

"Really, I am fine. Totally over it." I gulped down the rest of my glass of wine. "More wine?" I said reaching for the bottle that was sitting on the table between us. My attempt to change the subject was futile, I knew that Cassie wasn't going to leave this idea alone.

"Jenna. You were at dinner with his parents and yours to celebrate your college graduation. Everyone, including you, thought Brett was going to propose that night with your families there. Instead of finding a ring in your dessert, when the check came, that bastard announced, *in front of everyone*, that your relationship was just not working and it was time to move on now that graduation was over."

I closed my eyes as Cassie spoke. "Please don't remind me. I don't want to relive that moment."

"Sweetie, he broke your heart and it broke you for months after that. You were too distraught to start law school and had to take a year off before going back this fall. I get it, and it was the right decision at the time, however, you stopped living that night and have just been a shell of your former self ever since."

I opened my eyes and took a big gulp of wine. Twirling the stem of the glass around in my fingers for a moment before I looked over at Cassie. "As fun as this trip down memory lane is–"

"Jenna," Cassie interrupted. "You've had your life plan as long as I have known you. You planned to get married, have a successful career as a kick-ass attorney and have a big house in the suburbs with lots of little kiddos running around. Your life is not going according to your plan, so you have stopped living it," she said bluntly.

For the second time that day, I could feel the tears building under my eyelids. The worst part was that as much as it hurt to hear, I knew she was right. "I have only ever had this plan to work towards. Without the plan, I don't know what to do or where my life is going. I *need* to have a plan." My voice was barely a whisper as I said the words I didn't want to hear out loud.

Cassie scooted closer to me on the sofa and took both of my hands in hers. "Jenna honey, let me be the first to tell you that this life plan you have is just not working and it is time to move on."

I couldn't help but laugh even as tears were running down my face. "Actually, you are now the third person to tell me that."

"Well, third time's a charm, right? Plus you don't need a life plan. You have a super fantastic, one-in-a-million friend like me to help you out." Cassie let go of my hands and started waving hers all around herself striking different ridiculous poses.

"Oh yeah? What do you suggest, oh wise one? Teach me your ways," I joked.

By then we were both laughing hysterically. That was one of the great things about Cassie. She always seemed to know what I needed to hear and was not afraid to tell me.

Cassie was bouncing up and down in her seat and clapping her hands. "So I have an idea. You have been so closed off and shut down that you have not allowed yourself any new possibilities or experiences. From now on, when something presents itself, you are only allowed to say "yes." You cannot turn anything down. Well, unless it is totally unsafe, illegal, or something I wouldn't do. Force yourself outside of your comfort zone. Actually, on second thought, better just go with unsafe and illegal as your boundaries. Those are much stricter boundaries than just opening it up to something I wouldn't do."

I groaned at Cassie. "That sounds like something straight from Oprah or from some flowery self-help book."

Cassie looked at me over the top of her wine glass. "I'm sure it is. I didn't say it was an original idea, but you have to admit, it is a great idea for you. Think about it. What do you have to lose?"

I sipped my wine while I rolled everything over in my mind. "You do have a point there," I agreed. "I have no job, no love life, no friends - other than you..."

"Hey! Careful what you say next there! I am such an awesome friend. Why would you need a bunch more?" Cassie waved her arms around pretending she was offended by what I'd said.

"Ha ha, Cass. Listen. This may just be the wine, and my overly taxed emotions from today speaking, but I am in." Cassie was right, what did I have to lose at that point? I already felt like my life had gone down the toilet and if I wanted things to change, I needed to do something different.

Cassie let out a squeal of excitement as she grabbed me into a big hug. "You're really going to do it?" She asked.

I took a deep breath. "Yes. I will do it. I will start saying 'yes'."

Chapter 4
Nick

I shuffled through the massive stack of paperwork on my desk and told myself that I had to get through at least half of it before I could call it a night. Permits, building plans, contracts, payroll... fuck, I really needed to get a full-time assistant to help me keep all this shit organized. Blaine Construction had just grown too big for me to try and keep doing it myself.

That last thought brought a smile to my face. Who'd have thought a few years ago when I started Blaine Construction that I'd be sitting in the corner office of my new company headquarters, thinking about how much I needed to hire a full-time assistant? I had worked damn hard to get there, that was for sure. Blaine Construction had been my sole focus for those past several years and all my hard work was really starting to pay off.

The business plan was simple; hire locally and work exclusively with local contractors to build top-quality housing in all price ranges. Hiring locally and working with local contractors helped keep the employment rate up in our community. When people were employed, they spent money, which stimulated the economy. When people are employed and the economy is good they buy things like houses, creating increased demand, therefore creating more jobs. It was 'Good Business 101'. Recently, Blaine Construction had expanded into doing remodel work, which meant I'd bought up some of the more run-down houses in the area and fixed them up to resell. It kept my contractors and employees busy when we were in between building jobs and helped to restore parts of the community that were in need of repair. I'd recently moved into a condo that was remodeled by Blaine Construction and it was a really nice place (if I did say so myself).

I had grown up in the community, and I really wanted Blaine Construction to be a homegrown business that local folks would get behind and support. That meant Blaine Construction did everything from sponsoring little league teams, to having employee-led highway clean-up events, to hosting a community haunted house every Halloween. I personally attended every event so that I could to get the company name out there. My next big project was getting a Blaine Construction Scholarship started for each of the local high schools for a student that wanted to go to college and study architecture or business management. Making all that happen meant that I fucking worked non-stop, but Blaine Construction was on the cusp of hitting it big, which would make all the sacrifice worth it.

I pressed my hands into my exhausted face before picking up the next piece of paper off the stack. I *really* needed an assistant to help. From somewhere in the mounds of paper, my phone started to buzz. I quickly located it under the stack I had just been working on and pushed the answer button.

"Hello, this is Nick speaking."

"After all the time we have been friends, that's is how you greet me? You're an asshole, Nick." I immediately smiled as I recognized the voice of my best buddy, Baxter. We had been friends since high school, when we played baseball together, now mostly he called me and I told him I had to work. Things had changed a lot the last few years.

"Give me a break, I didn't look to see who was actually calling." I put the phone on speaker so I could continue to file papers while talking to Bax.

"Well, you are going to be glad that I called." I could hear lots of noise in the background as Bax shouted through the phone. I glanced at my watch and saw what time it was. Given that it was Friday night, I knew he was already out somewhere.

"Tell me why it is that I am going to be glad that you called because so far you are not giving me much to work with." That was a lie, I knew Bax and I knew exactly why he had called.

"Nick Blaine, have I got a deal for you," Bax said in his best salesman voice. "I am down at The Bulldog on fifth street. The game is on, there are several pitchers of beer, and a couple orders of wings on the way. Yours truly and a few other upstanding gentlemen are here and there are more ladies at our table than there are guys. Get your ass down here!" Bax sounded like he was already a few drinks into the evening.

"It does sound like an enticing offer, but I am going to have to pass, Bax." I finally had all of the shit on my desk separated into piles that kind of made sense.

"Just a minute. I'm going to step outside where I can hear you better because it sounded like you just said you were passing on tonight." I could hear a rustling noise on the phone and in a few minutes, Bax was back on the line, minus the background noise. "Alright, I'm outside now. Tell me I heard you wrong and that you are not fucking saying no to coming out tonight."

I sighed. "You heard me right. Not tonight, Bax."

"Wait, are you still at work?"

I hesitated before answering. I was not in the mood for a lecture. "Yes, I am. I have shit that has to get done."

"Not on a Friday night you don't. Come on, Nick. There is more to life than just working. There are really hot ladies at our table Nick. Like seriously fucking hot. When was the last time that you actually went out with someone that had tits?"

"Listen, Bax, you know I am not looking to date or for a relationship right now. I don't have time for all of that shit and the drama that goes with it. And the last person I went out with was that blonde you set me up with. You know, the one that only wanted to know about my company and how much money I made. No, Bax. Just no," I said flatly. I knew his game all too well.

"Dude, you live alone and it was months ago that you went out with her. I set you up because it had been months since you had gone out with anyone before that. Come on, Nick. You are twenty-eight years old, you are not totally unfortunate looking, and your personality is tolerable. You could seriously hook up with just about anyone you wanted to." I could tell he was exasperated, as per usual, he just didn't get it. Work was my focus and it was paying off.

I laughed, "'Not totally unfortunate looking' and 'tolerable personality.' Thanks, Bax. I don't think anyone has ever paid me such a huge compliment before."

"Don't let it go to your head you salty son-of-a-bitch. Someone has to keep you from a life of complete celibacy since left to your own devices, you seem bound to head that way."

"Listen, Bax. We have been through this before. I have other priorities right now, and those do not include any type of relationship. I'm over the random hookups. My choice and I am totally fine with it. Bachelor life suits me and I intend to keep it that way."

"That may be the stupidest fucking thing I've ever heard you say, Blaine. Fine, if you want to continue to live alone in your new, fancy condo and have a life of nothing but the gym, work, and eating takeout, be my guest."

"Sounds perfectly fine to me."

"You're an idiot. You know, someday, despite all your best efforts to the contrary, you are going to meet some girl who is going to flip your world upside down and I am going to just sit here and laugh and say 'fucking told you so.' How about that?" He joked.

"Not going to happen, Bax. I have no time or interest in that shit," I said, after all, I knew myself and what I wanted and I wasn't going to be swayed by one of Bax's 'hot babes'.

I decided it was time to shut down my computer and get ready to leave. I could come in on the weekend to get caught up on this paperwork.

"Suit yourself. Just means more ladies for me tonight now that you won't be around. Have fun at the gym, alone. And going back to your condo, alone. And ordering takeout, alone."

"You're an ass, Bax," I said as I grabbed my gym bag and headed towards the front door.

"An ass that is getting laid tonight. Unlike you, my friend. You are just an ass. A lonely, lonely ass," Bax said with a laugh.

"Night, Bax."

"We 'll be here for the rest of the night if you change your mind." I could hear the background noise start to pick up again as it sounded like Bax was heading back inside the bar.

"Thanks, man. I'll catch you later."

"Later." He clicked off the line.

My whole life for the past several years had been dedicated to Blaine Construction. That meant there were many Friday nights spent in my office doing paperwork rather than dating or any of the other things that single twenty-eight-year-olds did. Truth was, I was fine with it. I dated plenty in high school and college, but as I worked on growing Blaine Construction, I found I just didn't have the time or energy to play the dating game. There was too much bullshit that came with it and I had to keep my priorities straight. Plus, I never seemed to meet anyone I really wanted to invest the time and energy into for a relationship.

I locked up the building and started to walk across the parking lot. It was a perfect night. The sky was clear, the air was crisp and everything around me was quiet. I decided I would much rather go for a ride on my Harley than hit the gym. My Harley was the first big purchase I made for myself when Blaine Construction started to make money and I was damn proud of it.

I smiled to myself as I threw my gym bag on the back of my bike and climbed on. That was one of the great parts of being single, I could do whatever the fuck I wanted, whenever I wanted. The engine revved to life and I was itching to hit the road, to just go wherever the night took me. I pulled out of the parking lot relishing in the breeze hitting my face, the purr of the engine, and the fact that I had no plan about what was going to happen next. No way was I ever going to give any of that up and be tied down to another person.

Chapter 5
Jenna

The next morning, I awoke with a splitting headache, and my mouth was so dry it felt like I had been sucking on socks all night. I rolled over to look at my phone and saw it was almost noon.

I shuffled out to the living room where Cassie was sleeping on the sofa. Wine bottles and pizza boxes from the night before littered the coffee table and floor. We had decided to celebrate the new plan of saying yes for the rest of Friday night... and into Saturday morning.

"Cass, wake up. It's almost noon," I groggily mumbled to the pile of blankets on my sofa.

"Fuck! Why do I feel like I got hit by a truck?" the pile of blankets mumbled back. I saw Cassie's hand reach out and grab her dark-framed glasses. In college, when Cassie had to get glasses, she did it in typical Cassie fashion and got wild, thick black frames that had a slight cat-eye shape to them. With her bright red hair and funky wardrobe, they totally worked for her. Cassie poked her head out with her glasses on, opened her eyes, and looked around the living room. She let out a giggle followed by a moan. "I see why now."

Cassie sat up, pushed her glasses on top of her head, and rubbed her eyes. Her red hair was sticking out in all directions and her makeup was smudged across her face. "What do you have planned for the rest of the day?" she asked as she stretched and yawned simultaneously.

"I am going to make us some coffee and we can go from there." My slippers padded softly into the kitchen where I flipped on the coffee pot. I always set it up at night before I went to bed, it was part of my nightly checklist. One of the many mental checklists that I operated off of daily.

"After that task is completed, what is next on the checklist for the day?" Cassie shouted from the living room. She knew me too well.

I tossed some bagels into the toaster while the coffee brewed. "Well, I guess my first priority is to find a job. I should have one last paycheck coming from the law firm, but then after that, I have nothing. I need to find something quickly, even if it is only temporary."

It wasn't until after the bagels were toasted and loaded with cream cheese, and the coffee was done brewing, that I realized Cassie had been quiet the whole time I'd been busy in the kitchen. Quiet with Cassie was never a good sign.

"Cass? What's up? Why are you being so quiet?" I asked hesitantly as I walked into the living room with plates of bagels and mugs of hot coffee balanced precariously.

"Thanks, babe," Cassie said as I handed her a mug of coffee and put the rest on the coffee table. "Are you still serious about only saying yes?" She asked, grabbing a bagel.

I settled into the opposite side of the sofa from Cassie and deeply inhaled the scent of my coffee before bringing the mug to my lips and drinking greedily. I could feel the steamy caffeinated beverage immediately start to slice through my hangover and clear up my foggy mind. After my third drink, I looked at Cassie, "Why, yes, I believe so."

Cassie laughed. "Stop messing around you goofball! I am being serious!"

"So am I!" I laughed back. "I am serious about the saying yes plan! You are right, it is time for some changes in my life." I tried to nod for added emphasis but it hurt my head.

Cassie had this look on her face, the one that always terrified me a little. It usually meant she had some kind of devious plan that I was not going to like but was going to be roped into doing because she was my best friend. "Well, in that case... I think I have a solution to your lack of job situation."

"What did you have in mind?" I took a bite of my bagel and immediately mentally patted myself on the back for obtaining the perfect level of toasting with the exact right amount of cream cheese. Perfection in a bite.

Cassie held up one of the pizza boxes from the night before. There was a brightly colored piece of paper taped to the top. "I don't get it," I said looking at her in total confusion. "What does a pizza box have to do with my finding a job?"

"It is not the pizza box itself, but what is on the box." Cassie tapped her bright red fingernail on the paper taped to the box. I leaned forward to read the boldface font across the top out loud.

"Looking for a job? You are in luck! Pete's Pizza is now hiring delivery drivers. All schedules available, no experience required. Apply in person at Pete's Pizza." Cassie sat there with a huge grin on her face. It slowly dawned on me where she was going with this. "Oh no! You have to be kidding me! Pizza delivery driver? No way, not going to do it." I shook my head at her for added emphasis – hangover be damned.

"Jenna," Cassie gave me a disapproving look. "That is not how this goes. You are supposed to say yes when a new opportunity presents itself. You need a job and this flyer is literally asking you to apply."

I could feel my anxiety start to rise as I nervously twirled my hair around my fingers. "The whole job consists of constant interactions with strangers. And making small talk. Two things I hate. Not doing it, Cass. I don't even like talking to the checkout clerk at the grocery store."

Cassie smiled at me sweetly and batted her long eyelashes. "A stranger is just a friend you haven't met yet," she sing-songed.

"Do you have any idea how creepy that sounds?" I tossed a throw pillow at Cassie as she burst into laughter. "I'm having second thoughts about this..."

"No way! You do not get to back out now, Jenna Morgan! You need a job and the opportunity for a job is presenting itself. You have to say yes. This can just be temporary until you find something else. Or who knows? You might really like it and can stay until you go to law school in the fall. Or did you forget you will be moving away and leaving me for three years to attend that big fancy school you were accepted into?"

I had no doubt Cassie intended for that last part to be lighthearted, but just like she knew me too well, I knew her too well. There was some well-founded, deeply-rooted fear in Cassie about the people she loved and cared for leaving her. My voice grew soft as I looked directly at Cassie. "We will still visit each other and there is always the phone and texting." I gave her a big smile, "Plus, I will be busy studying and you will be busy becoming this area's premier and most sought-after real estate agent."

The slight hint of worry on Cassie's face was quickly replaced by a big smile. "Do not try and flatter me into changing the subject. Although you are right, I am pretty stellar at my job." Cassie winked at me and we both started laughing.

Cassie was a natural at sales and had already become one of the top-selling agents at the real estate agency she worked at. We often talked about working together at some point in the future. She would make the sales and I would specialize in providing legal services for real estate transactions. We would make a really great team.

"Back to the actual subject we were discussing," Cassie said with a wave of her hand. "Go take a shower and get changed. You have a delivery job that you are saying 'yes' to and will be applying for later."

I sighed and finished the last of my coffee. "Fine. I guess I need to start at some point. Yes, I will apply for the delivery job at Pete's Pizza."

"Great! What are you going to say when they offer you the job?" Cassie raised an eyebrow at me as she prompted me for an answer.

I rolled my eyes at her. "Yes. I will take the job." I put on a fake, cheerful smile, inwardly dreading saying yes and disliking this plan already.

"Good girl!" I see my work here is done. Call me later today and let me know how it goes!" Cassie stood up and took her dishes into the kitchen. She grabbed her purse, gave me a quick kiss on the cheek, and walked to the front door.

"You might want to fix your make-up smudges and tame your hair before you go," I warned Cassie as she had her hand on the doorknob.

Cassie turned to me with a smirk. "Oh, Jenna darling, my appearance and arrival home in the middle of the day will give the neighbors something really juicy to talk about. I am considering it my good deed for the day to get them all riled up."

I laughed. "Okay, well good luck with that."

"Good luck with your interview!" Cassie shouted as she walked out the front door. "You are my favorite!" she shouted when the door was almost closed.

"I love you too!" I shouted right before the door clicked shut.

I sighed and headed to the shower. I had a job to apply for whether I liked it or not. I was starting to question the wisdom of my decision to be a part of this crazy saying yes plan. So far I had gained one hell of a hangover and a job application to be a pizza delivery driver. Twenty-four hours before I would have never believed that was where my life would be, but I guess that was the point.

Chapter 6
Jenna

Later that afternoon I stood outside Pete's Pizza trying to psych myself up to go in. I was freshly showered and wearing dark jeans with a black V-neck sweater; my hair was freshly curled and in a loose ponytail. I figured it was time to take a break from the suits and heels I wore at my previous job.

The outside of Pete's was nothing super fancy, but the pizza was legendary. Pete's was a standalone building with huge picture windows in the front that had the restaurant's name painted across them in big white letters outlined in green. The lettering matched the green and white striped awning. It was both a family restaurant and a hot spot for the college kids since it was within easy walking distance of campus. I had eaten there several times growing up and I could see that the decor inside hadn't changed since I was a kid. There were still tables with red and white checked tablecloths and a big counter next to the cash register where you picked up orders to go.

I took a deep breath as I put my hand on the front door. "A stranger is just a friend you haven't met yet," I said silently to myself. "You are saying yes to new opportunities. Don't think about it, just say yes." I added my new mantra to Cassie's words from earlier, which were all still swirling and clamoring round in my head. Any other time I had gone to a job interview, I had spent weeks preparing and researching the company ahead of time. I was a planner, not a just-jump-in-and-go-for-it person. The fact I was walking in cold to ask a stranger for a job was so far out of my comfort zone I was not even really sure how to act.

I took another deep breath and pulled open the door as the bell announcing my presence softly jingled. There was a very kind-looking man with grey hair wearing a short-sleeve, white button-down shirt, and a black tie loosely around his neck standing behind the counter. He gave me a warm smile, "Welcome to Pete's Pizza. How can I help you today?"

"Hi, my name is Jenna and I saw this flyer taped to one of your delivery boxes," I held up the brightly colored flyer and tried to calm my nerves. "I wanted to apply for the delivery position, please."

"I'm Pete, the owner," the man said. "Let me just get someone to take over up here and I can sit down with you and talk about the job. Why don't you go ahead and take a seat at the table in the corner?" he said kindly, gesturing to the table at the back, where we wouldn't be disturbed by customers coming and going.

"Thank you." I breathed a sigh of relief as I headed to the table and sat down. The relief was only temporary, as I realized I had only just made it through the front door. I still had to actually interview for the position.

"Hey, Mike! Come out here and watch the front for me, would you? I am meeting with someone about the delivery job," Pete shouted into the kitchen.

"Sure thing!" a voice shouted back from the kitchen. I watched as a guy about my age came out of the back and took over at the cash register. He had light brown hair that was a little on the shaggy side and was wearing a black Pete's Pizza t-shirt with tan cargo shorts. He looked more like he belonged on a surfboard than behind the cash register at a restaurant. The guy, who I assumed was Mike, looked in my direction and smiled. Even from where I sat I could see he had kind eyes and that his smile was genuine and friendly. I nervously smiled back.

"Now," said Pete as he settled into the chair on the other side of the table. "I have just a few questions for you so let's get started."

The interview was only a few basic questions, so it went by fairly quickly. We seemed to be ready to wind our conversation down when Pete leaned back in his chair and crossed his arms. "I have just one last question for you. I don't know how else to say this, so I am just going to come out with it. Why do you want this job? You're not the typical applicant I get for this position. Usually, it's high school kids or someone that is looking for a first-time job who has no employment experience. You have years of work experience and are a recent college graduate that has been accepted into law school. You seem a pretty unlikely candidate who might have better options someplace else." I could see he didn't mean it unkindly, if anything, he looked curious.

I took a deep breath. I'd known that question would be coming and I had already decided to answer it honestly. I looked Pete straight in the eyes as I started my response. "I thought I knew what I was doing and where I was going in life, however, the universe has recently thrown me some curveballs. I decided to take some time to re-evaluate how I make choices, what it is I am doing and where I am going. I need an income while I do that and this seems like a great fit"

Pete nodded his head slowly, "I can respect that and I appreciate your honesty. The job is yours if you want it."

I smiled at Pete, relieved that the interview was over and that I had survived it without any awkward mishaps. "Yes! I would like the job. Thank you." I smiled, maybe this 'saying yes' thing was really going to pay off, I already had a job, after all.

"Great. You can start on Monday. See Mike before you leave today and he can get you the new hire paperwork and some uniform shirts in your size." Pete reached out to shake my hand. "Welcome to the Pete's Pizza team."

Chapter 7
Jenna

I survived my first week at Pete's Pizza and my first week of saying yes. I had to admit, I was actually really starting to like the job. I had some pretty cool co-workers and it was usually so busy that time flew by. Plus, I discovered the tips were really nice and quickly got used to always having cash in my purse.

"Hey, Jenna! In five minutes I'll have two more deliveries ready for you," my co-worker Steven shouted out. Steven was twenty-one years old and a total punk. Like, he literally had a bright pink mohawk, several piercings and I had never seen him wear anything other than all black. I figured the fact that the Pete's Pizza uniform shirts were black, with only the Pete's logo on them, suited Steven just fine. Oh, and don't try to call him Steve. I made that mistake on the first day.

"Sounds good! I'm ready, Steven!" I shouted back.

My other co-worker, Kimmy came back into the kitchen. "We're really slammed out there tonight! A game just finished up at the college and everyone's here for a slice and a beer. Plus, the phone's been ringing off the hook with deliveries. It's crazy!"

Kimmy was the same age as Steven, but unlike Steven and his black-cloud personality, Kimmy was like a bright and shiny rainbow. She was always happy and bubbly and wore nothing but bright colors with her uniform shirt. That day she was wearing bright red shorts with matching red sneakers and knee-high socks, the kind with the stripes at the top. Her long, dark hair was streaked with turquoise highlights and pulled up into two big buns on the top of her head which looked almost like ears. Somehow it all just worked on her. I, on the other hand, just wore jeans and tennis shoes with my uniform shirt, with my brown hair pulled back into a low ponytail.

"That's good right? Extra tips, plus it makes the time go by fast." I looked over my shoulder at Kimmy as I pulled down some empty pizza boxes for Steven.

"You know it girl!" Kimmy shouted back at me as she grabbed the pizza Steven had just finished cutting up and disappeared through the door back out to the front of the restaurant.

"Jenna! Order up! Hustle back because I have another round of deliveries coming up soon!" Steven handed me a stack of boxes.

"You got it!" I said as I smiled at Steven and grabbed the delivery boxes. I really liked my co-workers and, actually, the requirement to say yes had forced me to get to know them quickly, when otherwise I would have been far more likely to hang out in the background. It felt great to have some new friends in my life and they all seemed to be genuinely good, caring people.

I made the first delivery to a frantic-looking mom at a two-story house in a newer development. She explained her daughter was having a sleepover and her house was full of hungry girls as she shoved a wad of cash at me and grabbed the pizza boxes out of my hands.

I headed to my second delivery which was just a few blocks away in an area with newly remodeled condos. I slowed down as I tried to navigate through the parking lot and watch the letters on the buildings at the same time. "Let me see... where is building G?"

I finally located the building and rang the doorbell. I was looking down at the pizza box checking the order when the door opened. I didn't even bother looking up before I spoke. "Hi. I have a delivery from Pete's Pizza for Nick."

"I am Nick."

I froze for a second. It was the deepest, sexiest sounding voice I had ever heard. I slowly lifted my gaze upwards and almost dropped the pizza box. Leaning against the doorway was the most beautiful man I had ever laid eyes on... and I could see almost all of him since he was only wearing a pair of black athletic shorts hung low on his waist. My eyes greedily took in his chiseled abs before they roamed up a little further to his broad chest and strong arms covered with black ink tattoos. Even just standing there with his arms crossed, his muscles rippled. I continued to slowly gaze all the way up to his deeply intense brown eyes. His dark hair was cut short and there was a slight hint of stubble that graced his model-perfect face.

I could not stop staring and am pretty sure my mouth was hanging open as I blatantly checked him out. I was trying to think of something to say when I noticed his mouth curve into a big smile. It was then that I realized, as much as I was staring at him, he seemed to be checking me out as well. My cheeks instantly flushed a deep shade of pink.

"Hi. I... uhmmm... I have a delivery for you," I stammered. Smooth, Jenna. Real smooth.

"Yes, you said that." Nick continued to smile at me with an easygoing hint of laugher in his voice. The smile reached all

36

the way to those beautiful brown eyes which had me mesmerized. My brain felt scrambled as my heart started to beat faster. I was at a total loss as to what to say other than apparently just repeating myself. Real smooth Jenna!

I flushed another shade deeper. I didn't want to act like a total idiot, so I decided it was time to just get out of there. Plus, I knew they were busy and needed me to get back to the restaurant. I tried to refocus myself. Stop looking at the beautiful man. Why am I here? His smile is so perfect. Money. That's right, he needs to pay for this. The super sexy man named Nick needs to pay for his pizza. "Uhhhhh... that will be $22.47, please." My head was spinning and all attempts to refocus myself on the task at hand just found me focusing even more on Nick.

Nick chuckled as he grabbed some money from a table just inside the door and handed it to me. "Yes, sorry. I guess I do need to pay you if I want my pizza." He just kept looking at me with those beautiful eyes and a half-smile on his face. I felt a nervous giggle escape from my lips.

I handed Nick the pizza box and neither one of us broke eye contact. As soon as I realized we both had our hands on the box, I quickly pulled mine away and shoved them into the pockets of my jeans. I slowly smiled at Nick as I took a few extra moments to just bask in standing there with the hottest guy I had ever seen in real life. When I decided that I couldn't stand there any longer without totally making it super weird, I gave him one last smile and said, "Thank you and have a good night Nick. Enjoy your pizza... Nick." I just liked saying his name, it sounded so good.

"Thank you. Although I don't think my night is going to get any better than this moment right now." Nick winked at me and smiled again which made my heart start to flutter. What was it with this guy? I had never been so dumbstruck by another person before. Come to think of it, I had never felt a flutter quite like that. It was crazy. I had to get out of there... and he winked at me! He winked at me and it was so dang hot I thought I might melt into a puddle on the sidewalk. I had to get a grip on myself.

"Well, good night," I said quickly as I turned and started to walk back to the delivery car. My face must have been as red as pizza sauce, I felt so flushed.

I had only made it a few steps before Nick shouted at me. "Wait! What's your name? It doesn't seem quite fair that you know mine, but I don't know yours."

I turned and without even thinking about it first, gave him a big smile and said coyly, "Well, that is not something I just give out to anyone."

Nick looked surprised, but there was no way he was as surprised as I was by what came out of my mouth. Who was I? I didn't flirt and play cute with strangers. Especially an insanely handsome stranger. An insanely handsome stranger that had my heart racing and my palms sweating. I suddenly realized... all I had to do was say yes. Yes, I will flirt with a handsome stranger. Just say yes, Jenna.

I let out a giggle at the baffled look on Nick's face. A few beats passed before his face slowly morphed into a half-cocked grin. Hot dang, he was even sexier when he smiled. I couldn't help but flash him my biggest and brightest smile back. Hopefully, it looked seductive and not like I was having a stroke. It was really hard trying to be calm and coy when in reality, I felt like I was going to hyperventilate and pass out. How did people do that on a regular basis? No wonder I was single. It was difficult to flirt with sexy strangers… especially strangers named Nick who answer the door wearing nothing but a pair of black shorts.

"Well," Nick said slowly, never losing his grin. "What should I call you then? You know, in case I want to have another pizza delivered."

"You can call me Pizza Girl," I said with a laugh and a wave as I got into the delivery car and drove off. I had no idea where that came from, but it just seemed to fit the moment. As I pulled away, I looked in the rearview mirror and my stomach did a flip-flop when I saw that Nick was out on the sidewalk holding the pizza box with a big grin on his face as he watched me drive away.

Chapter 8
Nick

As I stood up from my desk to stretch, I decided to go ahead and leave work a little early. Well, early for me, which meant it was a few minutes after seven o'clock. I had finally broken down and placed an ad for a full-time assistant following last Friday's late-night slog through paperwork. I was shocked with the number of applications I had received and was trying to sort through all of them to set interviews for the week ahead. I was also in the process of putting together bids for a few big projects that could really propel Blaine Construction forwards. One of the projects was a multi-year, multi-phase sub development and every construction company in the area was chomping at the bit to be a part of it. The other was for a smaller development that consisted of very expensive luxury homes. That one looked to be a very demanding job with a tight timeline, but it was one that would be incredibly beneficial in setting Blaine Construction apart from other construction companies. I couldn't take my eyes off the ball for one second, getting the contracts was pivotal to our success and growth.

I decided I was going to go for a run to try and clear my head and loosen myself up after sitting behind a desk all day. I was eager to get someone hired to manage the office so I could spend more time out at the job sites, which is what I really enjoyed. Sitting behind a desk all day made me feel trapped... and I had been feeling trapped way too much lately.

I could feel more and more of the tension disappear with each thud of my running shoes on the pavement. I continued to push forward until all of it had completely melted out of my body. As I ran through a residential neighborhood, I couldn't help but feel a sense of pride as I noted all of the houses I passed that Blaine Construction had either built or remodeled. It made all the late hours and sacrifices worth it, seeing how much the company had grown in such a short time.

I finished out my run and decided to order a pizza from Pete's Pizza for dinner. Pete's had the best pizza in town by far and had been a favorite of mine since college. When I called to place my order, the girl from Pete's said that they were really busy and delivery might take a little longer than usual. That was fine by me since it'd give me time to take a quick shower first.

Either I lost track of time, or the delivery arrived sooner than expected because I had just stepped out of the shower and started to dry off when I heard the doorbell ring. I quickly grabbed a pair of black athletic shorts and went to answer the door. When I opened it I had to do a quick double-take at the woman standing on the other side.

She was not what I expected at all.

Luckily, she was looking down at the pizza box she was holding and not paying me any attention as I stared at her, trying to get my shit together. When she finally looked up, I literally lost my breath for a moment.

She was absolutely fucking gorgeous.

I just openly stared, taking her all in. Her brown hair was pulled back into a ponytail, but there were random pieces that escaped and framed her face. She had full pink lips that I instantly wanted to kiss, sparkling blue eyes, and flawless creamy skin that was starting to flush pink around her cheeks and neck. It didn't look like she was wearing any makeup which just showcased the fact she was naturally and effortlessly beautiful. I couldn't pull my eyes away from her.

It was then that I realized she was also checking me out. Judging by the flush on her face and the fact her lips had parted slightly, she liked what she saw. This totally fueled my cocky side and I decided to take full advantage of the fact that I was standing there without a shirt. I crossed my arms to flex my biceps slightly. Did I do it just to see if I could get a reaction out of her? Absolutely. Was it kind of an arrogant dick thing to do? Absolutely. In my defense, I work my ass off at the gym regularly... it's one of the few things that I actually do, other than go to work. As this beautiful woman stood in front of me and checked me out, I decided to take full advantage of all those hours busting my ass. Suddenly every workout I had ever done became worth it when she gasped a little and parted her lips even more as her eyes landed on my upper body. I couldn't help but smile.

I would have just stood there and stared at her all night if she hadn't reminded me that I needed to pay for my pizza. As I grabbed the cash I'd left on the table by the door earlier, I tried to think of something clever to say to her. I was totally out of practice with flirting or even being around a beautiful woman... it had been a really long time since I had felt anything even remotely close to how she made me feel. There was something about this woman on my doorstep that had me completely and utterly rattled. My pulse was racing and I felt like I was back in junior high trying to talk to a girl for the first time.

I handed her the cash and she handed me the pizza and I swear we had a moment. I didn't think that kind of shit was actually real, but we both seemed to be frozen staring at each other for... I don't even know how long, but I know it wasn't long enough. Even the Pete's Pizza t-shirt and jeans she had on couldn't hide the fact that there were some luscious curves under her clothes. I was just over six feet tall and I seemed to tower over her as she stood there in her tennis shoes... fuck... tiny, curvy, beautiful, and she kept blushing which I found to be oddly adorable on her... everything about her drove me fucking wild.

When I told her that there was no way my night was getting any better, I meant it. Fuck, my entire week couldn't get any better than that moment. As she turned to leave I was so distracted by the fact that her cheeks had flushed an even deeper shade of red I almost let her slip away without even asking her name.

Imagine my surprise when the little minx wouldn't tell me. As I stood on the sidewalk and watched her drive away, all I could think about was how much I wanted to see her again. My pulse continued to race and I could feel the big goofy grin plastered across my face that I wore all the way back into the house.

Once I was back inside, I turned on the game and sat down to eat my pizza. I couldn't even pay attention, all I could think about was Pizza Girl. The more I thought about her, the more conflicted I became. There was no question that I was attracted to her, more so than I had been to any other woman in... well maybe ever. There was just something about Pizza Girl that drew me in from the moment I opened my door and first laid eyes on her. Problem was, I didn't have time for distractions... that included dating. Blaine Construction was really starting to take off and there were the big new projects I needed to focus on landing. I had employees that depended on me and I had spent the past several years solely focused on getting Blaine Construction to the place it almost was... things were at a real tipping point. Any one of the big jobs I was looking at would be the thing that would send Blaine Construction over the edge and to where I envisioned it. I needed to stay focused on what I was doing and not get distracted by anything outside of work... especially brunette bombshells that randomly showed up on my doorstep delivering pizza.

I tried to push Pizza Girl out of my mind for the rest of the evening, but by the time I crawled into bed, I had already decided that I had to see her again. I had no idea how to contact her other than by ordering another pizza. I chuckled to myself as I laid in bed thinking of her beautiful blue eyes and what it would be like to kiss those perfectly pink lips. Looks like I'd be having Pete's Pizza delivered for dinner again the next night.

Chapter 9
Jenna

A few nights after my delivery to the hottest man I had ever laid eyes on, I was with Cassie at High Five for drinks and appetizers. The popular bar was fairly busy for a weeknight. Normally it was not my scene, but when Cassie asked me to meet up with her, I had to say yes. It ultimately worked out to be alright since hanging out with Cassie was a welcome distraction... I hadn't been able to stop thinking about Nick.

"You know, I am really starting to feel like an absolute genius. I should win some type of award or have a monument named after me," Cassie said as she looked at me and popped a nacho chip in her mouth. "At the very least, I should have my name on a park bench. Or my picture on a stamp."

"Oh really? Why is that?" I raised an eyebrow at her and took a sip of my cocktail.

Cassie leaned forward with a big smile on her face like she was about to divulge a huge secret. "Because my spectacularly brilliant plan is working. More perfectly than even I thought it would. I'm proud of you babe." Cassie leaned back in her chair and crossed her arms with a smug expression on her face.

"What are you talking about?" I asked, not quite sure I was following.

Cassie rolled her eyes at me. "Why the saying yes plan, of course! It has only been a few weeks and look at how many things in your life have changed. Look how much *you* have changed!" She exclaimed triumphantly.

I thought about it for a moment before I responded. "I guess you're right. I have a job that is actually fun, where I can just show up, put in my hours, and be done. I don't want to do it forever, but it pays the bills for now. Plus the tips are pretty great."

"Yes!" Cassie shouted, loud enough that a few people sitting around us turned to look. It didn't even phase Cassie as she kept on talking, "Plus you've made new friends. When I stopped by the other day during your shift, it was great to see how well you were all getting along. I know it has been hard for you to step out of your shy shell and make new friends in the past. I'm seeing a real change for the better and it's only been a few weeks!"

"True," I nodded in agreement. "The group at Pete's Pizza are totally unlike any people I have ever met before. They work hard, but they also have fun and genuinely seem to enjoy what they are doing. Weird thing is, I haven't known them for very long, but I already feel like they have my back. I have to admit, I was not looking forward to this job, but so far I am really glad that I did it."

"See! You just had to put yourself out there! Plus, I like this more confident, less stressed, and dare I say, more carefree version of you. Not having a plan looks good on you, babe. Keep saying yes."

I laughed and took another sip of my drink. I had to agree. I felt better than I had in a long time. Although there were times I started to worry about not having a plan, I just kept reminding myself to say yes and take the experience. This was for now, not forever. It felt really good to be more relaxed and not constantly worried about things that ultimately were beyond my control.

"Speaking of saying yes, my work friends, Mike, Steven, and Kimmy invited me to go out dancing with them Thursday night. They said to invite you along as well. What do you say? Want to join us?" I asked as I looked at Cassie hopefully. I really wanted her to come. Going to a club and dancing was way outside of my comfort zone. Having Cassie there would be a huge help.

"Hell yeah!" Cassie shouted and banged her palm on the table causing people to turn and look at us again. "I would not miss you at a dance club for anything! How many times have I tried to get you to go out with me and you said no? Let me answer that for you. About sixty hundred billion and twelve. I am such a fan of you saying yes!"

"I am not even sure that is an actual number, but I get what you're saying." I laughed. "It should be fun, but I am a little nervous. I think I've only been to a dance club once before and that was with Brett."

"Well, Brett is a stupid bastard who wouldn't know a good time if it came up and bit him on the ass. Prepare to have your mind blown, girlfriend! You, at a dance club saying yes— this is going to be my best night ever!" Cassie was clapping her hands and literally bouncing up and down in her seat. I laughed at how excited she was. It was true that Cassie loved to go out and I usually stayed home. Thursday night was going to be way out of my comfort zone, but I was ready. As Cassie pointed out earlier, so far saying yes was working well for me.

"Where are we going to be shaking our booties on Thursday?" Cassie asked as she took a sip of her drink.

"Ummmmm... I think it's a place downtown called The Star." I saw a weird look flash across Cassie's face but it was there and gone so quickly part of me wasn't sure it had actually happened. "You still want to go, right?" I asked hesitantly. I wasn't sure if I was reading too much into that look or if it really was nothing.

"It's going to be the best night ever," Cassie answered as she took a big gulp of her drink. I raised my eyebrow at her, wondering what was up since she hadn't exactly given a yes or a no answer. Cassie set her drink down and a mischievous look came over her face as she leaned forward. "Speaking of best nights ever, any more deliveries to your pizza hottie with the beautiful brown eyes?"

I blushed as Cassie wiggled her eyebrows at me. Of course, I had told her about the delivery to Nick. I hadn't been able to stop thinking about him since that night. There had been multiple fantasies of him holding me in those strong arms, me kissing his perfect lips, and licking that finely sculpted chest. My favorite fantasy was of him peppering kisses down my neck and continuing to move further down my body until...

"Hey! Earth to Jenna!" Cassie waved her hand in front of my face. "Wipe that drool off your chin and answer me! You better not be holding out critical information about another encounter!"

"Nothing like that." I paused as I stirred my drink with my straw. "I haven't been back to work since that night. We had some schedule changes which meant I had a bunch of days in a row off. I am back at work tomorrow night."

"Well, you better keep me posted if you just happen to make a delivery there again tomorrow night." Cassie got a big smile on her face as she chewed on a nacho chip. "You know this is the start of a great porno movie, right?" She chuckled saucily.

I choked on the sip of the drink in my mouth and started coughing as I nervously looked around to make sure no one overheard her. I knew my face was bright red. "Cassie! You can't just say stuff like that!" I exclaimed, flustered. It was true, after all.

"Why not?" Cassie shrugged. "You have to admit it is pretty perfect. Super hot delivery girl just happens to deliver a steaming hot pizza to an ultra sexy guy wearing nothing but a pair of gym shorts. Throw in some cheesy music and the story practically writes itself."

I started laughing uncontrollably. Cassie batted her eyelashes and spoke in a super high-pitched, sugar-coated voice as she stuck her chest out. "Oh my! What other services would you like me to deliver? I just love the taste of great big sausages!"

I threw my napkin at her as tears rolled down my face from laughing so hard. "Stop it! You're too much! I can't take you anywhere!"

"Admit it, you adore me and my totally twisted sense of humor."

"You are right, Cass, I do. Seriously though, I'm sure that I am never going to see him again. What are the chances of that actually happening?"

As much as I hated to admit it, the thought of not ever seeing Nick again made me feel kind of sad, which felt strange since I had only been around him once and for just a few minutes.

Cassie took a sip of her drink and smiled at me. "I don't know... but if it does, remember to just say yes."

Chapter 10
Nick

It had been four days since the night of Pizza Girl. I had ordered pizza from Pete's every goddamn night since then and much to my disappointment, and increasing frustration, every night she was not the delivery driver who knocked on my door.

The guy with the bright pink mohawk had just delivered my pizza for the second night in a row and I think he could tell I was frustrated when I opened the door. I may have even lost my cool for a moment and asked how many damn delivery drivers worked at Pete's. I had eaten so much pizza those past few days, I didn't even want the stuff. I just wanted to see her again.

I decided that instead of letting the latest order go to waste, I would give Bax a call. He picked up on the second ring.

"Alright, where did you find Nick's phone at and how much of a reward are you looking for to give it back?"

"What the hell are you talking about, Bax?"

"Well, it's just been so long since you called, I figured no way was it actually you. I thought someone found your phone and scrolled through the contacts until they found the one that said Sexy Single Stud and decided that was the best number to call."

I started laughing "Do you actually spend time sitting around coming up with stupid shit to say or does it just come to you in the moment?"

Now it was Bax's turn to laugh. "It comes to me in the moment. Some would say it's my superpower."

"You are so full of shit. Listen, I just had pizza delivered. Why don't you come over and help me eat it?"

"Hawaiian with extra jalapenos?" Bax asked.

"Is there any other kind?" I replied.

"I will be there in ten minutes. Actually, make that fifteen. I'll stop and pick up a six-pack along the way."

"Sounds good, man. See you when you get here."

True to his word, Bax was ringing my doorbell exactly fifteen minutes later. It wasn't too much longer after that we were sitting out on the balcony, both of us enjoying a cold beer and a slice of pizza.

"So what's the occasion tonight?" Bax asked as he helped himself to another slice of pizza.

"No reason." I took a drink of my beer and avoided eye contact.

"Bullshit," Bax said with his mouth full of pizza. "First of all, you are the worst fucking liar I know, Nick Blaine, and secondly, you never do anything without a reason."

I chuckled. He had me pegged on both of those points. "I've ordered pizza from Pete's several nights in a row and I am getting tired of it."

"You do realize that there are a whole shit ton of other places to order food from right? This town is full of restaurants and most of them deliver. So why Pete's?" Bax looked at me suspiciously. He knew me too well, damnit.

"Yeah, well..." I stammered.

"Seriously, Nick! How do you negotiate all of those deals for Blaine Construction when you have such a shitty poker face?"

I sighed. "Fine. A few nights ago I ordered pizza from Pete's Pizza and there was this delivery driver and she..."

Bax got a huge grin on his face. "Did you just say *she*? Are you ordering pizza from Pete's to see her again? You dirty dog, Nick! I knew you wouldn't live like a monk forever!"

"It is not like that," I said quickly.

"Sure it's not," Bax said with a knowing look as he took a sip of his beer. "What's her name?"

I looked at him a little sheepishly. "I don't know. I asked, but she didn't tell me."

"Jesus, Nick! Have you lost all of your game? How the hell did you not even get her name?" Bax exclaimed.

"She just said to call her Pizza Girl."

Bax raised his eyebrow at me. "Pizza Girl? Huh. Not the strangest thing someone has ever asked to be called... So how many times have you ordered pizza since then in hopes of seeing Pizza Girl?"

I hesitated. "Every night for the past four nights." Bax started howling with laughter. "Shut up you asshole. It is *so* not funny. I'm starting to think I imagined her."

"I'm not laughing at you, I'm laughing *with* you," Bax said wiping tears of laughter from his eyes.

"Well, I don't find anything about this very fucking funny," I snapped.

Bax slowly stopped laughing and put both of his hands up. "You are right. I am totally laughing at you. It's just, you've been so focused on one thing forever, and you've been so adamant for so long that the single life is your calling. Then, Pizza Girl blows in, and suddenly you're ordering pizza multiple nights in a row, just trying to see her again."

"Yeah, well, there was just something about her. I can't explain it, but I just really want to see her again."

"You've got it bad for her," Bax chuckled.

"I don't have anything for her... I just..." I couldn't say what it was, I just wanted to see her again.

"Hey, dude. You don't have to justify anything to me." Bax paused and took a drink of his beer. "So, how long are you going to keep ordering pizza from Pete's hoping she's the one that delivers?"

I thought for a moment. That was a good question. "A week," I decided. "I am going to give it a week and if I don't see her again, well, then that will be the end of it."

"The end of it, huh? Well, here's to hoping that sometime in the next three days Pizza Girl graces your doorstep again." Bax held his beer out to me for a toast. As I clanked my bottle against his, I couldn't help but hope I would see her again and that Pizza Girl had not disappeared for good.

Chapter 11
Jenna

The night after I had drinks with Cassie, I was back to work at Pete's Pizza. It was another busy night and all of us hustled and bustled around the place as we tried to stay on top of deliveries.

"I have another order for delivery!" Kimmy shouted as she walked back into the kitchen. "It is the 'Hawaiian pizza with extra jalapenos guy again. I swear he's called and ordered the same thing every night for the past week. He must really like the pizza here."

Mike looked up from the pizza that he was cutting. "That is so strange. I've delivered to that guy a few times this week and he always seems so disappointed that his pizza has arrived."

"Is that the guy in the fancy new part of town?" Steven chimed in. I delivered there two nights in a row and the guy seemed a little off. He was asking weird questions about how many delivery drivers we had."

"Yes! That's the one!" Mike turned to me. "Hey, Jenna if you want Steven or me to take this delivery, we will. I don't want you to be in an uncomfortable situation with some weirdo."

"That's really nice of you Mike. Thank you for looking out for me, but I'm sure I'll be fine." I grabbed the boxes of pizza that were ready for delivery off the counter.

Mike's forehead creased in concern. "You have my cell phone number. If you get there and something feels off, call me straight away."

I nodded my head at Mike as Kimmy came back into the kitchen. "Here is the GPS with the delivery addresses programmed in for you. Be safe!" Kimmy set the GPS on top of the boxes that were already in my hands.

"You guys are the best. Thank you. I'm really glad to have all of you looking out for me," I said, I meant it too. It felt good to know I had people who genuinely cared about me. All of the employees at Pete's were great to work with, but I considered Mike, Steven, and Kimmy to be my friends, too.

"Well, we care about you. Be safe, Jenna," Mike said simply, before he turned to put a pizza in the oven.

"I'll be back soon!" I shouted as I went out the back door and headed to my delivery car.

The night air was warm so I rolled the windows down as I drove to make this last delivery. The wind blew through my hair and I couldn't remember the last time I felt so at ease with everything in my life. Could it really all have been from just opening myself up by saying yes when I previously would have said no? Was it really that easy? Had I been that tightly wound?

I mindlessly followed the directions from the GPS until I turned on to Hudson Street. Suddenly everything started to feel really familiar. "Oh, no, no, no... this is where Nick lives!" I mumbled out loud to myself. I pulled over and quickly looked up the complete address. Sure enough, it was building G. I felt a wave of disappointment flash through me.

"Of course. The one guy I am wildly attracted to turns out to be a total crazy person. I feel so stupid." I banged my head on the steering wheel a few times as I continued to talk to myself in my parked car. I was really losing my marbles.

There is no way both Mike and Steven are wrong about this. Both of them said there was something off about the guy they were delivering to. Well, there goes a whole week of fantasizing about what it would be like to see him again.

I took a deep breath as I pulled out my cell phone to call one of the guys and see if they could come and do the delivery. My finger was hovering over the call button for Mike when I paused. "Wait, why are you saying no to this? So the guy is a little weird. It's just a pizza delivery. It is not like I am going to spend the rest of my life with him. It will be a five-minute interaction and then it'll be done." I started to feel inspired by my own pep talk. "Put on your big girl panties and say yes to the delivery, Jenna!" I shouted to myself a little louder than intended.

I was fired up and ready to go. I pulled the delivery car away from the curb and drove the last two blocks to building G. Before I got out, I continued my pep talk. "What's the worst that's going to happen? Realize the guy I have been fantasizing about non-stop is a total weirdo? A weirdo that eats pizza every single night and has awkward interactions with delivery drivers? I can handle that!" I told myself.

I took one last deep breath as I summoned up my newfound confidence and marched up to building G, knocking firmly on the door.

I was a confident, badass woman and I was ready for anything! Cassie would have been so proud of me. I made a mental note to tell her about my pep talk later... only maybe I would leave out the part where I was actually talking out loud to myself in the car.

The door suddenly swung open and Nick was on the other side. I don't know what I was expecting because, obviously, I knew he lived here, but I let out a tiny gasp as his brown eyes raked over me. He seemed to be frozen with his hand on the door as he took me in. My hair must have been a wild mess from driving with the windows down, and I knew I had some spills on my uniform shirt. I mentally facepalmed myself for not taking a quick look in the rearview mirror of the delivery car before walking to the front door. Yet another smooth move, Jenna.

We both just stood there for a few seconds until I accidentally blurted out, "You're even more handsome than I remembered. I'm not sure how that's even possible." As soon as the words fell out of my mouth, I knew my face turned red. Dang it, I was so not ready. I couldn't even keep my thoughts inside my head.

Nick had a look of surprise on his face. I'm not sure if he was surprised to see me, or was surprised at what I had just blurted out. Maybe it was both. My eyes quickly ran up and down his body. No wonder my mind had turned to mush.. He was wearing a pair of well-faded jeans and a white t-shirt that clung to his chest. It looked like his biceps were about ready to rip out of his sleeves. I had never wanted to be a t-shirt more in my life. I don't even know if that's a thing, but as we stood there, I would have literally given anything in that moment to be that shirt wrapped around that man.

"Uhhhhhh… I stammered quickly trying to save the moment from being totally ruined by my awkwardness. "I have a Nick. I mean a Pete order. No, dang it! Nick pizza. Ahhhhhhhh! I mean I have a delivery here for Nick. A pizza. From Pete's Pizza. For Nick. That you ordered."

Well, that was smooth. My cheeks burned as they flushed even brighter. I was so very, very not ready. Just about the time I was ready to drop the pizza box and take off running, Nick's face slowly lit up with the most brilliant smile.

I was afraid my panties were going to burst into flames while I stood there with sweaty palms and a death grip on the pizza box. I don't know how it was humanly possible, but he was even sexier when he smiled.

"Pizza Girl! You have no idea how glad I am to see you! I was starting to think I had imagined you."

Nick's deep, smooth voice rumbled through me and soaked into every molecule of my body. Did he just say that he was glad to see me? I must have heard him wrong. "I'm sorry, what did you just say?" I asked, blinking in confusion. Maybe I should have just left it alone and pretended what I heard was correct, I should get out of there before I embarrassed myself even further.

"I was starting to think that this incredibly beautiful pizza delivery girl who showed up at my door a week ago was just a fantasy I made up. Glad to see you are, in fact, very real." Nick continued to smile at me as he crossed his arms and leaned up against the door frame casually. Damn he was smooth.

"Why would you think that?" My question came out as a breathy whisper. Nick's eyes were smoldering and looked directly into mine. I felt like I was on fire everywhere. I wondered what his body could do to me, if his eyes on me made me feel this hot and bothered.

Status of panties = full-on melted.

"Well, you see this beautiful pizza delivery girl left without giving me her name, and the only way I could figure out how to see her again was to order another pizza."

"Well, I guess this is your lucky night," I smiled back at him and gave him a wink.

Wait, what? What was I doing? Was I flirting with him? Suddenly a red flashing light went off in my head as I remembered Steven and Mike's concerns that Nick was a creepy pizza driver stalking weirdo. Slow down, Jenna! Slow down!

I mustn't have given any indications that my mind was racing a million miles a minute, because Nick continued on. "Actually, luck had nothing to do with it. I have ordered pizza every night from Pete's Pizza since I last saw you hoping to see you again." He had a trace of a goofy smile on his lips as he spoke.

I laughed. "That is a whole lot of pizza considering that was almost a week ago." Maybe he wasn't a totally creepy pizza driver stalking weirdo after all. I liked that option much better, so that was the one I went with.

"You're telling me. Don't get me wrong, I like pizza as much as the next guy, but pizza every night for a week has forced me to spend a whole lot of extra time in the gym." Was he flexing as he said that, or was it my imagination?

"Well, it certainly looks like you've put that gym time to good use." I was blatantly staring at Nick's body as I spoke.

Who was this wild, wanton woman I was turning into? I don't think I had ever flirted like that before. It was a good thing there was at least a pizza box between us. I couldn't trust myself to be any closer to him. Not when I wanted to climb him like a spider monkey.

Nick grinned and flexed his arm muscles a little, or was it a little more? It was hard to believe how toned he actually was. I had to take a deep breath and clench my legs together as I unconsciously licked my lips. I was a hot mess. A hot, horny, awkward mess.

What the hell was I doing? Why did this man have me so twisted around and turned upside down?

Chapter 12
Nick

There she was. She was really there standing right in front of me and fuck... her hair was all wild and her face was flushed. I couldn't help but wonder if that is how she would look after a night of hot sex. I was about to mentally smack myself for the thought when I noticed that she was blatantly checking me out. I couldn't help the thrill that coursed through my body.

I decided to seize the moment and flex my arms for her a bit to see if I could get any more of a reaction. It had worked well the last time. Kind of a selfish bastard thing to do, but the way she looked at me made me feel... well, it was unlike anything I had ever felt before.

When she gasped and licked her lips, I almost lost it right there on the spot. I hoped she didn't notice I was harder than a high school boy on prom night after hearing her breathy little gasp and watching the tip of her tongue slide across those perfect pink lips. There was just something about the beautiful, slightly awkward pizza girl with a brilliant smile that made both my body and mind react in ways that seemed totally beyond my control.

Part of me couldn't believe I had so easily told her I ordered pizza every night for a week, like a creeper, just trying to see her again. She didn't seem totally freaked out by it, so I decided to just own it.

"I have to say, getting to see you again has made a week of pizza and extra gym time worth it. This was the last night I was going to order and hope to see you. Your co-workers seem nice, but it was a real disappointment to see one of them every night instead of you." I hoped it came across as nonchalant. She didn't need to know how very real the nightly disappointment had been.

"We had some shift changes and I have been off for the past several days." She smiled softly and I couldn't help but wonder if she had thought about me at all during that week. I quickly reminded myself not to be an arrogant asshole and that, of course, she wouldn't be thinking about me. I was just one of many deliveries she made in a night... fuck, it had never even occurred to me that she might have other guys that were interested in her. Or a fucking boyfriend. God, I hated that idea. A lot.

I didn't want her to leave, so I tried to keep the conversation moving. "That explains why you weren't delivering. I didn't want to be a total creep and ask for you, but I was starting to get desperate." I mentally kicked myself. Good job, Nick. Way to point out that you are, in fact, a creep and desperate. Fuck, it had been a long time since I tried to flirt with someone... maybe Bax was right and I had lost my game.

Pizza Girl laughed and it was such a beautiful sound I instantly wanted to hear it again. "There may have been mention at the pizza shop of an increased number of deliveries to this address over the past week. I am flattered it was partially because of me and not just because of a Hawaiian pizza with extra jalapenos." Those lips, that smile!

Now it was my turn to blush. I ran my hand through my hair. It was a nervous habit I had done all my life and continued even now that my dark hair was cut short. "Yeah...

I guess after a few nights it becomes rather obvious something is up. I hope your co-workers don't think I'm some kind of nut job." I had only been thinking about seeing her again and had not fully considered all the ramifications of my plan, now I probably had strangers thinking I was crazy. Nice move, Nick.

Suddenly an awful thought hit me. This was exactly why I couldn't be involved with anyone... I had been so distracted just trying to see her again, I didn't think about anything else. I was so close to launching Blaine Construction into the next level I couldn't get distracted and lose my focus. I had worked too hard and already given up too much to fuck it all up. I had only seen her twice and already Pizza Girl was a distraction. Hell, I hadn't been able to stop thinking about her since the last time I saw her. That was not good.

"I wouldn't worry about it too much," Pizza Girl said with a chuckle.

I raised my eyebrows at her. "That is just a polite way of saying they do." I tried to push all of my previous thoughts out of my head and just focus on the moment, on this beautiful girl standing in front of me.

Pizza Girl smiled at me. God, that smile was enough to make my heart skip a beat every time I saw it. "Well, it was nice to see you again. Thank you for ordering one more night," she said softly.

As much as I wanted her to stay, I also realized she had to get back to work. Plus, I didn't want to push the creep factor any further by trying to get her to stay longer. "So Pizza Girl, what do I owe you?"

Her brows knitted together in confusion. "Excuse me? After all that, you owe me something?"

"For the pizza," I said as I reached in the back pocket of my jeans for my wallet. I knew exactly how much it was since I had ordered the same damn thing every night for the past week. Any reason to keep talking to her was a good one though.

"Right," her cheeks flushed. It was adorable how she blushed so easily. "Sorry about that. Looks like it's $22.47."

As I handed her some money, I realized I still didn't know her name and that I had better ask before she left. "Here you go. Do you have a name other than Pizza Girl?"

She hesitated for a moment. "Yes."

"Am I going to find out what it is?"

"Yes."

"Well, what is it?"

"Not tonight..." she seemed hesitant or uncertain of her answer. I wasn't sure where she was going with it either.

"Wait, you're not going to tell me your name tonight?" What was she doing?

"Yes, that is correct." She looked up at me through her lashes as she gave me a small smile.

Oh, Pizza Girl, you little game-playing minx. I looked at her and smiled. Game on. "Good thing I like challenges and don't give up easily, Pizza Girl," I tried to say in my sexiest voice. God, flirting with her just felt so good and so right... I couldn't think of a time I'd felt like that with anyone else.

Pizza Girl quickly shoved the pizza box at me and as she did, our hands touched. I swear I felt a physical spark pass between us just from the small contact. The air around us felt electric and we both looked up into each other's eyes. The way she looked at me left no doubt in my mind that she felt it too.

We just stood there, both holding on to the pizza box, neither one of us wanting to let go. The only sound was from both of us breathing heavily, lustily.

Suddenly Pizza Girl's eyes grew big and she let go of the box. "Good night, Nick. Enjoy your pizza."

"I think I am going to need to take a cold shower before I eat this pizza." I'd intended for that as a joke, but as soon as I said it, I realized I was actually completely serious.

Pizza Girl's face flushed again and I couldn't help but smile. "Am I going to see you again?" I asked her. My heart was racing as I waited for her answer. I wasn't liking the idea of this being the last time I saw her.

"Yes. You know where to find me," she said with a coy smile.

"Alright, Pizza Girl. Until next time. Know that I will not be able to get you out of my mind until I see you again." That last part just kind of slipped out, but I knew deep down that it was true.

"Likewise," she responded softly. "See you later, Nick."

I watched her as she turned and walked down to the sidewalk and out to her delivery car. As soon as she got into the car I heard a squeal and immediately went down to the sidewalk to make sure she was okay. My heart was thudding in my chest at the idea of something happening to her.

When I got to where I could see her again, my heart just about burst. She was in the car with the windows rolled down squealing and doing a little dance as she sat in the driver's seat. Given the big smile on her face, I assumed it was a little happy dance. It was so damn cute I couldn't help but chuckle.

Suddenly she stopped and let out a loud groan. From where I was standing, I could see her close her eyes and lean her head against the back of the seat. Slowly she rolled her head to the side and opened her eyes. When she saw me standing there, her face turned the brightest shade of red I had ever seen.

I guess she didn't realize I was still outside and that the windows on her car were rolled down.

Not wanting her to feel embarrassed I quickly said, "Glad to know that we're on the same page, Pizza Girl. Drive safely tonight and I will see you again soon."

There was an instant look of relief on her face followed by a big smile as she gave me a little wave and started up the car. I stood there on the sidewalk and watched her as she drove away.

Fuck. Part of me immediately wanted to see her again and part of me knew I had absolutely no business seeing her again. I sighed. I wasn't sure how exactly we were going to see each other again, but at least I knew where she worked. I guess only time would tell how things were going to play out. I turned and slowly started walking back up towards my condo.

Although, honestly, deep down I knew exactly how I wanted it to play out.

Chapter 13
Jenna

"I am pretty sure that the purpose of the saying yes plan is not for you to manipulate me into doing something like this." I raised my eyebrow at Cassie and folded my arms across my chest.

Cassie waved her hand at me like I was the one being ridiculous. "My idea, my rules. I offered to get you ready for tonight and you said yes. I have wanted to give you a makeover for years and you have never let me. Now, hold still so I don't burn your ear with the curling iron," Cassie instructed firmly, ignoring my protests.

I sighed as Cassie wrapped another section of my hair around the curling iron. "That's because I don't need a makeover. I am totally fine with my style as is. It's a Thursday night and we are meeting up with my work friends. How fancy do we need to be?" I continued.

Cassie was standing behind me and looked at me in the bathroom mirror. "You never get a second chance to make a first impression. Your first impression tonight needs to be a totally hot babe who is single and ready to mingle." Cassie laughed and did a little shimmy before picking up another section of hair and wrapping it around the curling iron.

I snorted. "I'm impressed you managed to put two clichés together like that."

"Stick with me babe, I'm going places." Cassie put down the curling iron and spun me around in the chair so I was no longer facing the mirror. "Now, close your eyes so I can start your makeup."

I closed my eyes and could hear Cassie rummaging around in her makeup bag. She had rolled her eyes earlier when she looked at my small collection of makeup and chastised me for only owning neutral shades of everything. "Speaking of hot babes," Cassie said as she started putting makeup on my eyes. "You had any more deliveries to Panty Melter Nick?" She asked. I could practically hear her eyebrows shimmying up and down suggestively.

"No, there haven't been any orders since the last one. I guess a week of pizza every night was his limit." Just because I hadn't seen him again, it didn't stop me from thinking about him more than was probably healthy. But I wasn't going to tell anyone about that, even Cassie.

"Well, tonight I guarantee you are going to be catching the eye of several eligible, and possibly ineligible, gentlemen with this fabulous makeover courtesy of yours truly. Now, hold still while I get some mascara on these eyelashes," Cassie said bossily.

"Cassie, really this is too much. I don't need a full-on makeover," I protested. Truth was, I was a little worried about what she was doing make up wise, since I couldn't see anything. Wild and over the top worked on Cassie who considered red lipstick, high heels, and leopard print to be the foundation of any good outfit. It totally suited her but, I preferred a more subdued look. I preferred neutral tones and simplicity in my fashion choices and for my makeup.

I opened my eyes and Cassie was standing in front of me with one hand on her hip, while the other was pointing at me with a tube of mascara. "Honey, yes you do. You are a vivacious twenty-three-year-old, but you are hiding behind your clothes. Your favorite color is gray. Gray is not a color, it's a shade. The shade of sadness and despair. It has no place in your life and it definitely has no place at the club tonight."

Now it was my turn to roll my eyes at Cassie. "Fine. I will play dress up for tonight, but you should know that this is for one night only."

"We'll see about that. Now, pucker up those totally kissable lips and let me paint them red. As soon as I'm done, I want you to put on the dress I laid out on your bed. No peeking at the final result until you are back here in the bathroom. Now, go." To emphasize her point, Cassie smacked me on the booty. I laughed and went into my bedroom.

Cassie had gone through my closet earlier to pick out something for me to wear as part of the makeover, which is why I was completely surprised to see a bright red mini dress laying on the bed. I didn't own anything that bright or that revealing. I shouted out to Cassie who was still in the bathroom putting on her own makeup. "Cass? This red dress isn't mine. Where did it come from?"

"It's one of mine that I brought with me and you are going to wear it tonight. All of your dresses are either conservative work dresses or flowy, flower print summer dresses. Not appropriate for tonight," Cassie shouted back.

I leaned out the bedroom door and shouted down the hallway. "I am not sure there is anything appropriate about the dress that's on the bed!"

Cassie poked her head out of the bathroom. "You are my favorite, but you need to stop bitching and put on the damn dress!"

I stuck my tongue out at Cassie and went back into the bedroom where I shimmied into the red dress. It only came down to my mid-thigh, which was much shorter than anything I had ever worn before. The front came down to a deep V that showed just a little bit of cleavage. The back was also a deep V that came to a point right above my butt leaving my back completely exposed.

"Are these red heels next to the bed for me as well?" I called out to her, picking up the strappy sandals doubtfully – how was I meant to walk in them, let alone dance?

"Yes! Do you think I would make you go barefoot? Strap those puppies on and get in here!"

"Alright!" I started walking down the hallway towards the bathroom. "I'm coming back in! Get ready to see me looking ridiculous!"

I walked into the bathroom and Cassie gasped. "Oh sweetie, you don't look ridiculous. You look amazing. You are so beautiful! Look at yourself in the mirror and tell me what you see."

I turned around and looked at myself in the full-length mirror. I gasped at the reflection staring back at me. "Oh my goodness, Cassie! I don't know what to say. You're like my fairy godmother!"

Cassie pretended to wave a wand at me as I continued to soak in my reflection. "Well, what do you think?" she asked, admiring her handiwork.

My hair had been transformed into soft waves that ran down my back and framed my face. My makeup looked professional and accentuated my features without looking overly made up... I had no idea my lashes could look so long! I will admit, I had been a little worried about the cherry red lipstick, but it perfectly matched the color of the dress. The dress... well, it looked amazing. It hugged all of my curves and looked like it had been made just for me.

"Cass... I look beautiful... and kind of sexy," I whispered. I was completely taken aback at my appearance, I hadn't known it was possible. I didn't feel as uncomfortable as I thought I would with make up like this on, and dressed in such a revealing outfit.

Cassie came over and stood next to me. "You are beautiful no matter what you wear, but what you see right now in the mirror has always been there. You've just been hiding it behind ponytails, sensible shoes, and conservative gray clothes. You are beautiful inside and out. All I did was make your outside match your inside a little bit more."

I hugged Cassie. "Honestly, I never thought I could look like this. Cass, I look and feel amazing! I don't think I have ever felt this way before. Thank you, Cass." Tears started to form in my eyes... I felt so overwhelmed.

"Ahhhhhhhhhh! Don't cry! You'll ruin all of my hard work! I am happy you finally said yes to me doing this for you."

"Now, I just got a message that our Uber is out front." Cassie bowed at the waist. "Your chariot awaits my fair princess. Let's get you to the ball before you turn into a pumpkin!"

Chapter 14
Jenna

I could feel the music pumping the second we stepped foot in the club. To the left was the bar and some tables and to the right was a DJ and a huge dance floor that was already full of people. It was only the second time I had been somewhere like this and I just tried to stay calm and take it all in. The flashing lights, the loud music, and all the people crowded into the bar area and on the dance floor overwhelmed my senses. I wondered for a fleeting moment if I should even be there and what exactly I had said yes to.

I leaned into Cassie so I could shout into her ear. "Is it always this loud?"

"Yes, grandma," Cassie shouted back. "It's a dance club. How can you dance to music that you can't hear or feel?" She added, laughing a little.

"Right. Silly me. Let's go find the rest of the crew." I scanned the tables and quickly located my friends at a booth in the back corner. My friends. I liked the sound of that and couldn't help but smile at the thought of the new friends I'd made already thanks to 'saying yes'.

Mike seemed to spot us at the same time and waved. When we made our way over to the table he stood up so we could sit down. "Hey! Glad you guys could make it! Did you have any problems getting in?" He asked, as we moved to join them.

I shook my head. "Not at all. We gave the bouncer our names just like you said to and he let us right in. He didn't even make us pay the cover charge." There had been an awkward moment when I tried to give the bouncer money and he looked at me like I had lost my mind before waving Cassie and me in.

"My roommate is the DJ here tonight, so I got you both on the guest list," Steven said casually.

"Wow! Thank you, Steven. I had no idea you were so connected in the club scene," Cassie said with a smile as she slid into the booth next to him.

Steven laughed right as Kimmy came back to the table with a tray of drinks. "I am afraid that is the extent of my influence but glad I could use my powers for good instead of evil." He joked, returning her smile.

"Alright, guys! Let's get this party started! Tequila shots for everyone!" Kimmy shouted as she started handing out drinks. "To new friends and new beginnings! Cheers!"

Everyone licked their wrist and poured on some salt as Kimmy passed out the drinks. I just went along with everything since I had no idea what it was for. After everyone clinked their shot glasses together, I saw that you lick the salt off your wrist, take the shot and then bite on a piece of lime. I looked around nervously and then followed suit. "Wow! That burned a little! I've never done a tequila shot before!" I said as I coughed and tried to keep my eyes from watering.

"Stick with me, babe!" Kimmy shouted as she let out a bubbly laugh. "By the way, you look so smoking hot tonight; every guy in this place is checking you out! Who knew there was such a hottie hiding under that uniform shirt and jeans?"

I blushed and laughed nervously. "This is all Cassie's handiwork," I told Kimmy. "She was my fairy godmother, transforming me into a princess for the night."

I looked over at Cassie and noticed that Mike was now sitting across from her staring. He glanced at me and quickly looked away. I swear his cheeks looked a little flushed. "Hey everyone!" Mike suddenly shouted. "Let's go and dance!"

I hesitated. I was really not one for dancing. I always felt out of place and like I had no idea what I was doing.

Cassie had a gleam in her eye and a big grin on her face. "Well, Jenna, what do you say about hitting the dance floor?"

I took a deep breath. "I say yes. Yes, let's go."

"Wooooooooo hoooooooo! Let's do this!" Kimmy shouted as she turned towards the dance floor.

We had been out on the dance floor for several songs when it began to get noticeably more crowded. I was genuinely having a great time, but I started to feel overwhelmed by all of the gyrating bodies and flashing lights. I danced over to Cassie and grabbed her arm.

"Hey, Cassie? I am having a lot of fun, but I need a little break. I'm going to go to the restroom."

"Do you want me to come with you?" she asked, as she continued dancing.

"No, I'm fine. How about I meet you back at our table in a little bit?"

"Sounds good babe! I'm glad you're having a good time!" Cassie shouted as she lifted her arms over her head and swayed her hips in time to the music.

I slowly started to make my way through the crowd of people and off the dance floor. When I reached the bar area, I finally felt like I could breathe again and continued walking towards the restroom.

Apparently, I wasn't paying attention to where I was going, because the next thing I knew, I crashed into what felt like a brick wall. Strong hands grabbed onto my arms to keep me from falling over.

"Oh no! I am so sorry! I am such a klutz! Are you okay?" I exclaimed. How did I constantly find myself in these embarrassing situations?

The brick wall did not immediately respond but left his hands on my arms. I couldn't help but notice that he smelled amazing... like something spicy and male with a hint of leather from the jacket he was wearing. I slowly lifted my eyes up to the face attached to the strong chest I was nestled up against.

When my eyes met his, I let out a gasp. I knew those deep brown eyes.

Chapter 15
Nick

I am not sure what possessed me to actually agree to go out to a dance club, especially on a Thursday night. The day before, when some of the guys on my crew asked me, it seemed like a good idea. I invited Bax, and of course, he thought it was a great idea. The closer I got to the club, the worse it all sounded. However, I'd promised I would be there, so I pulled my motorcycle into the parking lot and started to walk towards the front door.

Inside was a group of guys from my crew who were all in their early twenties. Apparently, some local DJ was playing that they had all heard of. They also thought it was the premiere place in town to go and try to meet women. Neither of those things interested me in the slightest, however, since we were in between jobs and the new one wasn't starting till Monday, I had agreed to go out with them.

I heard the music before I even made it all the way to the club. As I got closer, I saw Bax waiting for me out front. As soon as Bax saw me he started giving me shit. "So you'll go out with your crew to a club, but you won't go out with me anywhere in town. I see how you roll Blaine, and I'm going to have a moment of truth with you; my feelings are hurt." Bax immediately started laughing as we got in line at the front door. "I'm just fucking with you. I don't really give a shit how it happened, I am just glad to see you out. Actually, how did this happen?" He asked in amazement.

"We're meeting up with a group of guys from my crew. They're in between jobs right now and invited me out. They've invited me a few times before, and I was starting to feel bad about how many times I'd said no, so this time I said I'd come. It sounded like a much better idea yesterday."

"So you feel bad when you turn them down, but not when you turn me down?" He asked, mock hurt on his face.

"You got it," I smiled at Bax. We had always had an easy friendship that was mostly us constantly giving each other grief about one thing or another. It had gone on for so long, I couldn't even remember exactly how it started.

"You are an asshole, Nick."

"You're just figuring this out?" I shot back, smiling. Right then, it was our turn to go in. The bouncer checked our ID and we paid our cover charge. As soon as we stepped into the club, I saw my group of guys at a table on the far side of the club by the dance floor.

"They're over there," I nodded my head in the direction of the group.

"I'm going to grab a drink at the bar and meet you over there. Do you want anything?" Bax shouted at me. The music in the place seemed incredibly loud and it was packed with people, making it hard to talk. I just shook my head no in response, no sense in shouting over the noise, I'd have no voice in under an hour for sure if I even tried.

As Bax made his way over to the bar, I headed over to the table with my crew. "Nick!" they all greeted me as I pulled up a chair to take a seat.

"We weren't sure if you were actually going to make it tonight," said Clay, one of the carpenters.

"Yeah, we were going to give you another half hour before we officially called it," teased Kevin. Kevin was working on his apprenticeship to become an electrician. All of the guys at the table laughed.

"Yeah, yeah," I laughed along with them. "Congrats! You guys got me out on a Thursday night." I put my arms up in surrender, smiling.

"I should really be thanking all of you for that," said Bax as he came up behind me with a drink in his hand. "I'm Bax, Nick's fun friend. Please don't judge me by what a stick-in-the-mud he can be." Bax nodded his head in my direction.

"I think I like you already, have a seat," Clay said pointing to an empty chair across from him.

"Thank you," Bax said, taking the empty chair. "Nick used to be fun. We used to go out all the time, but then a few years ago he stopped, so I've had to carry on alone." He grinned at the boys.

"Poor you," I rolled my eyes at Bax. It was true though. When Blaine Construction started to take off, it became my entire focus... and had remained that way until a beautiful brunette pizza delivery girl showed up at my doorstep. I still didn't even know her name, but she had me starting to think that maybe Bax was right... maybe there is more to life than work. Maybe it was time to stop being alone all the time.

I quickly tried to push the thoughts of her out of my head. I didn't even know how to contact her other than by ordering a pizza from Pete's and to keep doing that would definitely put me into complete creeper territory. I had already pushed that envelope by ordering pizza every night for a week just to try and see her again. No doubt her co-workers were weirded out by the nightly deliveries of the same pizza.

As the night went on, I had to admit I was having an okay time. It still was not really my scene. Bax on the other hand seemed to dance every song with a different woman. He just had a magnetic personality that drew people in. He was fun to be around and therefore almost everyone loved him. It was part of the reason he was so successful in all the different sales jobs he'd had over the years. He was also a firm subscriber to the theory of 'work hard, play hard.' Bax was one of the hardest working, most dedicated people I had ever met, and somehow, he also seemed to always achieve the perfect balance of work and fun. I, on the other hand, had never been able to make that balance happen. For me, it was always all or nothing.

I glanced at my phone and noticed it didn't seem to be getting any service. Kevin must have seen me looking at it because he leaned in. "For some reason, the reception on this side of the club is really shitty, but if you go over by the bathrooms, it's fine."

"Thanks, I might actually head over that way for a few minutes. I'll see you in a bit." Kevin nodded as I got up and walked across the club. Even though it was after normal business hours, some of the suppliers and clients I worked with were in different time zones and I always liked to have access to my phone and email.

Kevin was absolutely right. As soon as I got to the other side, my phone had full service. I was standing there looking at it and not paying attention to anything else when suddenly a lady ran right into my chest. The phone flew out of my hand

and, instinctively, I reached out to grab the woman who had smashed into me to keep her from falling. I grabbed her upper arms and helped steady her.

When it became clear the only thing hitting the ground was my phone, I realized the woman had nestled up against my chest and I was still holding her arms. Even in heels, her head did not come up close to my chin, but I still got a whiff of her strawberry shampoo. It was the best damn thing I had smelt in a long time.

The woman slowly started to lift her head so I could see her face. When her eyes met mine I couldn't believe it. The blue eyes I was looking into had been in my thoughts during the day, and my dreams at night, for the past several weeks. She looked different though... probably because she was at a club and not delivering pizzas, but it was definitely her.

"Pizza Girl?" I asked as I still held on to her arms. It was like I just couldn't make myself let go of her.

Chapter 16
Jenna

"Nick?" I asked in a breathy voice, startled and pleasantly surprised.

I was trying to think of something clever to say, but it was like my brain had short-circuited. Nick continued to hold my arms and keep me nestled to his chest. The skin on my arms sizzled from his touch and I could feel my breath start to quicken as my heart raced.

"Are you okay?" He asked, as his gaze remained transfixed on me. "I was looking at my damn phone and not paying attention to what I was doing." He let go of my arms and bent down to pick up the phone he had dropped when I crashed into him. My skin already yearned for him to touch me again.

"Are you okay? Is your phone okay? I didn't break it when I ran into you, did I? Oh gosh, I did! I am so sorry, that is totally my luck. I will replace it for you." I realized I was talking about a mile a minute and not even taking a breath as I rambled on. I stopped and told myself to get it together and be cool.

Nick stood up and turned his phone over. "Totally fine. I have learned the hard way in my line of work to invest in a good screen protector and case. My phone has taken far worse falls than this." He said, wiping the phone after it's contact with the floor.

"Oh, good!" I breathed a sigh of relief. Unsure of what to say next, I just blurted out the first thing that came to mind. "So you're here. At a club. On a Thursday night." How did people make small talk? I wondered if there was a class online or something like that I could take to teach me how. Clearly, it was a set of skills I did not possess. What if I was too old to learn? Was I destined for a life of awkward conversations now that I was saying yes and trying to put myself out there more? Maybe it was just a side effect of putting yourself out there?

My thoughts were interrupted by Nick's chuckling. "Yeah, I have to admit this is not really my scene, but I promised some guys from my crew that I would come out with them tonight since we are in between jobs right now."

His crew? In between jobs? Who talked like that? Oh, Jesus! He was a drug dealer! Or a bank robber! Those were the only logical explanations. I knew he was too good to be true! My eyes got wide as I started to feel a rising panic.

Nick seemed to sense my apprehension as he quickly elaborated. "I work in construction. We do remodels and new builds. Right now we are waiting on some subcontractors to finish up so we get a few days off in the meantime," he explained, smiling.

"Of course! That is totally what I was thinking!" I giggled nervously. Okay, so maybe being a drug dealer or bank robber were not the only logical explanations.

Nick ran his hand through his hair and seemed to be a bit nervous himself. "So what are you up to tonight? Are you here with someone?" Now, I might be absolutely clueless about making small talk... actually, I had started to doubt my abilities for human interaction as a whole when I was around Nick, but even I could see the hopeful look in Nick's eyes as he read into the greater meaning behind the question. My stomach did a little flip-flop. I couldn't help but smile.

"I'm here with some friends from work and my friend Cassie. This is not my usual scene either." I tried a casual laugh as I looked up at him.

Nick let out a breath and a look of relief flickered across his face. "Good. Going out with friends is good. You looked like you were on your way somewhere when I bumped into you. Am I interrupting anything?"

"No! Not at all! I am glad I ran into you. Literally ran right into you... I mean I was on my way to the restroom and then going back to meet my friends at our table," the words tumbling out of my mouth in a breathless stream.

"Well, maybe I could wait for you and walk you back to your table?" Nick seemed almost hesitant as he asked, which made my heart flutter. Damn, he's cute.

"I would like that. I'll be right back." I tried to sound cool as I responded. Really what I wanted to do was let out a squeal and jump up and down clapping my hands. But I had the embarrasment of our last interaction in my mind and needed to at least try and keep it together this time.

I rushed to the restroom with a giant, goofy grin on my face. Part of me did not expect him to actually be waiting when I returned, but there he was, standing in exactly the same spot. I stopped for a moment just to take all of him in. Nick was clearly over six feet tall and wearing a pair of faded jeans, a black t-shirt, and a black leather jacket with black boots. He looked like a model with a sexy bad boy vibe. I involuntarily licked my lips as I stood there staring at him.

Right at that moment, Nick looked directly at me and a huge smile broke out on his face. It felt like the rest of the room melted away, leaving only the two of us. He started walking towards me and I felt my knees go weak as I took a few steps in his direction. "Hi," I said when I was close to him.

"Hi." Nick stepped in even closer until we were standing so close that our bodies were almost touching.

"Thank you for waiting."

"You are worth waiting for. I can't believe I did not say this earlier, but wow, Pizza Girl, you look... incredible. You are so beautiful in your delivery shirt and now, in that dress." His eyes burned into me lustily.

My face had to be flushed and about as red as my dress. "Thank you," was the only thing I could think of to say back. My mind was overloaded just being that close to him and when he told me I was beautiful in his deep sexy voice... well, I'm kind of surprised I even managed to squeak out a thank you.

"Should we get you back to your table with your friends? I don't want to steal you away from them." Nick's arm brushed against mine and left a trail of goosebumps in its wake.

"Ummmmm... yes. That would probably be a good idea. I'll bet they are wondering where I am." I had lost all concept of time and didn't know how long I had been gone. It must not have been too long, or Cassie would have sent out a search party.

"Lead the way," Nick said as he put his hand on my lower back. I sucked in a gasp of air as he touched my bare skin. I silently told myself to remember to thank Cassie for making me wear the backless dress. I was seriously going to need to stop wearing panties around this guy because, if he could melt them or cause them to burst into flames with nothing but a look, I was afraid of what could happen to them when he actually touched me. The way my body responded to him was insane.

"Holy shit! Jenna! There you are! I was about ready to send a search party out for you! What the hell happened?" Cassie was shouting over the music as she started walking towards Nick and I.

Cassie took about three steps and stopped, as the worry on her face was replaced with a smirk. Her eyes looked over me and locked in on Nick who was still walking behind me with his hand on my lower back.

"Oh! Now I see exactly what happened." Cassie raised an eyebrow and her smirk turned into a full-on grin. "Well, Jenna, are you going to introduce us to your new friend?"

Nick bent down until his mouth was right next to my ear. I could feel his warm breath on my cheek and smell a faint hint of mint as he whispered to me, "Jenna. I like it. Much sexier than Pizza Girl."

Oh. My. God.

Status of panties = dripping wet.

My heart was racing so fast I thought it might burst out of my rib cage. "Cassie, this is Nick. Nick, this is my best friend, Cassie." Nick kept one hand on my back and reached the other out to shake Cassie's. It thrilled me that he remained touching me the entire time.

"Nick! Nice to meet you." Suddenly Cassie got a strange look on her face. "Wait a minute! Are you panty-melting pizza Nick?" My eyes flew wide open and I made a strangled, gurgling noise in my throat. Forget thanking Cassie for the amazing dress. I was going to murder her and hide the body thanks to her big mouth.

For the second time tonight, I wondered how it was that I kept finding myself in these horribly awkward situations.

Chapter 17
Jenna

While I stood there and silently wished for the floor to open up and swallow me whole after Cassie's comment, Nick just threw his head back and let out a big, deep laugh. "Well, I don't know that I have ever been described quite that way before. I will own up to the pizza portion of the description. It's hard not to be a Pete's Pizza fan when it's delivered by Jenna." Nick looked at me and winked when he said my name. Hearing my name on his lips was so hot I kicked myself for not telling him earlier.

Mike stepped forward and extended his hand. "I am Mike. This is Steven and Kimmy."

"Hello!" Kimmy waved from the booth where she was sipping a drink that was almost as bright pink as her dress.

Steven nodded his head in Nick's direction, "Hey."

"Nice to meet all of you," Nick said. "Do all of you work with Jenna?"

Mike eyed Nick suspiciously. "Yes. Are you the daily order of Hawaiian pizza with extra jalapenos? The one that was ordering pizza just to see Jenna?" Mike crossed his arms over his chest.

Jesus! Why did I tell my friends anything? So they could bring it back up at the most inopportune times?

Nick chuckled and ran his fingers through his hair. "Guilty. I wasn't sure how to see her again. I figured the best way was to try and get another pizza delivered."

"I see," said Mike as he continued to stare at Nick. Things were getting awkward. I knew Mike meant well and was looking out for me, but that was not how I had pictured things going. I felt I had to do something quickly, so I blurted out the first thing that popped into my head. "Nick works in construction."

"Wait a minute! I thought you looked familiar! Are you Nick Blaine?" Cassie suddenly seemed even more excited.

"Yes, I am," Nick said with a small smile.

"Well, how about that? I am Cassie Charles. I'm a realtor. I've sold some of the houses your company built and some of the condos you remodeled over by Hudson Street. That is going to be a really nice area when you are finished."

"Thank you, I think I've seen your name on several of the listings over there. Nice to meet you and put a face to the name." Even though Nick was talking to Cassie, he stayed right next to me the whole time. His hand was still resting on my back and he was slowly drawing small circles with his fingers on my bare skin.

Cassie seemed pleased that Nick recognized her name. "Nick, I really appreciate the work your company does and that you only use local subcontractors and hire local crews. I grew up here and Blaine Construction has really put a bunch of people back to work. It's been great for the town!" She said enthusiastically.

Nick seemed to beam at Cassie's statement which, in turn, made me happy. "Thank you! I grew up here too and have no intention of leaving. This town just needed a push forward."

Cassie nodded her head happily in agreement.

"I'm here with some of my crew tonight, I should go back and check in with them. It was nice to meet all of you." He added, before turning to face me. He reached down and squeezed my hand. "It was especially great seeing you, Jenna. I plan on seeing you again soon."

"I would like that," I said, giving Nick my biggest smile so he would know I really meant it.

"Until then..." Nick squeezed my hand again and disappeared into the crowd.

He'd barely left the table when Cassie shouted, "Holy shit! I had no idea Panty Melter Nick was Nick Blaine! You go girl!"

I turned back to Cassie, after watching Nick disappear into the crowd. "I had no idea either. What do you know about him?" I asked, now we had a full name to go with that face, those eyes, and that body.

"I've only heard good stuff. Treats people well and really seems to care about this town. Blaine Construction supports all kinds of community events. The company is known for quality work and is in demand. All of my top commissions have been from his property sites."

"Wow! He sounds almost too good to be true." I glanced back over to where I had seen him last, but he was no longer there.

"Well," said Cassie in a very matter-of-fact tone, "he probably has hookers buried in his basement and his junk is super tiny. Oh, and I bet he kicks puppies and baby rabbits."

"Cass! Stop! You're crazy!" I laughed.

"You know I'm just kidding! In all seriousness, I've never heard a bad word about him from anyone."

"I think he's suspicious," Mike chimed in.

"You think everyone is suspicious," Steven shot back. "Who wants another drink before we head out?"

"Count me in!" Cassie raised her hand.

Steven looked at me and I nodded, "Yes, please!"

"I'll help you grab the drinks, Steven," said Kimmy as she slid out of the booth. I turned to watch Kimmy and Steven disappear into the crowd.

I sat at our table and looked out over the crowd. What a night it had been. I was so excited I had run into Nick. Just like the previous times we'd met, we parted with a desire to see each other again, but no real plan on how that was going to happen. I sighed and played with the cocktail napkin sitting on the table in front of me.

Suddenly, out of the corner of my eye, I saw Nick walking back in my direction. My heart started racing. What was he doing?

Chapter 18
Nick

As I made my way through the crowd back to our table, I was already kicking myself for walking away from Jenna. I had her name but realized as I was walking that I didn't have a phone number or any way to contact her again other than through Pete's Pizza. Damnit, I really had lost all my dating skills over the past few years.

I sat down at the table and rubbed my hands over my face. I had no idea what the fuck to do when it came to her. I liked being around her... maybe a little too much for someone I had only seen a few times. There was something about her that grabbed a hold of me the very first minute I laid eyes on her and had not let me go since. If anything it just gripped me tighter every time I saw her.

"Hey, buddy, where did you disappear to?" Bax pulled up the seat next to me.

"She's here. I ran into her."

"Who is... wait ... oh fuck... you're not talking about Pizza Girl are you?" Bax asked excitedly, looking around at the crowd.

I turned and looked at Bax. "Yeah. Her name is Jenna. She's here with a group of friends."

"Holy shit," Bax let out a low whistle. "What are the chances of that?" he laughed. "If she is here somewhere in this club, then why the fuck are you sitting with this sausage party?" He asked, elbowing me lightly in the ribs.

"I don't know what to do about her," I admitted.

"What do you mean you 'don't know what to do about her?' I know it's been a while since you've been with someone, but the basic, fundamental principles remain the same. Boy meets girl. Boy likes girl, boy pursues girl. Boy takes girl back to his fancy new condo. Boy and girl have mind-blowing sex. Has it really been so long since you used your dick that you don't remember how it works? Do I really need to go over this with you?" Bax tried to give me a stern face but was also clearly trying not to laugh at my predicament.

"You are an idiot," I sighed.

"Admit it, that was pretty funny."

I raised my eyebrow at Bax. "That's not what I meant at all. I don't have time to be pursuing someone or going through the ridiculous process of dating. My sole focus right now is Blaine Construction. I've worked too hard and have too many people counting on me to get distracted and start letting shit slip. Ever since I met her, I haven't been able to stop thinking about her and it's making me crazy. Jesus, Bax I ordered pizza every night for a week just hoping I would see her again. Who does crazy shit like that?" I spluttered, exasperated at who I was with Jenna on my mind. What would happen if she was more than just an idea, if she and I were real?

"A guy who is interested in a girl," Bax said with a shrug of his shoulders. "I think you're making this way more complicated than it needs to be."

"My life is complicated. I don't know how it is going to fit in with someone else's life," I said honestly.

"Why are you trying to mesh your lives together right now? Just have some fun. Listen, Nick, you and I have been friends for a long time and I have never seen you like this over a girl before. That tells me that there must be something really special about this chick and I don't know why you're fighting it so hard. You've done an amazing job with your company, but it has consumed your life for the past few years. You can't keep working this like this forever... it's just not a sustainable, long-term plan for anyone. Go back and talk to her. Ask her out. See what happens. Stop being an asshole about all of this and give yourself a chance to have someone good in your life."

I rubbed my hands over my face again and leaned forward with my elbows on the table. "I hate to admit it, Bax, but you may have a point."

"And that, my friend, is why I am in sales. I can convince anyone   of   anything. It's part of my charm," Bax winked at me and I snorted at him. "So what are you going to do?"

"I don't know..."

Bax interrupted me with an obnoxiously loud noise that I think was supposed to sound like a buzzer. "Wrong answer. Try again."

I sat there in silence as I went back and forth in my mind about what I was going to do. "Ok, let me ask you this," Bax interrupted my internal war, "How do you feel when you're with her?"

"Good," I responded quickly.

Bax looked at me like he was expecting more. "Nick, I'm trying to help you. Stop being a total dick, and making it difficult, giving me one-word answers. Try again, only tell me what   you   like   about   her."
"I like flirting with her and seeing her blush. I like that she's a

little awkward... it's actually really adorable on her. She seems to have a good sense of humor and has a loyal group of friends, which makes me think she is a good friend to them. She is the most beautiful woman I have ever seen and every time I am around her all I want to do is kiss her. I like how I feel when she is around... like all the other day-to-day bullshit I deal with doesn't really matter. I like the way she looks at me with her big blue eyes... like she really cares about me. Not about the fact that I own a company, not about any of that other stuff..." I trailed off when I realized that Bax was staring at me with his mouth slightly open.

"Jesus, dude. This is probably the most feeling I have ever heard you express about anything. Ever. It's honestly a little weird."

"I thought you were trying to help me figure out what to do."

"Right, I just need a minute to actually process Nick Blaine having all of these feelings. You threw me off." Bax shook his head like he was trying to clear it. "If you never saw her again after tonight would you be okay with it, or would you always be wondering 'what if?' What if I had just stopped acting like such a douche canoe and actually talked to her? What if I hadn't fucked everything up? Let me tell you, brother, living in the 'what if' zone is not a good place to be."

"I don't know, there is a lot to consider..." I started to say.

"Stop acting like a jackass and answer the question," Bax interrupted.

I thought about his question carefully before answering, "I would not be okay never seeing her again. She would be a 'what if?'" As soon as I said it out loud, I realized it was completely true. I wanted to see her again. I wanted to get to know her more and see if the crazy feeling between us was actually the beginning of something. I didn't have to figure everything out that night, I could just go with it and see what happened.

Bax cleared his throat. "Which makes me ask again, Nick, if she's somewhere in this club, then what the fuck are you doing sitting over here and not with her?"

I thought for a second. "You're right Bax." I stood up. "I am going to go and find her. Catch up with you tomorrow?"

Bax jumped up from his chair and thrust his fist into the air. "Go get your girl!" he shouted.

I sighed and shook my head. "Too much, Bax. Too much."

Bax laughed. "It just felt like the perfect moment for a cheesy, eighties movie line. Go. Call me tomorrow," he said, slapping my arm good naturedly.

I nodded my head and took off through the crowd. I only hoped I wasn't too late and she hadn't already left. I was relieved when I caught a glimpse of her across the room in her red dress.

As soon as my eyes landed on her, I knew exactly what I was going to do. I took a deep breath and walked up to her.

"Jenna, I don't really do this kind of thing, but do you want to get out of here?" Jenna's mouth opened slightly and she looked completely surprised. I had a moment of panic thinking I had totally misread the entire situation.

"Well, Jenna," Cassie said grinning like the Cheshire Cat. "He asked you a question. What's your answer going to be?"

Jenna paused for what felt like ever before she finally smiled and said, "Yes. My answer is yes."

I didn't even realize I had been holding my breath until she answered. I reached my hand out for hers and intertwined her fingers with mine. I looked right into those beautiful blue eyes and told her with complete sincerity, "Good. I'm glad your answer is yes." Everything else seemed to disappear and it was only the two of us standing there holding hands and smiling at each other.

"Alright, you two crazy kids. Why don't you get on out of here and don't do anything I wouldn't do!" Cassie's voice brought me back to reality.

Steven laughed. "I have not known you for very long and even I know that is a very short list."

Cassie flashed him a big smile. "So true my friend, so true! You only get one life so you might as well make the most of it and seize every moment."

Mike glared at me before looking over at Jenna, but I was too happy to give a shit. "Be careful Jenna," he said. "You have my number if you need to call for any reason."

I looked Mike directly in the eye, "Don't worry, I'll take good care of her and get her home safely." He really needed to back the fuck off.

Jenna quickly added, "Thank you for looking out for me, Mike. I appreciate it." Mike gave her a slight head nod.

"Ready?" I asked Jenna. She quickly nodded her head.

"Good night everyone and thank you for a really fun night. I will see the three of you at work tomorrow and Cass, I'll call you in the morning," she said, waving goodbye to her friends.

Jenna turned back to me and we started walking towards the front door. I put my arm around her and she looked up at me and smiled before moving her body closer.

I knew at that moment, without a doubt, I had made the right choice to go back and find her. Jenna had me under her spell and I quickly realized, much to my surprise, I was just fine with that.

Chapter 19
Jenna

The cool night air hit me as soon as we walked outside. Nick had his arm around me, but I couldn't help letting out a shiver. Cassie and I had left my place in such a rush that I'd forgotten to grab a jacket on our way out.

Nick must have felt me shiver because he immediately asked, "Are you cold? Here take my jacket." Before I could respond, he'd shrugged out of his leather jacket and draped it around my shoulders. It was huge on me but it smelled like him and I instantly felt wrapped in his warmth.

We continued to walk down the sidewalk to the parking lot hand in hand. The realization hit me that we might have very different expectations about where the night was headed. I needed to find out quickly. I couldn't think of a smooth way to bring it up, so in typical Jenna fashion, I just blurted out the first thing that came to mind.

"I'm not going to sleep with you tonight. I don't do that. I mean I don't leave places with men I just met and go somewhere to... you know. I am not saying it is never going to happen but it is certainly not going to happen tonight. Maybe after I get to know you a little better... if we see each other again..."

We had stopped in the middle of the sidewalk and Nick looked at me with a confused expression on his face. Great. I had totally blown it. He was going to laugh at my crazy outburst and everything would be over before it even began. I took a deep breath and started talking again. "I totally understand if you want me to just leave now if you were thinking that's what we were leaving to go and do. I can call an Uber..."

Nick smiled at me. "Jenna, please stop and take a deep breath for me."

"Okay," I whispered.

"My turn to comment on the subject?" It looked like Nick's eyes were shining with amusement, which was not helping to settle my nerves.

"Yes, I'm sorry." I looked away from Nick as soon as the words were out of my mouth.

"Hey," he said gently, putting one finger on my jaw and turning my head back towards him. "Do not apologize. You have nothing to apologize for. I can tell you in all honesty that was not the reason I asked you to leave with me tonight. Don't get me wrong, I have fantasized about what it would be like, but not tonight and not like this."

"Okay... now I feel awkward and embarrassed. I didn't mean to ruin the moment." As embarrassed as I was, I was not letting the fact that Nick said he had fantasized about me escape my notice. I was taking that little golden nugget of information and tucking it away to analyze later.

Nick looked at me with sincerity in his eyes. "You didn't ruin anything and you have nothing to be embarrassed about. It's an important conversation to have."

"Okay," I said with a small smile, still not sure if I had killed the mood or not.

"The reason I wanted to leave with you tonight is that I wanted a chance to talk to you and get to know you more. That is virtually impossible inside of a club, with all of the people and music. I thought we could go somewhere and talk. Does that sound like something you would like to do?" He seemed so sincere, I was starting to like him even more.

I smiled at him and clutched his jacket around me a little tighter. "That sounds great. Thank you."

"You're in the driver's seat, Jenna. We are not going to do anything you don't feel comfortable with. Okay?"

"Okay." I smiled a little wider, it was nice the lengths he was going to, to reassure me and make me feel comfortable. Hot and sweet, how did I get this lucky?

Nick had a mischievous smirk on his face. "Now, that said, I was hoping to kiss you at some point tonight. How do you feel about that?" Nick's voice had grown huskier as he moved closer to me. He put his finger under my chin and tipped my head up until I was looking directly into his eyes. Even under the faint light of the street lights, I could see his eyes had grown darker and were filled with lust. It made my head spin. I liked that feeling. I liked it a lot. I liked being with him.

"Jenna?" Nick whispered waiting for my answer.

I continued to stare into his eyes and out of nervousness and excitement, I started to chew on my lower lip. Nick's gaze instantly fell to my lips and I could hear his breath catch. It was thrilling to see him look at me like that. Like he desired me. "Yes," my voice was so breathy that I barely recognized it.

Nick smiled and reached down to gently take my hand in his as we resumed walking. "Good," was all he said. It was only a little further until we reached the club's parking lot. "Here we are."

"Wait? What? We're here? Where's your car? I don't see a car here..." I started to get nervous as I glanced around at the mostly empty lot.

"I didn't drive my car tonight, I have my Harley with me. Have you ever ridden before?" Sure enough, Nick was standing next to a big, badass-looking motorcycle. I felt panic rise in my throat. I had never been on a motorcycle before. My mother's voice rang clear as day inside my head; *'Those things are nothing but a death trap!'*

I found my voice and managed to squeak out an answer. "No. I never have."

Nick gave me a big grin. Damn that sexy grin of his and the fact it made my brain all scrambled and my lady parts scream with excitement. "You ready for your first ride? You can wear my helmet." Nick pulled a big black helmet off the back of the bike and handed it to me.

Now it was Cassie's voice in my head telling me to say yes and be open to the experience. I took a deep breath and tried to muster up some confidence. "Yes?" I squeaked out.

Nick raised his eyebrows at me. "That sounded more like a question than an answer." Okay, so maybe I hadn't been able to muster up any confidence. The idea of riding his motorcycle was only slightly above 'absolutely terrifying' in my mind.

"Ummmmm... Yes," I said trying to sound at least a little more confident than before.

Nick paused and looked at me for a moment, I'm sure the look on my face was one of absolute panic. "Jenna, the words coming out of your mouth are yes, but everything else about you is screaming no. What's going on? Talk to me." Damn he was good, everything about him seemed so right, so strong, so reassuring.

I sighed. I felt like I was in the midst of another potential mood-killing moment and if he didn't already, Nick was soon going to regret asking me to leave with him. "Alright. Here is the total truth." Might as well just throw it all out there so he could leave without wasting any more of his time. "My life is kind of a mess so I have been trying to be more open to new experiences and opportunities by saying yes when I would normally say no."

"Ahhhhhhhh... I see." Nick rubbed his chin for a moment. Here it comes... the 'this is just not going to work' moment. I braced myself for what he would say next. "So riding the bike would usually be a no-go, but you're trying to be open-minded about it. Fair enough. If you really don't want to ride, that's absolutely fine. We can call an Uber and I'll just pick up the bike later. Remember, I told you we're not going to do anything you're not comfortable with."

It took a moment for Nick's words to sink in, since they were not at all what I expected. Any concerns I had seemed to melt away as Nick spoke. I realized he really was being considerate and respectful of me and my feelings. It made me feel... well it made me feel safe and like I could trust him.

"You know what? Let's do it. I trust you. Yes, I would like to ride your motorcycle with you, Nick."

"You sure?" He asked, looking intently at me, trying to filter out the truth from my words.

"Yes! Yes, I am. Let's go!" I pulled the helmet on and Nick went over a few of the basics about riding with him. I climbed on the back of his bike and wrapped my arms tightly around him as I pressed my front up against his back. My dress rode all the way up my thigh, but I didn't care. It was one of the most thrilling moments of my life.

The engine roared to life. "Ready?" Nick asked. I gave him a thumbs up. "Alright, hang on tight, here we go!"

I let out a little squeal and clutched on tighter to Nick as the motorcycle began to move. Nick chuckled as we pulled out of the parking lot and started to drive down the road past the club.

I, Jenna Morgan, was riding a motorcycle holding on to the most handsome man I had ever seen.

When did this become my life?

Chapter 20
Jenna

I'm not sure what was more intoxicating. The feeling of the wind on my skin and the sheer power of the motorcycle between my legs, or the warmth of being pressed up against Nick's incredibly muscular body and breathing in his deliciously spicy scent. Either way, I was hooked.

We rode towards the outskirts of town. It wasn't long until the houses were further and further apart. We turned and went up a winding road before Nick pulled the bike over on a bluff and turned off the engine.

"Here, let me help you." Nick grabbed me around the waist and lifted me off of the motorcycle.

"Woah! You just lifted me off that thing like I weigh nothing! "I was momentarily surprised. I don't think anyone had ever just picked me up like that before.

Nick laughed and reached for my hand. "Come on. There's something I want to show you."

Nick and I walked across the parking area and over to the edge of the bluff. I couldn't help but gasp when I looked out to where Nick was pointing. "Oh my goodness! Look at all the lights! You can see the entire town from here. Nick, it's so beautiful!"

Nick wrapped his arm around me and pulled me closer to him. "This is one of my favorite spots. In the daytime, it feels like you can just keep looking out forever, but at night, all the lights from town look almost magical."

I snuggled into Nick's side a little more. I seemed to fit just perfectly up against him and couldn't get enough. "How did you find it?" I asked as I continued to gaze at the twinkling lights in front of me.

"I don't remember exactly." I was pressed so tightly up against Nick I could feel his deep husky voice vibrate through me. "It seems like I have always just known about it. I grew up here and with the type of work I do, I'm constantly looking for new building sites. There isn't much of this area that I haven't seen."

"Thank you for sharing this with me. It's really special."

We stood there in comfortable silence before Nick finally said, "Can I ask you something?"

"Of course," I answered quickly, not having any idea where Nick's question was going.

"What is the deal with you and Mike? He seems very protective of you. Is he an ex-boyfriend or something like that?"

I was so surprised by the question and the hint of insecurity in Nick's voice that it took me a second to regroup and respond. "Oh no! Nothing like that at all. I've only known him since I started working at Pete's Pizza. He's just really protective. Poor guy lives with four younger sisters and his mom, I think it's just in his nature to be protective of people he cares about."

"How much does he care about you?" Nick asked. Was that jealousy I heard in his voice? It couldn't be. Nick and I had only just met... he couldn't be jealous... could he?

"Strictly friends. I promise, nothing more," I assured him.

"Good to know," Nick said, sounding relieved before he quickly changed the subject. "So, tell me more about this 'saying yes' thing you were talking about earlier."

I turned and slid from Nick's side to his front so I could look at his face. He brought both of his hands down to rest on my hips as I brought mine up and put my palms on his chest. I looked into his eyes for a moment before I took a deep breath. "I'm going to lay it all out on the table. You can choose to do what you wish with the information."

Nick wrinkled up his face a little. "Ok, this sounds rather ominous."

"More like a big mess. Or to use one of Cassie's favorite phrases, it might even be 'total dumpster fire' level." Nick was listening intently and so I continued on. "For as long as I can remember, I have had this plan about what my life was going to look like and where it was going. I took great comfort in that plan and have stuck to it. A little over six months ago, my plan started to crumble, and about a month ago, it blew apart."

"Okay," Nick said slowly. "So what kind of crumbling are we talking about?"

I quickly continued, determined not to lose my nerve. "I was in a relationship almost the entire time I was in college that abruptly ended the day I graduated. At the time, I was lost and heartbroken, but now, with some distance, I see that it was toxic and I am much better off without it."

Nick's voice was a low growl as he pulled me a little closer to him. "Just so we are clear, I have no idea who this guy is, but I already hate the fucker for whatever he did and the way he treated you."

I gave Nick a small smile. I did not doubt what he said was the absolute truth. "Thank you. My life went on pause for a while after the breakup. I was enrolled to start law school last fall, however, I ended up deferring it for a year and am going to start this fall instead."

"Wow! You are going to law school! That is incredible! Congratulations! Is it close by?" The enthusiasm in his voice was so genuine, making me like him even more and wanting to share even more with him.

"It's about a four-hour drive from here." I briefly paused before I continued with my story. "After the breakup, law school was still part of my master plan and so was working at a very prestigious law firm. I got an entry-level clerical job at my fantasy law firm and was hoping to work my way up through the ranks there. About a month ago, I suddenly got fired from that job."

Nick was quiet for a few seconds. "Do you mind if I ask what for?"

I shook my head. "I don't mind, but I am not sure what for. They just said it was not a good fit. It was still within my probationary period, so there was not really anything to be done about it."

Nick pulled me into a hug. It felt so perfect and so right. "That sucks," he said talking into my hair as I buried my face into his chest. "I'm sorry that happened to you."

I pulled my head back and looked back up at him. "After that, Cassie suggested I make some changes in my life, so we came up with the 'saying yes' plan. Basically, any time something comes up that I would have previously said no to, I need to say yes and see what happens. The idea is to be open to new experiences and opportunities." I thought it was going to feel weird telling Nick everything, but I actually didn't feel that way at all. Maybe it was the fact that he seemed genuinely interested... or maybe it was because he was so freaking sexy I had lost my mind standing near him. Honestly, it was probably a heavy mixture of the two, with a little boost from the drinks I'd had at the club earlier.

"So, how is this 'yes' plan working out for you?"

I gave Nick a coy smile and decided to be bold. "Well, I'm here with you right now, so I would say pretty good."

Nick leaned in and kissed me on top of my head. "I am glad to hear that," he said in his husky voice and it was like a current zinged through my body. I could still feel the spot where his lips touched me and for a fleeting moment, I considered never washing my hair again just to preserve the kiss.

"In all seriousness," I said, as I tried to keep myself focused on the moment and not fall off into a series of highly naughty thoughts about where else Nick could kiss me. "I think it's going pretty well. It's how I landed the job at Pete's and through Pete's I've made some new friends, who I really like and who I have a lot of fun with. I'm usually pretty quiet and have a harder time meeting new people, so it is a pretty big deal for me."

"So what other new experiences have you had as the result of saying yes?"

"Well, going to the club tonight is something I would have likely said no to before. Same thing with the outfit I am wearing. Way outside of my comfort zone. Cassie played fairy godmother tonight and gave me a bit of a makeover."

Nick leaned in so he was whispering in my ear. "I do have to say I admire her work. You are incredibly beautiful. When I ran into you at the club you took my breath away. There was no way I wanted to let you out of my sight once I laid eyes on you." A shiver ran all the way through me from my head to my toes and back up to my head again... only this time it was not from the cold air. Nick's breath was warm on my cheek and the intimacy of the moment made my pulse race.

"Thank you," my voice was barely above a whisper. I don't think anyone had ever talked to me like that before and I was not quite sure what to say.

Nick moved his head slightly until his lips were almost touching mine. "Jenna?" he said, his breath growing unsteady.

"Yes?" I whispered back.

"I want to kiss you right now. Is that okay?"

"Yes."

"Is that a real yes because you want it to happen or a yes because it is part of the 'yes' plan?" Nick whispered against my lips. I could feel his grip on my hips tighten and I was about ready to explode with desire for him.

I wanted it. Badly. So badly that if it didn't happen soon, I would pass out from need. Was that even a thing? If not, I was going to become the first documented case. "A real yes," my voice was still barely a whisper.

That was all it took before Nick's mouth came crashing down on mine. I let out a soft moan and grabbed the front of his t-shirt with both hands. Nick wrapped one arm around my waist pulling me flush against him as the other hand came to the back of my neck and his fingers wound into my hair.

I had never been kissed like that before. It was so... I don't know if there is a word in the English language to express how freaking amazing it was. I considered myself to be ruined for all other kisses, since no one was ever going to kiss me like Nick Blaine.

After a few moments, we pulled apart, both of us breathing heavily. I looked up at Nick through half-lidded eyes and reached my hand up to my lip. They felt swollen from his kisses and it was the best feeling I had ever felt.

Chapter 21
Nick

"Wow," Jenna whispered as her hand reached up to her mouth and she traced her lips with her fingers.

Holy fucking shit, 'wow' was right. I struggled to get my breath back under control along with the rest of me. I don't think I had ever been that impacted by a kiss before. Yeah, I had kissed my fair share of women, but it was always just kind of a means of getting to the next thing. Though with Jenna... holy fuck. It was like an event in and of itself. My head was spinning and I couldn't think of the last time I was so turned on. Her soft lips pressing against mine as she clutched my shirt in her hands like she was holding on for dear life. And when she moaned... holy shit, when she moaned into my mouth, I about lost it right there on the spot.

I cleared my throat. "Wow is right." Lamest fucking thing I could have possibly said, but I still couldn't quite think clearly. There was something about Jenna that scrambled my thoughts every time I was around her and after that kiss... man, I didn't know if I was ever going to quite recover from that kiss.

We just stood there holding on to each other as we tried to catch our breath. The only sound around us was our rapidly beating hearts. The fact she seemed to be just as impacted by that kiss as I was only made the whole thing hotter.

I started doing multiplication tables in my mind, trying to distract myself in an attempt to get my head and my dick back under control. *9 x 9 is 81. 8 x 8 is 64. 7 x 7 is 49...*

Suddenly a thought occurred to me. I was in the perfect situation. Jenna was going to law school in the fall, which meant her time in town was limited... she was only going to be there for a few more months. We could hang out and have some fun, but there was an expiration date on it. There was no doubt we were attracted to each other, but I had other shit going on in my life that I couldn't be distracted from in the long run. A short-term distraction, that I could manage. Just enough to get her out of my system and then she would go to law school and I would go back to focusing solely on Blaine Construction.

No attachment, no expectations, and when the expiration date came, a clean end to things. It really couldn't be any more perfect. I just had to figure out how to make it happen.

"So, the 'yes' plan is all about having new experiences and new opportunities, correct?" I asked, trying my best not to sound too excited about what I was thinking.

"That is the idea." Jenna nodded. Her voice still had a breathy quality to it which made every nerve in my body sizzle.

"Are you going to be here until you leave for law school in the fall?" I needed to stay focused on the matter at hand and not think about how her tongue darted out and lightly licked her bottom lip as she nodded her head. I blinked my eyes trying to stay on target. "Then, when it's time for school to start, you are moving to be closer to school, right?" Dammit, Blaine! Stay cool!

"That's what I am planning," Jenna confirmed, nodding her head. It was going to be perfect. The perfect plan.

"I have an idea," I said with a smile, as trying to contain myself grew more and more difficult. I couldn't believe my luck.

Jenna smiled. "Does it involve more kisses with you? If so, then I'm all in." She blushed as soon as the words were out of her mouth. Jesus, it drove me wild when she blushed.

"That could definitely be arranged." I chuckled and wiggled my eyebrows at her which only made the blush deepen. I had to keep talking or else I was going to start kissing her again and get distracted. I jumped right in. "How about, during the time you are here, I help you say yes to some new experiences. Before you go, we can cross off some of those things that you have always wanted to do, but so far have not."

Jenna studied my face for a moment. "What's the catch?" She asked quizzically.

"No catch. I like you Jenna, and I like spending time with you. The last few years I have been so focused on getting my company up and running it's left virtually no time for doing anything outside of work. This will be great for me too... I can get out and have some fun with you before you leave. It will be a nice break from working all the time. So what do you think?"

I couldn't help but look at her expectantly as she mulled it over. Her face broke into a huge smile. "Yes! I am all in!"

"Is that a real yes or a yes plan 'yes'?" I teased.

Jenna laughed and lightly swatted me on the arm. Even the light brush of her fingers against my bicep left my skin aching for more of her touch. "It's a real yes!"

"Good," I was relieved. It was going to be great. Just fun with no mess. "As much as I don't want this night to end, I should probably get you home, princess, before you turn into a pumpkin. It's getting late."

"When will I see you again?" Jenna asked hesitantly. I almost asked her if she wanted to come home with me, but I didn't want to push things too far, especially in light of our previous conversation outside the club. It was pretty clear the whole night had been filled with things that were outside of her usual activities. Plus, I really did want to see her again and I didn't want it to just turn into a one-time hook-up.

"Do you work tomorrow night?" I asked.

Jenna frowned. "I do. I work for the next few nights."

I didn't want the night to end without a plan to see her again. "How about lunch tomorrow? I can pick you up at noon." I quickly tried to think of what I had in my schedule for the next day, and luckily, because it was Friday and we were between jobs, it was a pretty light day.

Jenna's face immediately brightened and I felt my heart skip a beat. "I would like that." Her smile was one of the most beautiful things I had ever seen.

"Good. Let's get you back on the bike and take you home." I helped Jenna climb back on and I slid in front of her. She wrapped her arms around my stomach and pressed herself up against me, resting her head on my back. Dammit, she felt good. I was so pleased I had more of this in my immediate future. More of her.

Everything was going to work out great. Spending time and having fun with a smart, beautiful woman for the summer. She had her plans and I had mine, so when the time came, we would go our separate ways. Since there was an end date in sight and she was going to be working full time, being with Jenna would not distract me from Blaine Construction. There was no way there were any downsides.

When we got to Jenna's apartment, I walked her up to the front door and made sure she got in safely. We kissed goodnight and repeated our plans to meet the next day.

As I walked down the steps to her apartment building and back to the parking lot, part of me missed her already. If I missed her after only spending a few hours with her, what was it going to be like after spending a few months together?

I shook my head as I fired up my bike and pulled out of her parking lot. That just was not going to be an option. I was not going to fit into her plans to go to law school and she was not going to fit into mine with Blaine Construction. We were only going to fit together for a short window of time, and when the window closed, that was going to be the end.

Chapter 22
Jenna

I woke up the next morning and smiled as the memories of the previous night flooded my mind. I rolled over and grabbed my phone. I noticed that there were a few new text messages.

Mike: *"Just wanted to make sure that you made it home last night. Let me know if you're OK or if I need to kick someone's ass."*

Cassie: *"I hope you are waking up wrapped around a handsome hunk of panty-melting hotness. If not, give me a call. I need details about last night. If you are, get off your fucking phone and take full advantage of that hot man in your bed."*

Nick: *"Good morning, beautiful. Can't wait to see you today."*

My smile just grew bigger as I read through each of the messages and realized all of those people cared about me. I sent a quick response to Mike to let him know I was okay and one to Nick that I was excited about our lunch date.

I called Cassie who picked up on the first ring. "Well, well, well. Good morning sleeping beauty. I'm going to guess that since you're calling me, you and Nick are not in bed together eating pizza after working up a huge appetite?"

I laughed. "Nope, I am in bed alone and starving. No man and no pizza with me."

"So what happened after you left last night wild woman, Jenna?"

"Well, he took me for a ride and we went to a bluff overlooking the city then..."

"Wait!" Cassie interrupted. "What do you mean he took you for a ride? Like in the hot, dirty sense? Took you for a ride on his bicycle? Bought you a pony ride? I need clarification and details. Give me details!"

"On his motorcycle."

I could feel Cassie smiling through the phone. "Shut. The. Front. Fucking. Door. You rode on his motorcycle with him? I thought riding a motorcycle was something you said you would never do! What happened to my best friend who swore all motorcycles were nothing but, and I am quoting you directly here, 'a death trap'."

"Well, your best friend said yes and hopped on the back of Nick's motorcycle." The excitement of the evening was coming through my voice as I thought about riding behind Nick, pressed against him with the wind in my hair. Maybe I could get a leather jacket? I was never a leather jacket-wearing kind of woman, but maybe after my night with Nick, I could be!

"I'm glad I was already sitting down for this conversation or I may have just passed out. So tell me, biker momma, what did you think?" I could hear Cassie take a sip of her coffee.

"It was amazing. Unlike anything I have ever experienced before." I smiled to myself... it wasn't just the motorcycle ride that I was referring to. I absentmindedly reached my hand up and touched my lips.

"I am going to take a moment, Jenna Morgan, and point out that it is unlike anything you have ever experienced before because you never allowed yourself to have these experiences before. That is the magic of saying yes instead of saying no and living under a rock."

The comment about living under a rock rubbed me the wrong way. "You know I wasn't always like this, Cassie," I snapped back, a little harsher than I intended.

"Woah there momma. Like what? A wild, wanton goddess on the back of a motorcycle?" Cassie teased. I knew she was trying to make up for the under a rock comment.

I sighed. "No, Cassie. Unsure of myself. Afraid to try new things and step out of my comfort zone. It's just after..."

"I know, sweetie and I am sorry if I pushed the joking too far," Cassie's voice was soft and I knew it was a sincere apology. "I don't want you to spend another second thinking about that limp-dicked, loser ex-boyfriend of yours. Enjoy this moment and what you shared with Nick last night. Don't let the king of darkness steal away your happiness."

I ran my fingers through my hair and climbed out of bed as I continued to talk to Cassie. I needed some coffee. I padded down the hallway and into the kitchen. "You're right. Sometimes it is just hard. We were together for almost four years. You can't just erase that in a few months."

"I would like to erase him. Permanently." Cassie had a bit of a snarl to her voice. She had never liked Brett and when the break up happened... well, Brett had better hope that he never crossed paths with Cassie. I turned on the coffee maker as Cassie continued, "Now I need to cleanse my brain after this terrible turn in the conversation. Tell me more about hot Nick and his motorcycle."

"He kissed me, Cassie. It was so electric and the single best kiss of my life. I don't think any other kiss can possibly ever be as good as that one. I can still feel him on my lips." I closed my eyes and leaned against the counter as I pressed my lips together. I could still feel the warmth of his body pulling me closer while his fingers clutched my hair.

"I'm happy for you, babe. You should, and deserve to, be kissed like that all the time."

"None of this would have happened if you hadn't convinced me to make some changes and start saying yes. Thank you, Cass. How was the rest of your night?" I reached up and grabbed a coffee mug.

"It was good," Cassie said. I could instantly tell she was trying to hide something.

I poured some of the coffee into my mug. "That's it? 'Good?' What happened after I left, Cassie Charles?" I tried to use my stern voice so she would know I was onto her. Cassie was uncharacteristically quiet on the other end of the line. "Cass?" I asked, starting to worry a little.

"Mike gave me a ride home last night. We sat in his car in my driveway and talked for almost two hours. It was really nice," Cassie blurted out very quickly. I don't think she even stopped to take a breath.

I was surprised at such behavior from her. It was very un-Cassie-like. "Why didn't you invite him inside?" I asked as I poured some cream and sugar into my coffee.

Cassie let out a heavy sigh. "Because Mike is a nice guy and not my type. I would chew him up and spit him back out before he even knew what happened. Staying in the car just seemed like a much safer option than going inside where there is a bed, a sofa, a countertop in the kitchen, a shower, a dining room table... you get the idea."

Suddenly it hit me and I almost dropped my coffee cup in complete shock. "Wait!" I shouted. "Do you like Mike?"

"He is cute, I'll give him that, but he is just so incredibly... nice. Plus I think I scare him a little," Cassie said with a chuckle.

"You scare a lot of people when they first meet you," I pointed out, only half kidding.

Cassie's chuckle turned into a full-on, loud burst of laughter. "It is one of my more charming personality traits. Enough about me and nice boy Mike. When are you going to see Nick again?"

I smiled as my stomach fluttered. "For lunch today. He's picking me up at noon."

"It's a little after eleven right now. You had better get that cute ass of yours in gear if you want to be ready on time. Wear your yellow sundress with the spaghetti straps and the little flowers on it."

I was suddenly hit with a sense of panic realizing I only had an hour until he was going to be there. I didn't realize I had slept in so late. I grabbed my coffee and started to head back to my bedroom. "Yikes! I need to get moving. Cass, that dress is too short."

"It is not too short, just be sure you wear some pretty, lacey panties. You'll be fine."

"Too much, Cass!" I frantically started flipping through everything in my closet.

Cassie laughed. "I'm hanging up now. Have a good time on your date!"

I quickly jumped into the shower. Once I was done, I pulled my hair on top of my head in a messy bun while swiping on some mascara and lip-gloss. I stood in front of my closet still unsure about what to wear. Finally, I grabbed the yellow sundress and threw it on. I didn't have time to question my decision since it was noon and there was a knock on my door.

He had arrived. It was happening. I was going on a date with Nick. I smiled as I opened the door.

Chapter 23
Jenna

"Hi," I said as I opened the door. Nick looked at me and smiled. I just about melted into a big puddle on the floor.

"Hi. You look amazing, Jenna. Like a ray of sunshine. How did you know I have an absolute weakness for a beautiful woman in a sundress?" Everything he said was perfect. How did he do that?

"Lucky guess," I smiled. I would have to remember to thank Cassie later for the dress suggestion. So far she was totally winning with outfit suggestions. Maybe I needed to think about upgrading my wardrobe a little...

If I looked like a ray of sunshine then Nick looked hotter than the whole dang sun. He was wearing a long-sleeve, gray Henley shirt with the sleeves pushed up and his tattoos peeking out. His brown eyes were hidden behind his aviator sunglasses, but I could feel them raking over my body.

"You ready to go?" He asked, holding his hand out to me.

I placed my hand in his. "Yes. Where are we going?"

"It's a surprise. Do you like surprises?" The way Nick said that made me think he was talking about more than just where he was taking me for lunch.

"Ummmmmm... I am just going to say yes." Actually, I really never liked surprises. I've always wanted to know what was going on so I could plan accordingly. However, saying yes was about opening myself up to new experiences so I was going to go with it... even if that experience was a surprise.

Nick smiled and let out a deep laugh at my answer. "I think you're going to like this one."

We walked hand in hand down to the parking lot where I looked around for Nick's bike. "Are we walking? I don't see your motorcycle."

"No bike today. I'm on my lunch break from work, so I have my truck. The bike doesn't work well on construction sites." Nick walked over to a brand-new-looking shiny, black pick-up truck. He opened the passenger side door and helped me get in. Then walked around to the driver's side and climbed up into the seat.

Nick's eyes were twinkling at me and he had a sexy, half-cocked grin on his face that seemed to bring the temperature in the cab of the truck up about twenty degrees. "Buckle up. You never know how wild a ride it is going to be," he said with a wink.

The double meaning of his words was not lost on me. I clenched my legs together and wiggled in my seat as I buckled the seatbelt. I turned to Nick and gave him a flirty little smile. "Looks like I'm ready for your wild ride, Mr. Blaine. Question is... how ready are you?" I was flirting again – who was *this Jenna?*

For once, Nick was the one blushing. I was loving every second of it. "Your seatbelt Mr. Blaine. You are not buckled up. How can you be ready for this ride?" I gave Nick an overly innocent look and waved my hand towards his seatbelt still hanging by the door. Nick let out a whoosh of air followed by a deep chuckle. I smiled back. "That red on your cheeks is a good look on you."

Nick shook his head. "You never cease to surprise me."

"There's a lot about me you don't know." I intended for that statement to come out flirty, but instead, it just sounded solemn. A heavy feeling filled the cab of the truck. I tried to recover quickly so as not to ruin the moment. "Speaking of surprises, where are we going for lunch?" Good job, Jenna. He already said where we were going was a surprise and he wasn't going to say. I mentally cringed and tried to look straight ahead out the window.

Nick stared at me for a minute not saying anything while I tried to do everything in my power not to make eye contact with him. I started to panic that with one statement I had ruined everything. All of my old insecurities started to flood back in full force as I sat there, just waiting for him to tell me he had changed his mind and to get out of the truck. My chest started to tighten and I could feel beads of perspiration break out on my forehead. My hands felt clammy and I didn't know what to do with them so I rested them in my lap, trying to keep them still and not overly fidgety. Damnit, that was embarrassing.

Finally, Nick spoke and I let out a breath that I didn't even know I was holding. "Hey, what is going on right now? Is everything okay?" Nick spoke softly as he took off his sunglasses. He had a look of genuine concern in his deep brown eyes. Despite his tenderness, my chest felt heavy and I felt like I was having trouble breathing.

"I'm sorry," I stammered, still not able to make eye contact with him for more than a brief second or two at a time. "I spoke without thinking. If you want me to get out and go now, I will totally understand." I looked down at my hands which were fidgeting in my lap, despite my best efforts to calm myself.

Nick turned so he was facing me. "Don't apologize. You have nothing to apologize for. Everything seemed to be all good and then suddenly you checked out and looked genuinely panicked for a few minutes. If this is too much, we can do something else. I don't want you to get out, and you haven't ruined anything." He was so calm and his tone was so reassuring.

Gosh, he was so sweet and I was such a big hot mess. The only thing I knew was that I did not want to ruin everything and I did not want him going anywhere. I started to feel the hot prick of tears under my eyelids. I was so embarrassed for acting like that. I hadn't had a panic attack in months.

So I did the only thing I could think of. "Yes," I said in a small voice.

"Yes, what? Yes, you want to do something else?" Nick asked in that same gentle tone he had used earlier.

"No! Not that! I am sorry. Gosh, I just can't seem to get this right." I paused and took a shallow shaky breath. "Yes, I want to go to the surprise with you. I am sorry that I am acting this way. It has just been a long time since I have done anything like this and I am obviously really rusty." I turned to face Nick and tried to give him a small smile. He reached out and took hold of my hand. He held it so gently and rubbed his thumb across my palm. Suddenly the weight was lifted and I felt I could breathe again. I could also feel myself slowly starting to relax a little.

"You sure?" Nick asked, still holding my hand.

"Yes, absolutely. Let's do this."

Chapter 24
Nick

We drove in silence. I kept sneaking glances over at Jenna and figured that after what had happened, I would follow her lead. If she needed some silence I would give that to her.

I wasn't exactly sure what happened, but I did know seeing her like that triggered something deep within me. I suddenly had this insanely strong urge to protect her and do whatever I could to help her get through whatever was happening. The only other time I felt a surge of protectiveness like that was the night before when she mentioned how toxic her last relationship was. I could only guess, but I would bet money that the look of panic on her face had something to do with that fucker ex-boyfriend she'd mentioned.

My hands clenched around the steering wheel until my knuckles turned white. The thought of someone mistreating her made me so angry. I glanced over at Jenna who had her head pressed up against the passenger side window with her eyes closed. She was so incredibly beautiful, smart, and funny. There was also a very innocent and awkward quality about her which I found quite endearing. I couldn't believe how strongly I felt after spending such a small amount of time with her. I had never felt that way about anyone before... Jesus, I don't think I had ever had so many feelings before, period.

Part of me started to worry that my plan of spending time with her and then having it end when she left for school was going to be harder than I thought. The longer I was around her, the more I wanted to be around her. I liked how easy it was to be with her. To flirt with her and make her blush or laugh. To talk to her. When I was with her I wasn't Nick Blaine, owner of Blaine Construction... person responsible for everything and everyone. I wasn't the guy who had invested several years of his life in his business and now felt like he was being impossibly pulled in a bunch of different directions. When I was with her, I was just a guy who liked a girl and was pretty sure that the girl liked him back. The bottom line was, it just felt really good to be with Jenna.

I pulled into the parking lot of our destination and when the truck stopped, Jenna blinked her eyes open. "Where are we?" she asked in a soft voice.

"The park." I smiled at the confused look on her face. Everything had been last-minute planning because I had been unexpectedly stuck on the phone with investors that morning. A few new projects were going on in the area and I was talking to people at each one.

"The park?" she asked looking around.

"Yep. Hang on just a minute." I jumped out of the truck and opened her door, helping her out. It was a beautiful day. The sun was shining, it was a perfect temperature, and all of the flowers were in full bloom, the leaves of the trees were lush and green and swaying gently in the light breeze. Jenna started smiling as she looked around and my heart instantly did a little pitter-patter. I hoped that being there was helping her to feel better.

'This is only temporary', I told myself. *'Only until she leaves for law school. You are not going to disrupt her plans*

and she is not going to disrupt yours', I continued. *'She is going to be moving and you are going to be staying here. It won't work beyond this short time together.'*

I was pulled out of my own head by Jenna's excitement. "This place is so beautiful! I have been here before, but I don't think I ever really appreciated it." Her eyes grew big as I pulled out a picnic basket and blanket from the back of the truck. Jenna let out a little squealing noise and clapped her hands together. "Are we going to have a picnic here, at the park?"

"Yes, and it sounds by your excitement level, this was a good choice."

Jenna laughed; the sound was beautiful and warmed my insides. "This was a great choice! I have never been to a picnic like this before! Thank you, Nick! Thank you so much!"

Her excitement made me feel incredible... that I was able to do something for her to make her so happy. I immediately started to wonder what else I could do for her to keep that smile on her face.

Who was I? When did I turn into a guy who got so excited doing something to make someone smile? When did I turn into this guy who cared so much about how another person felt?

When Jenna first delivered a Hawaiian pizza with extra jalapenos, that's when. As much as I wanted to try and deny it, I had been mesmerized by her since the very first moment I laid eyes on her. That was a dangerous thing. I had a lot on the line with so many different deals in the works for Blaine Construction and there were a whole lot of people counting on me for employment. I had to stay focused on everything I was doing to keep all of the balls I was trying to juggle up in the air.

For the moment, though, I was just going to enjoy my time with her. I leaned forward and kissed Jenna softly on the lips as I balanced the blanket and picnic supplies in one hand and reached for her with the other. "Well, in that case, would you like to go on a picnic with me, Jenna?" I smiled knowing what her answer would be.

"Yes! I am saying yes!" Jenna burst out enthusiastically.

I gestured ahead of us with the hand holding the basket. "There is a rose garden just up to the left. I thought we would put the blanket out there and eat. It's usually a quiet place during weekdays."

We rounded the corner and Jenna gasped. It really was an incredible sight. There were, what looked like, hundreds of roses in every color growing as far as the eye could see. Jenna turned to me. "Wow! This is so beautiful! I'm speechless! How do you know all these amazing places?"

I spread out the blanket and started to get the food out. "My mom belongs to a gardening club and one of their big community projects is caring for this rose garden. I spent a whole lot of time here as a kid playing while my mom tended the roses."

"I like the idea of little Nick running around here," Jenna said with a giggle.

I waved her to the blanket. "Come sit down and eat. I wasn't sure what you liked, so I got a few different kinds of sandwiches. There's also iced tea or lemonade and I have some fruit in here as well." Thank god there was a great deli between the Blaine Construction office and Jenna's apartment. I even bought the picnic basket there. Brilliant marketing on the part of the deli owners.

"Nick!" Jenna gasped again as she sat down on the blanket. "This is so absolutely perfect. Thank you. I can honestly say no one has ever done anything like this for me." Jenna crawled forward on her hands and knees across the blanket and gave me a soft kiss on the lips. "You are pretty amazing."

I couldn't help myself, I put my hand on her cheek and pulled her in for another kiss. She moaned softly and leaned into me. "You are so beautiful," I whispered to her. "Plus I am a huge fan of those little moans that you make." She blushed and gave me another soft kiss before pulling back and busying herself with getting a sandwich. I could tell, by the flush that remained on her face and by the fact that her hands were shaking as she unwrapped a sandwich, that the kiss had an impact on her. I liked that. I liked it a lot. Fuck, I just liked her a lot.

Jenna carefully unwrapped the sandwich and took a bite. As she ate, she looked around the park. "So tell me about little Nick running around in the rose garden."

I chuckled. "Not too much to tell. I was always way more into baseball than roses, so I usually wandered off to the baseball diamond on the other side of the garden."

"Do you still like baseball?" Jenna asked before taking another bite of her sandwich.

"Absolutely! I played all through high school and still make a point of taking in a handful of games every season."

Jenna took a drink of her lemonade before responding. "I have never been much of a sports person, so I don't really know too much about it."

I suddenly got very excited about the idea of introducing her to baseball. "Well, we need to do something about that! There's a big game in a few weeks. We should go." She smiled back at me like she was unsure if I was asking her or just casually bringing it up. "Let me rephrase that, Jenna. Will you go to a baseball game with me?

She smiled. "Yes!"

She looked so excited, it really pulled at my heart. I couldn't explain it, but I didn't need to. I liked being around her and I might as well enjoy the limited amount of time we had. "Man, I could really get used to this saying yes plan." I shot Jenna a grin as I took a bite of my sandwich.

She lowered her gaze and looked up at me through her lashes. "Oh yes?" she teased. "What other ideas did you have in mind?"

The way she said it was so fucking sexy there was only one thing on my mind. I tried to gulp down some air. "You are all kinds of trouble." Jenna looked a little surprised by my statement. I lowered my voice and said, "Good thing I like trouble." There was that blush again on her cheeks that I liked so much. I couldn't help but smile.

The rest of our lunch went by rather quickly and, unfortunately, I had to get back to work. We packed up our picnic and were admiring the roses as we walked back to the truck.

"Thank you again for an amazing lunch and for sharing this beautiful spot with me." Jenna leaned forward to smell a rose. "Which of the roses are your favorite?"

"I've never really thought about it. I don't know that I could pick just one. How about you?"

Jenna stopped to smell another rose. "Oh, that's easy. The red ones. Classic, bold, beautiful."

"No rose is as beautiful as you." The words fell out of my mouth before I could stop them. I pulled her close for another kiss. There was something about kissing her that I had rapidly grown addicted to.

We reached the truck and were putting the picnic supplies in the back when I turned to her. I had to know when I was going to see her again. "So, we're going to the game in a few weeks, but I want to see you again before then. When can I do that?"

"I work the evening shift for the next few nights, but I'm free during the day," Jenna said with a smile as she stepped closer to me.

I reached out and put my hands on her hips. "I'll take it. I don't want this day to end, but I'm going to have to take you home so I can get back to work. I want to get a bunch of things done today so my weekend is free." It was a spur-of-the-moment decision to try and get things done before the weekend. I couldn't remember the last time I didn't work all weekend, but I would do it to spend time with Jenna. I was not the kind of guy to make spur-of-the-moment decisions and schedule changes, but I had done it twice now for Jenna. Part of me felt like I should be concerned I was losing focus, and part of me didn't give a fuck as long as I got to see her again.

"Big plans for the weekend?" she asked, giving me an eyebrow raise.

I leaned forward and kissed her softly. "Absolutely. You see, I met this amazing, smart, sexy, and completely irresistible woman. Ever since the first time I laid eyes on her,

I can't seem to stop thinking about her. I heard she might have some free time this weekend and I plan on spending every minute she will give me with her." If I wasn't going to work that weekend, I was going all in.

Jenna nodded her head and acted like she was really thinking about it. "She does sound pretty amazing. I think I would like to meet her. Maybe she and I could hang out sometime?"

I kissed her playfully on the nose. "Did I mention she has quite the sense of humor?"

"She sounds pretty perfect," Jenna said playfully with a laugh.

I looked into her eyes. I was beginning to think she was.

Chapter 25
Jenna

The next few weeks seemed to fly by. Nick and I saw each other almost every day. When we were not together, we were texting or talking on the phone. I really liked Nick and I really liked being with him. He was fun, smart, thoughtful, funny... and, well, he was just easy to be around. He was unlike anyone I had ever met before. Plus, he was so freaking sexy I sometimes had a hard time believing he was real.

I was in the backroom at Pete's Pizza on a break when I saw I had a text message from Nick. *"The baseball game is on Sunday, but are you free Saturday night?"*

I quickly wrote him back. *"What are you proposing?"*

"Dinner?"

I smiled. *"As long as it's not sushi again. Trying it once was more than enough for me. :-)"*

"LOL! Well, you said yes and tried it and didn't like it. No one ever said you would be batting a thousand."

"I see what you did there with the baseball reference. Very smooth."

"You're a quick learner...nice to know our baseball study sessions are working."

I blushed as I thought about Nick teaching me baseball. I tapped out a message back to him, smiling as I wrote: *"Well, I have a super hot teacher that hands out kisses for correct answers. You better believe I am going to study to get 100% on that test."* I wasn't going to tell Nick that I had read a few books about baseball since he asked me to the game. I wanted to have an idea about what was going on and I thought I could maybe impress him a little with my new baseball knowledge.

"Hey, Jenna! Is your break almost over? I've got some deliveries ready to go for you!" Steven shouted from the kitchen.

I sighed and sent Nick a quick message. *"I've got to go...pizzas to deliver."*

Nick responded back almost immediately, *"Dinner at my place tomorrow night? I want to cook for you."*

"You cook?!?!?!?! Oh, I am saying yes to this for sure!" Good grief! Sexy as all get out and he could cook! How did I get so lucky?

"Come over around 7?"

"Catch you then! (See what I did there with my own baseball joke?)"

"Very clever, Jenna. Now get back to work. Text me when you get home tonight after your shift so I know you made it safely."

"It will be really late. I'm closing tonight."

"Exactly why I want to know you made it home safely." I reread his last message a few times and my heart went pitter-patter each time. He often asked me to text him when I got home after working a late shift just to make sure I got home alright. I thought it was really sweet and made me feel like he really cared about me.

"Jenna!" Steven shouted. "Deliveries are ready!"

I slipped my phone into my back pocket and stepped into the kitchen where Kimmy was also waiting. "Here is your GPS with delivery addresses programmed in for you," she said as she handed me the device.

"Thank you," I said, taking it from her. My mind was still stuck on Nick as I thought about dinner at his place the next night. It seemed like everything had moved in a really great direction with him. I had developed some very strong feelings for him which made me excited to see where things between us were going to go.

"I see that dreamy look on your face... you were talking to Nick, weren't you?" Kimmy asked with a huge smile on her face, looking like she had just solved some great mystery.

I blushed. "Maybe..."

Kimmy leaned forward resting her elbows on the counter. "How is everything going with him? You two have been together for a while now, right?"

"It's great. He's great. It is so unlike my previous relationship that sometimes I feel like all of this might be too good to be true. Or maybe I should pinch myself and wake up."

"Aww, girl. You deserve to be happy and have a great guy in your life! What are you going to do when you go to law school in the fall? That's going to be here sooner than you know."

My stomach felt twisted up in knots the minute Kimmy said that. Although I tried to push it out of my mind, it was always looming in the background. I was going to be moving away to start school at the end of the summer. Nick and I had not talked about it at all other than that first night at the bluff when I told him about law school. I was too afraid to bring it up and I wanted to keep things the way they were... which was not going to be possible when law school started. Not only was it not possible from a practical standpoint, but since that night at the bluff, the plan was for this thing we were doing to last until I started school. I couldn't help but frown at the thought of not having Nick in my life anymore.

"I still don't trust him," Mike said as he took a pizza out of the oven and started to cut it into slices. I shook my head to clear my thoughts and tried to focus on what was going on around me.

Kimmy let out a huff and rolled her eyes. "Would you trust anyone that Jenna dated? You're just acting like an overprotective older brother right now."

Kimmy threw a towel at Mike as I picked up the pizzas for delivery. Kimmy got a mischievous look on her face. "Since you want to jump into other people's conversations, Mike, let's start talking about you. How is Cassie?" Kimmy raised her eyebrows at Mike and his face turned bright red. He mumbled something and walked out of the kitchen.

I stared at the door Mike walked out of before turning back to look at Kimmy. "What just happened?" I asked, full of confusion.

Kimmy smiled. "I think Mr. Romeo over there has the hots for a certain redhead. It's cute. He's worked here for a long time and I've never seen him with anyone. I was starting to think he just didn't date at all, but now I think it is because he gets so shy around women. Or at least around women that he's into. Specifically, Cassie. I think Cassie scares him a little, but I also think that he is totally into that."

I stopped and thought for a minute. "Huh, I guess it has been a little while since I talked to Cass. I need to call her and find out what's up." I tried to picture Cassie and Mike together.

Maybe I really did catch him secretly checking her out when we were at the club that night.

"I don't think anything's actually up. I think Mike is lusting from afar. He hasn't stopped talking about her since the night we were all at the club and he gave her a ride home. She stopped in here a few days ago to grab some lunch and I thought Mike was going to pass out. He was so nervous. He totally knocked her soda over and spilled it all over the counter." Kimmy was grinning ear to ear.

Steven glared at both of us. "Stop talking about him when he's not here. Jenna, if you don't get out of here right now, the pizza is going to get cold. If you deliver cold pizzas, I'm going to make you clean the bathrooms tonight."

I grabbed my boxes and did a mock salute to Steven. "Aye aye captain. I be on my way, matey."

Steven rolled his eyes at me as he tried to fight a smile. "You are such a dork. No wonder you fit in here. Get going and get your pizzas delivered."

I grabbed the boxes and headed out the back door to the delivery car. Cassie and Mike... I was going to need to talk to her and find out what exactly was up with that. They seemed like such an unlikely pair, but one that was just so crazy it might work.

While I was talking with Kimmy and Steven, I realized I had become one of those awful friends that gets a boyfriend and gets wrapped up in spending time with him. I couldn't even remember for sure the last time I spoke to Cassie and I didn't like that at all.

As bad as I felt about neglecting my friendship with Cassie, I also felt a little flutter in my stomach at the idea that I referred to Nick as my boyfriend. Is that how I saw what we were doing? We hadn't known each other for very long, but everything with him just felt so good and so right that maybe... I had to stop myself from going down that path and remind myself things with Nick were for now, not forever...

Chapter 26
Nick

"So, what has you sitting behind your desk with a huge grin on your face in the middle of the workday? Let me guess someone whose name starts with 'Jen' and ends with 'na'." Bax walked into my office and flopped into one of the chairs across from my desk.

I looked up at him. He was right, I had been texting with Jenna. We had been texting cheesy baseball references and I invited her to my place where I was going to cook dinner for her the next night. I had never cooked dinner for a woman... in fact, I was not really sure what made me throw that out there, but I liked doing things for Jenna, and cooking dinner for her seemed like something she would be into. I wasn't going to admit any of that to Bax. Instead, I scowled at him, "Who let you back here; and why are you here?"

Bax laughed. "See that is the beauty of it, my friend. No one. You still haven't hired an assistant so there is literally no one sitting at that front desk to stop me from just waltzing my wonderful self right back here to talk to your grumpy ass. I just stopped by to say hello, since I haven't talked to you for a while and this is the welcome I get." Bax leaned forward putting his arm on my desk as he whispered like we were sharing some great secret. "I'm onto you, Blaine. I know you're only pretending to be grumpy. I saw that smile on your face before you realized I was here."

I groaned. "I know. I need to get some interviews done and hire someone. I've just—"

"Been busy having pizza delivered?" Bax interrupted, making a gesture with his hands that he must have learned in a junior high locker room.

I glared at him. Actually, he was right, again. I had been so busy seeing Jenna every spare moment I could, that I hadn't set up the interviews for an assistant yet. Fuck. That was exactly the type of thing I was worried about happening if I got distracted by a... whatever it was that Jenna and I were doing. Hiring an assistant had slipped through the cracks while I drowned in paperwork and Bax waltzed into my office during the middle of the day. I needed to refocus.

Bax snapped his fingers in front of my face. "Hey, Blaine. Where did you go just now? I lost you. What is going on?"

"I don't know what I am doing, Bax," I admitted.

"Is this about Pizza Girl? Because I can give you some pointers. I have been told I am quite good at making the ladies happy if you catch my drift." Bax gave me a wink.

"You are an ass. Plus I am not even talking about that." I wasn't going to mention to Bax that we hadn't even done... that. I didn't want to pressure Jenna into anything; she was special so I was going to follow her lead and wait until she was ready. And take a fuck ton of cold showers between now and then.

"I don't know what I'm doing with her in general." I paused as I ran my hand through my hair, "I haven't interviewed for an assistant because I have been so wrapped up in spending every spare moment with Jenna. I have been distracted, Bax, and shit is starting to slide." I waved my arm over my desk which was once again covered in mounds of paper.

"So then, things are going well with Jenna?" Bax asked. I just stared at him, unsure of how to respond. "Feelings, Nick. I am asking how you feel about her. I know you don't like talking about or expressing or even acknowledging feelings, but..."

"I really like her, Bax. More than I should. She is leaving and I want to just pretend like that is not going to happen. I thought this was going to be easy... that we could just hang out until the expiration date when she left. I'm not so sure I can do that anymore."

"Fuck, Nick. We have been friends since high school and I can count on one hand, with fingers to spare, the number of times you have talked about your feelings and two of those spots belong to talking about Jenna. Once at the club and now. You really like her, don't you?"

I rubbed my hands over my face. "I can't, though. I won't do anything that could interfere with her going to law school. That was a plan she had in place long before she met me and I am not a part of it. I knew that going into this. I also can't do anything to interfere with Blaine Construction. I'm on the edge of really breaking through into the big time and I have worked too hard to get to this point just to let it slide away. I have too many people counting on me."

"So, what are you going to do?" Bax asked leaning back in the chair.

"Keep pretending like she is not leaving, and enjoy it right now, I guess." I shrugged my shoulders.

"Here's a super crazy idea; have you talked to her about any of this?"

"No," I admitted.

"Why? Because it would require Nick Blaine to talk about the fact that he feels real feelings for Jenna... what's her last name?"

"Morgan," I answered.

"Right, you might have to admit that you feel something for Jenna Morgan? Even crazier, you might have to actually tell Jenna you have these feelings for her." Bax looked expectantly at me. I was growing increasingly frustrated with the whole conversation and I think Bax could sense it. "Listen," he finally said. "When is the next time you're going to see her?"

"Tomorrow night. She's coming over to my place for dinner."

"You going to order Pete's Pizza?" Bax laughed. "Awww, come on. That was funny." He laughed at my grimace.

"I am going to make dinner for her."

Bax let out a low whistle. "Damn, Blaine. You do really like her. You've barely cooked for me before and I've known you forever. Until Jenna came along, I was your favorite person and you weren't cooking for me. Don't tell me you're making your dad's spaghetti for her."

"I was thinking about it..."

"You know that's my favorite! It has been since the very first time I ate at your house when we were in high school! What time are you eating so I can be there?" Bax joked and then suddenly turned serious. "Wait, have you ever cooked for a woman before? I think you're entering into some completely new and uncharted Nick Blaine territory with this."

"You are not invited," I growled. "And no, I have never cooked dinner at my place for someone that I am... with."

Fuck, what would someone call the thing between Jenna and me?

"Damn, Nick. I have never seen you like this before." Bax paused as if waiting for me to respond. When I didn't, he continued on, "Before you kick me out, I also want to offer my services to be on the interview committee for your new office assistant. I am an excellent judge of character, and a great friend willing to help you out."

"An excellent judge of character, huh?" I raised my eyebrow at him.

"Well except for a momentary lapse when I decided to be your lifelong friend," Bax laughed. "Now that one was funny." He said, laughing at his own joke.

I couldn't help but smile back at him. "You are an idiot, Bax. Are you really offering to help? You're not going to do anything weird like ask one of them out on a date in the middle of an interview or something like that, are you?"

"I am insulted you would think that... and disappointed in myself for not thinking of it first. No, I won't do anything 'weird,'" he said, making air quotes, "I am genuinely offering to help you. You are my friend and occasionally I try to do something nice to keep you around."

"Thanks, man. I really appreciate that." I was touched that Bax could see how overwhelmed I was and wanted to help me out.

Bax put his hand over his heart. "That may be one of the nicest things you have ever said to me, Nick Blaine."

"Yeah, well don't get used to it," I pretended to be looking at a stack of papers on my desk. Leave it to Bax to make a moment fucking weird and awkward.

Bax just laughed as he stood up and started to leave. "There is the 'devoid of any human feeling or emotion' Nick that we all know and love. I was worried you were getting soft on me for a moment. Good to see that the asshole is still strong in you." When Bax got to the door he turned around and said with a smirk. "Oh, by the way, Nick. I fucking told you so."

"What are you talking about?" I asked, genuinely confused.

"Remember when I told you someday, despite all your best efforts to the contrary, you were going to meet some girl who was going to flip your world upside down and I was going to just sit there and laugh and say 'fucking told you so.' Remember that, Nick?"

"Yeah..." I said slowly.

"Well, Nick, I am laughing and saying 'fucking told you so,'" Bax waved as he walked out the door.

Damn him. Especially because I was certain he was right.

Chapter 27
Jenna

The next night I was standing on Nick's front steps at seven o'clock on the dot getting ready to ring the doorbell. I was suddenly really nervous. Coming to his house seemed like a really big deal. Like something that people in a relationship did. Is that what we were doing? Dang, I needed to slow down. I wiped my sweaty palms on my jeans and said a little prayer of thanks that I was wearing my extra-strength deodorant.

I finally worked up the nerve and rang the doorbell. I could hear Nick shout from inside, "It's open! Come on in!" I opened the door and hesitantly stepped inside. "In the kitchen! Down the hall and to your right."

I followed the sound of Nick's voice and when I stepped into the kitchen there were pots and pans all over the stove with delicious smells coming from each of them. Nick looked adorable stirring something in one of the pots with a kitchen towel thrown over his shoulder. "Hi," I smiled at him. "It smells amazing in here. What are you making?"

"Sorry I didn't come to the door, I need to keep an eye on the sauce to make sure it doesn't bubble over. We are having pasta with red sauce. None of that shit from a jar. I make mine from scratch."

"Wow, handsome and handy in the kitchen. What other hidden talents do you have, Mr. Blaine?"

"Play your cards right and you just might find out tonight." Nick winked at me and I felt my entire body flush. He smiled and gestured to the other end of the counter. "There's a bottle of wine on the counter. Do you mind opening it and pouring us both a glass?"

"I'm on it." There was a wine opener sitting right next to the bottle. "Your place is really nice, Nick. Have you lived here long?" I popped the cork out and saw two glasses sitting there as well. It appeared Nick had already thought of everything. I don't know why I was surprised, it seemed like Nick was always thoughtful and prepared.

"No, only a few months. This was one of the condos we did some remodel work on. I needed a place to live, so I just opted not to resell this one. I've been working so much I haven't really had time to purchase much furniture or have it decorated, so it is still a little sparse." I glanced around and saw he was right. There was a black leather couch with a matching chair in front of a giant TV in the living area and a small table with four chairs near the kitchen. That was pretty much it. It looked like a stereotypical bachelor pad.

"Is there anything I can do to help with dinner?" I asked walking over to Nick with a glass of wine. I noticed when I went to hand him the glass, my hands were shaking. I am not sure if it was nerves or excitement. If I was being honest, it was probably a little of both.

Nick stepped away from the stove and gave me a quick kiss as he took the glass of wine. "We should be almost ready. If you would please put the salad on the table, that would be great. It's right there at the end of the counter."

"Thank you for doing this. I have never had anyone cook like this for me before."

Nick paused what he was doing and looked at me. "Previous boyfriends didn't cook? What a shame. My dad was the cook at our house growing up and he made sure I knew how to make at least a few dishes. Mom made sure I knew how to order takeout." Nick laughed his deep, sexy laugh.

"Well, I am grateful for that, since I met you delivering pizza to your house. Also, it is *boyfriend*. Singular. Not boyfriends," I said quickly. I took a sip of wine as I immediately regretted bringing up my past boyfriend.

Nick looked surprised but recovered quickly. "Really? You're so beautiful, smart, kind, and fun to be around, I figured there would be a trail of broken hearts behind you." I couldn't tell for sure if he was serious, joking, or probing for more information.

Whatever his motives were, I couldn't help but laugh at Nick's statement since it was light years away from the truth. "I didn't really date in high school and I met my ex-boyfriend during my first semester of college. We were together until graduation." I said simply, I really didn't want to talk about my relationship history.

"That is a really long time to be with someone. It must have been pretty serious." Nick was looking down at the sauce he was stirring as he spoke and I couldn't read his facial expression.

I squirmed a little and took another sip of wine. I really did not want to talk about Brett and all of the terrible things that made up our relationship. "I thought so... he did not. How about you? I assume there is a trail of broken hearts behind you." Initially, I had been trying to change the subject to something other than Brett, but as soon as the question came out of my mouth, I realized I really didn't want to hear the

150

answer. I didn't want to think about Nick being with anyone else... in the past or the future.

Nick paused and looked at me like he wanted to ask something. Luckily, I think he sensed my discomfort and changed the subject. "I dated in high school and some in college, but honestly, there hasn't really been anyone for the past few years. I have been focused on work and getting Blaine Construction off the ground which has not left much time for anything else."

Before I could think of something to say, Nick drained the pasta and placed it in a big bowl. "Alright, dinner is ready. Why don't you grab the basket of bread and we'll move into the other room?" Nick smiled at me and instantly any discomfort I had about the previous subject floated away.

Dinner was amazing. Nick was a really great cook and the conversation flowed easily. The past relationship conversation had been completely dropped, which was fine by me. I put my fork down on my plate and wiped my face with my napkin. "Nick, everything was so delicious! I don't think I could possibly eat another crumb. Can I help with the dishes?"

"Nah. We can just leave them for now. Why don't you grab your wine glass and we can go sit on the balcony? It's really nice out there this time of night."

"That sounds great." I was really enjoying the evening with Nick. I didn't want it to end...I was starting to think that the night wasn't the only thing I didn't want to end. I really wasn't sure what was going to happen when I went to law school. I decided to do the same thing I had been doing and push it out of my mind. I wasn't going to ruin the evening with thoughts about leaving.

Out on the balcony, I leaned against the railing and looked out over the neighborhood. "Are these all houses that Blaine Construction has built or remodeled?" Nick was sitting in one of the chairs on the balcony and I turned my head slightly towards him as I spoke.

"For the most part," Nick said casually, although the hint of pride in his voice was inescapable.

"That is really impressive."

"Not nearly as impressive as you are." I could hear Nick stand up from the chair and felt him walk up behind me. With one hand he brushed my hair away from my shoulder exposing my neck, while the other hand wrapped around my waist and pulled me tight against his muscular body. He started peppering soft kisses along my neck and lightly nibbling my earlobe. I couldn't help it... it felt so good that I let out a soft moan.

"Is this what you had planned for dessert?" I asked, tipping my head to the side to give him better access to my neck. There was no way I wanted him to stop what he was doing. Not when every nerve in my body felt like it was on fire and my heart was furiously pounding in my chest.

I could feel Nick's breath hit against my neck and cheek as he spoke in a low and sexy voice. "No, there's chocolate cake in the kitchen. Do you want me to stop and get you some?"

"Don't you dare stop," my voice was deep and breathy. I had never felt so good with someone before and there was no way that I wanted it to stop. I wanted to feel like that forever...

but then I quickly reminded myself that was not what this was... this was for now, not forever.

Nick let out a deep chuckle and spun me around so I was facing him. "You just looked so amazing with the soft glow of the sunset around you. I couldn't resist." Nick hesitated for a few moments as he seemed to be searching my face. I hoped that the internal conflict between my head and my heart was not evident on my face. "You are something special, Jenna," he whispered softly as he lightly touched my cheek.

I felt a warm glow start in my chest and spread throughout my entire body. I looked into Nick's deep, brown eyes and saw nothing but warmth and understanding. I stood on my tiptoes and he lowered his head so I could place a soft kiss on his lips. "Thank you. For everything. I am so happy you came into my life."

"Stay with me tonight, Jenna. We can move as fast or as slow as you want, but I don't want tonight to end. I want to hold you and wake up with you here tomorrow morning."

My heart fluttered as I pressed my body more firmly against Nick's. Everything felt so right and I didn't want the night to end either. I had been thinking about that moment ever since the first time I laid eyes on him, and I was ready. "Yes, Nick."

"You'll stay the night?" he asked, a smile overtaking his already handsome face.

"Yes," I said confidently as I smiled back at him. "I want nothing more than to stay here with you tonight. I am saying yes to everything. I want all of you, Nick. Tonight."

Chapter 28
Nick

I woke up the next morning tangled in my sheets with my arms wrapped around Jenna's deliciously warm and soft body. Jenna's back was pressed up against my front and it felt so damn good. I smiled as memories of the previous night filled my head. It was... well, it was amazing. Far beyond my wildest fantasies about what being with Jenna would actually be like, and trust me, there were many to choose from.

It was exactly how I wanted to wake up this morning. I could feel Jenna start to stir as she wiggled a little to snuggle up closer to me. I obliged and wrapped my arms around her tighter as I gave her a soft kiss on her neck. "Good morning, beautiful," I whispered to her.

"Good morning," she mumbled back, her voice still heavy with sleep.

"God it feels amazing to wake up with you here in my arms. A man could get used to this."

Jenna rolled over on her side facing me. I rolled onto my back so she could lay her head on my chest. I wrapped my arm around her as she cuddled up close and pressed her body to mine. I don't think I had ever actually 'cuddled' with someone, but holy fuck, if that was what it was like... well, I might have to consider it more often. I had never been a touchy-feely type of person, but Jenna was bringing out a whole other side of me that I had no idea even existed. I liked the person I was becoming around her. I liked doing things for her, spending time with her... fuck, I even liked lying in bed and cuddling with her. I gave her a little squeeze as I felt my heart swell just being here with her.

Jenna was lazily rubbing her fingers up and down my chest as she traced the outlines of my tattoos. "There is a woman in this bed that could get pretty used to this as well." She looked up at me. "You're extra cute with that sleepy look on your face."

I chuckled. "You kind of wore me out last night. And that other time last night. Oh and early this morning. Can't forget about that one."

"Well, all three of those times were pretty amazing and unforgettable. You do good work, sir." Jenna patted me on the chest and looked up at me playfully.

I grinned. "Well, just be sure to leave me a five-star review on Yelp and recommend me to all of your friends and family."

"Not a chance! I'm keeping you all to myself!" Jenna declared, laughing.

My heart skipped a beat at the idea of Jenna keeping me all to herself. Before I could get too lost in my thoughts about it I rolled over and started tickling her. Jenna let out a little shriek and started laughing hysterically. "Alright! Alright!" she gasped after a few minutes. Things between us were just so easy when we were together. I liked that we could share in playful banter after a night of hot and steamy sex. I never had anything like that before and well... it was the best of everything.

"Ha! Ha! Winner again! Now I shall collect my prize!" I leaned down and gave Jenna a kiss that started out slow and chaste but quickly turned hot and passionate.

"Man, if that is what happens when I lose, I'm just going to go on record now and say you can win every time," Jenna said with a hint of playfulness still in her voice.

"It's a mutually beneficial prize." I smiled at her and kissed her again. I didn't know how I could ever grow tired of kissing Jenna Morgan. I quickly reminded myself that I couldn't think like that... this... whatever it was... had an expiration date on it and we both had very specific plans after that date.

"Nick, I hate to even ask this question, but what time is it? Today is game day and I can't let all of my baseball studying go to waste."

I rolled over to grab my phone from the nightstand. "Looks like we slept in a little. Gates open in about two hours."

"I better get home so I can get showered and changed. Got to be ready for my first game! Big day!" Jenna made no attempt to move and instead stayed with her head laying on my chest with my arm around her. I really didn't want her to get up and even though I was excited to take Jenna to her first baseball game, I was cursing the fact it was that same day.

"Alright, how about I make you a deal?" I said as I absentmindedly twirled her hair around my fingers.

"I'm listening..."

"You can go home to shower and change then I will pick you up at one o'clock to head to the baseball field..."

"So far your terms seem to be agreeable, sir." Jenna was trying to act serious but she couldn't seem to stop smiling. The fact that I may have even played a small part in putting that smile on her face warmed my heart. Apparently, I had gone from 'Nick Blaine, guy with no feelings' to 'Nick Blaine, guy who has all the feelings at one time when it comes to Jenna.'

"... and when you are home getting ready, you should also pack an overnight bag." Now that I had Jenna in my bed, there was no way I wanted to spend the night without her. Plus, I happened to know she had asked for the whole day off of work to go to the baseball game.

Jenna sat up in bed and held the sheet up so it was barely covering her. Her hair was wild and her cheeks were flushed. She looked so fucking sexy I was seriously considering ditching the baseball game altogether. "The plot thickens. Where exactly do you think I am going with my overnight bag, Mr. Blaine?"

I almost lost my train of thought as I laid there staring at how beautiful she was. Fuck, Nick, focus on the conversation, not on how Jenna is biting her bottom lip and how the sheet is about slip off her left breast... I had to tear my eyes away from her before I completely lost my ability to speak. "Back here to my place after the game. Since you aren't working tonight, you should stay here again."

"Your deal is very interesting..." Jenna tapped her chin and tried to pretend like she was deep in thought considering my offer.

I decided to sweeten the deal a little more. "Did I mention the part where you won't need to pack any pajamas? You won't need to be wearing anything tonight for what I have planned." I gave Jenna a little half-cocked grin just so there was absolutely no question as to what my plans were.

"Yes! Yes! Yes! I am saying yes and accepting the terms of your deal in full. You are an excellent negotiator, sir." Jenna pounced on me and started kissing me as she giggled. "I need to stop kissing you or I am never going to leave and we're going to miss the game," Jenna said in between kisses.

"Missing the game could be an option…" I slid my hand under the sheet and started to brush my fingers up her leg.

"Nope!" Jenna shouted as she jumped out of bed and started putting her clothes on. "You have been looking forward to this for weeks and it's my first game. I will see you at one o'clock. Until then, you might want to take a nap and drink some Gatorade so you're rested and ready for tonight. I have a few of my own plans for you, Nick Blaine." Jenna winked at me and blew me a kiss as she walked out of the bedroom.

I was left sitting on the bed grinning ear to ear. I heard Jenna laughing down the hallway before I heard the front door click shut.

I flopped back down on my bed. How do you stop yourself from falling for someone? I needed to find out and I needed to find out fast.

Chapter 29
Jenna

At exactly one o'clock. there was a knock at my door. I was freshly showered, and dressed in a tank top and shorts ready to go. My super pale skin was completely lathered up with sunscreen. No way I was going to risk a sunburn when there were plans to be back in Nick's bed. Nothing was going to keep me from a repeat of the night before. I could feel myself blush just thinking about it. It was beyond amazing. The only other person I had ever been with was Brett and well... let's just say I had no idea until last night that sex could be so incredible. After one night with Nick, I finally understood why everyone made such a big deal about it.

I swung the door open and was momentarily stunned by Nick standing there leaning against my door frame. You would think by that point I would have been used to it, but every time I saw him I got butterflies in my stomach and my heart started racing.

He took his sunglasses off and smiled at me. "You look incredible. I'm going to have a hard time keeping my eyes off of you and on the game."

I could feel myself blush, just like I did every time he gave me a compliment. Which was a lot. I was starting to think that sometimes he said or did things just to make me blush. "Thank you. I wasn't really sure what to wear. Is this okay?" I spun around for him to get the full view.

"Well, you're missing something." It was then that I noticed Nick had one of his hands behind his back. He pulled it forward and handed me what he had been hiding. "If you are going to go to the game, you've got to wear a jersey for the home team."

"Nick! This is so thoughtful! I'm even more excited for the game now, thank you!" I quickly pulled the jersey on over my tank top and threw my arms around Nick, giving him a big hug and a quick kiss.

"I don't think I've ever seen a jersey look so good. Now I know I'm not going to be able to keep my eyes on the game."

I ran my finger down his chest and looked up at him through my lashes. "Maybe later tonight I could wear the jersey for you... and nothing else." Nick's eyes grew big and I am pretty sure his cheeks flushed a little. I even kind of surprised myself with that one. It was not something I'd normally say, but around Nick... well, I felt sexy and playful. Like a much better, more confident version of me. Being with him just made me feel really, really good.

Nick let out a low growl. "Now I'm not even sure we're going to make it to the game..." Nick dropped his lips onto mine and after a few seconds deepened the kiss and pulled me tighter to his body.

"We're going to be late," I murmured as the kiss started to intensify.

"Nothing good ever happens in the first inning..." Nick mumbled in between kisses.

I laughed and broke the kiss. "Let's go, stud! I said yes to my first baseball game and I don't want to miss any of it!"

"Alright, you win. Did you pack a bag?"

"It's sitting by the front door." I smiled and nodded my head towards the overnight bag.

"Perfect. It's so nice out I brought the Harley without really thinking about the fact you would have a bag. Do you mind swinging back here to pick it up after the game?"

"No problem! Now, take me out to the ball game and buy me some peanuts and Cracker Jacks." I patted Nick on the chest.

"Yes, ma'am! Your wish is my command." Nick bowed towards me with a grand sweep of his arms.

I laughed as we walked out the door. It all felt so right and so good. Of course, no matter how good it felt there was still a little nagging part of me that wondered if all of it was too good to be true, and how I was ever going to make it through everything ending when I had to leave for school.

***

"Nick! These seats are incredible! We're practically on the field, we're so close!" My excitement level had been off the charts since we entered the stadium.

Nick chuckled and put his arm around the back of my seat. "I'm glad you like them. Blaine Construction is a season ticket holder and I usually give the seats out to a different employee each game."

"Really? That is so cool of you! I bet the employees really like that." He was incredibly modest about it, but Nick was so good to all of his employees and incredibly involved in the community. It was no wonder that everyone wanted to work for him and that there was so much support locally for Blaine Construction.

"It's just a fun way to give recognition to someone who's been working extra hard and going above and beyond, plus it supports the local baseball team. Makes it a win-win." Nick shrugged his shoulders, as if to minimize what a neat thing it was, and quickly changed the subject. "Do you have enough to eat?"

I looked down at my lap which was heaped with food and laughed. "I think you literally bought me everything they have here! I have a hot dog, popcorn, a giant pretzel, nachos, soda, a bag of peanuts, and my box of Cracker Jacks. I think I'm all set."

"I wasn't sure what you liked so I got a mix of everything. I can help you out with some of that." Nick winked at me as I smiled and passed him a hot dog.

The energy in the stadium was contagious. A few innings into the game and I could totally see how people become sports fans. Nick talked about both teams and different players throughout the game. He really did know way more about baseball than I originally thought. I was really glad I prepared for the game by reading some books on baseball so I could follow along. Baseball was clearly something important to Nick and I wanted to be a part of it with him.

"So what do you think so far?" Nick asked as he tossed a piece of popcorn at me.

I pulled my eyes away from the field and could not stop smiling. "I am having so much fun! I can see why you are a fan. Thank you for inviting me along."

"Thank you for saying yes." Nick leaned over and kissed me on the cheek.

Soon it was time for the seventh-inning stretch. As we waited for the second half of the seventh inning to start, we watched the different fans in the crowd appear on the Jumbotron screen hanging high above us all.

"That is so nuts!" I said looking up at the huge screen. "I don't know how people can do silly dances and act all crazy when they are up there on the screen. I think I'd pass out from nerves if I was in front of the whole stadium like that."

Nick started laughing. "Well, then don't look up now!"

I looked up and saw me and Nick front and center on the huge screen. Before I could freak out, Nick grabbed me and planted a hair-raising, toe-curling kiss on my lips. I heard the entire stadium clapping and cheering for us.

Nick broke the kiss and I looked up at him in a daze. "Oh my goodness! I just got kissed on the big screen in front of an entire baseball stadium full of people!"

"Yes, you just did," Nick replied with a huge grin on his face.

"They were all cheering and clapping for us!" I was still stunned by the entire thing.

"Yes, they were," Nick said laughing.

I turned to face him. "Have you ever done anything like that before?"

Nick shook his head. "Nope. Never. First time for me as well," he said with a huge grin.

I smiled back at him. "Good. Just checking. Glad I could be your first."

Nick threw his head back and laughed before putting his arm across the back of my seat. He leaned in and kissed me on the top of my head. "Me too, Jenna. Me too."

Chapter 30
Jenna

A few days after the baseball game with Nick, I found myself at brunch with Cassie.

"Glad you could finally come up for some air and spend some time with those of us who are not panty-melter Nick." Cassie raised her eyebrows at me as she looked up from her menu.

"I'm so sorry! I have been a little wrapped up in spending time with him. I never intended to be one of those awful women who starts seeing someone and then ditches my friends. Please forgive me." I was feeling really bad about how little I had talked to Cass lately. I was glad she agreed to come to brunch with me so we could catch up and I could apologize.

Cassie waved her hand. "Buy me another mimosa and all shall be forgiven."

"Done!"

"That was super easy. Especially because I was never upset in the first place. I really just wanted another drink," Cassie said with a smirk.

I laughed. I felt good to be out with Cassie and to know no matter what, she would always be my best friend.

Cassie put down her menu and leaned forward. "So speaking of good old pizza guy Nick, how are things going with you two? If your texts and our phone conversations are to be believed, it sounds like you two are pretty hot and heavy."

I set my menu down as well. "Let's talk about you first, then me. I feel like I have been a neglectful friend and have no idea what is going on with you."

"Well, unlike other people at this table, I have not been lighting any sheets on fire lately with a wild, hot, passionate lover. Work has been keeping me really busy. I've had some really big sales close recently."

"Cass! That's awesome! Congratulations! I'm so proud of you!" I really was excited for Cassie. I knew she worked really hard and was very good at what she did. It had been her goal since the beginning of her career to eventually branch out and open her own real estate agency. I had no doubt that Cassie Charles Real Estate would be happening in the future.

"I have your Romeo and the houses Blaine Construction has been building to thank. Almost any project they work on is sold before completion. You need to keep Nick happy so he keeps building and I keep racking up the commission checks!" She said happily.

I knew a portion of each of those commission checks was going into an account Cassie had started to open her own agency. She opened that account with her very first commission check, and I was pretty sure I was the only other person that knew about it.

Cassie looked at me over the top of her champagne glass with a smirk. I laughed. "I'll see what I can do."

"Thank you, Jenna. I really appreciate you taking one for the team and keeping your hotter-than-sin lover happy. I'm sure that it is really difficult to wake up with that rock-hard, tattooed body in the morning after a night of screaming his name." Cassie rolled her eyes as I blushed.

"Cassie!" I hissed at her as our waitress came to the table to take our order.

"Alright! Alright! I'll quit talking about Mr. Hotness." She turned to our waitress. "I will have the strawberry waffles, please. Oh, and another mimosa."

"You got it," our waitress said as she wrote it down on her notepad and turned to me. "For you?"

"I'll have the same please." I was still a little flustered and wondering how much of the conversation our waitress had overheard.

"No problem." The waitress picked up our menus. "I'll get that in for you. Congratulations on snagging Mr. Hotness. He sounds like quite the catch." She winked at me and I think I turned a thousand shades of red. Cassie roared with laughter.

As the waitress walked away I tried to compose myself. "So what else is going on with you, Cassie?" I asked, taking a big drink of my water and attempting to change the subject.

"Not much else..." Cassie was looking somewhere over my shoulder and refused to make eye contact.

Now it was my turn to lean forward across the table. "Let me rephrase that. What is going on with you that you are trying to keep a secret?"

Cassie gulped down the rest of her mimosa. "Alright! You are relentless! I have been hanging out with a guy. He is really different from anyone else I have ever gone out with. I think I am starting to like it. And maybe starting to like him."

"Oh my God! Cassie! This is fantastic!" I shrieked. "Who is it? Anyone I know?"

"Yes," Cassie said quickly.

"Well, don't leave me hanging here! Who is it?"

Cassie paused for a few minutes. It was all very unlike her. The guy must have really meant something to her for her to be acting like that. "Mike," she said suddenly.

I was completely surprised. "Like Mike that I work with at the pizza shop?" Suddenly, I remembered the conversation with Kimmy in the kitchen about Mike and Cassie and everything started to make sense.

"Yes, that Mike. We've gone on a few dates now. Are you happy? You got it out of me." Cassie fidgeted uncomfortably in her seat. I wasn't sure if she was actually uncomfortable with the conversation or just being overly dramatic in her very Cassie way, it was very unlike her to be so reluctant talking about someone she was dating.

"I am super happy for you, Cass. I'm not going to lie, I am really surprised. You two are just such opposites. I never pictured you hooking up with Mike or someone like Mike." I looked at the soft smile that came across Cassie's face when I said his name and had to hold in my surprise.

"No, you are right about the opposite part. We are. I think there are times when I can be a little overwhelming and intimidating to him. Then, there are times when I'm weirded out by how quiet and genuinely nice he can be." Cassie paused and shrugged her shoulders. "Somehow it all just works."

"That's good, right?"

Cassie quickly nodded her head. "It is. You are also wrong about part of it." Cassie looked around and leaned forward like she was telling me a great secret. "There has been no hooking up. Nothing more than a goodnight kiss so far," she whispered to me, her eyes wide.

My eyes got big and my mouth may have dropped open a little. "Seriously? Now I'm totally shocked! I love you, babe, but you're the one that calls guys 'clingy' if they ask to see you again after a hook-up, and you have refused to see any guy past two dates for years." I was struggling to adjust to this side of Cassie, not that it was bad, it was just so different!

"I know," Cassie whispered. "I'm having a hard time wrapping my mind around this too. I feel like I don't know who I am anymore."

I shook my head, still in disbelief over the whole situation. Cassie had her heart trampled on a few years earlier and since then had been very strict about her dating rules. The fact that she had thrown all of them out the window for Mike was huge. "How did this all start?" I asked, leaning forward across the table, eager for the story.

I made myself comfortable as I prepared to hear about the beginning of Mike and Cassie. Judging by the smile on Cassie's face, it was going to be quite the story.

Chapter 31
Jenna

Cassie took a deep breath before she began. "Well, since you started working at Pete's I have developed a deep appreciation for how good the pizza is there. I've gone in a few times for the lunch special. Anyway, I stopped in after the night at the club and Mike was at the register. I tried talking to him and he could barely put two words together. He even knocked a soda all over the counter."

"Kimmy may have mentioned the soda spilling conversation to me," I said with a smile.

"Yeah. So after that whole thing, I thought the guy was a total klutz. But then I remembered how different he was when we sat in my driveway and talked for so long the night he gave me a ride home from the club."

The waitress appeared with our brunch. After she set the plates down in front of us, I looked at Cassie, "Keep going," I prodded. Man! This was so strange, she was usually so forthcoming – she must really like Mike!

"So I went back a few days later. Only that time he saw me walk in and ran to the back. He wouldn't come out. Steven ended up helping me." Cassie took a big bite of her waffle. "Holy fuck-on-a-stick this thing is good!" She exclaimed, a rapturous expression coming across her face.

"What does that even mean? You know what, never mind. Back to the story... how did you guys actually end up on a date?" I put a bite of waffle in my mouth and moaned. Cassie wasn't kidding about how good they were. "This is so good.

The waffle and the story. Keep going," I prompted, through a mouthful of deliciousness.

"Right. Well, I was starting to lose my patience with the whole situation. I mean you're either in or you are out, right? Make a decision and stick to it." Cassie took a bite and chewed thoughtfully. "These waffles are really fucking good. What do you suppose is in them that makes them taste so good? Magic? Unicorn tears?"

I ignored Cassie's weird waffle ramblings. I wanted to stick with the story about Mike. "I still don't see how you guys ended up on a date," I said, refocusing the conversation.

"I went a third time. Mike saw me come in and tried to dodge into the back again, only I shouted at him to stop."

I paused with my bite of waffle in mid-air. "You did not!" I gasped. I was both impressed and a little horrified that she was yelling at Mike in the middle of Pete's Pizza.

Cassie laughed. "Totally did. I make no apologies for it. He froze and so I went behind the counter to talk to him. He was too far away and I wasn't going to keep shouting."

Now it was my turn to laugh as I pictured the whole scene in my head. "No way! What did Mike say?"

"He didn't say anything. I went up to him and said, 'Do you want to take me out to dinner tomorrow night?' He nodded his head then I said, 'Good answer. Pick me up at seven and I will tell you then where I have decided we are going."

"This just keeps getting better and better!" I was talking with my mouth full but did not care about manners at all by that point. I was so completely engrossed in Cassie's story.

"Well, he just nodded his head again, so I patted him on the chest and said, 'See you tomorrow night and don't be late.'

Then I walked out of the restaurant. Mike showed up at my place the next night at seven o'clock on the dot and I told him he was taking me out for Mexican food. So that's what we did." Cassie took a big bite of waffle and smiled at me.

"I think you're my new hero," I said, leaning back and smiling at her.

"You mean I haven't been all this time?" She said in a voice of false hurt.

I held my hands up and laughed. "I stand corrected. You have been, this just reaffirms why you are."

"That's better. So yeah. There you go. We've been on a few more dates since then. He's really nice and it feels really good when I'm with him." Cassie had a big smile on her face as she took another sip of her mimosa.

I was stunned yet again. "I can't believe you just called a guy 'nice' and meant it as a compliment and not an insult. I also can't believe you've been on more than two dates with him and still want to see him. Is this a new record?"

"I know right?" Cassie laughed. "So now that you are up to speed on me, start dishing about you and Nick."

I swallowed the bite in my mouth before proceeding. "Things are really good. Being with him is just easy and fun. I feel like I'm a better version of myself when I'm around Nick. Saying yes seems to come naturally when I am with him."

"I'm so happy for you! This is the kind of romance you deserve to have. What's the plan for when you leave for law school?" Cassie looked at me expectantly and I squirmed in my seat. I'd known the topic was going to come up and I knew I did not want to talk about it. I hesitated on answering, hoping Cassie would change the subject. I should have known she wouldn't. "Jenna, please tell me you have been talking about law school with him and not just ignoring it. The start of school is right around the corner and this is not just something that will magically fix itself." She had a concerned tone in her voice, I knew she meant well but things had been so great, it was hard to worry about the future when I was with Nick.

I let out a big sigh. "I know. It is just that things are so good and I don't want to ruin anything. For a while, part of me hoped he could maybe come with me, but I see now, with his company here, that is just not possible. Plus, he has a few huge development deals in the works that will likely keep him super busy if they go through."

"You have got to talk to him, Jenna. You guys either need to commit and figure out how you're going to make this work or end it before you go."

I pushed my plate away. The conversation had my stomach churning and I wasn't hungry anymore. "I know you're right. It's just hard. There are lots of feelings mixed up in everything now, for the both of us. I didn't anticipate I was going to feel so much for him. This was just supposed to be a short term fling, but I don't want it to end when I go to law school... I just don't know if that will work, with the distance and the time studying will take up. Plus his work schedule. It's a lot to think about," I said, finally giving voice to the thoughts that had been chasing themselves around my mind the last few weeks.

"All the more reason to start this conversation now and figure out where things stand." Cassie's voice was soft and full of concern.

"I will," I sighed. "I'm just scared. What if I'm good enough to be with him now, but not good enough to try and work things out when I am gone? Cassie, I think I am really starting to fall for him."

"Oh, honey." Cassie reached across the table and put her hand over mine. "You are good enough. It is other people that act like shit. Have you given any more thought to setting up a session with a therapist?"

"Not really," I answered honestly.

"You have been through a hell of a lot over the past year, and the therapist I see is really great. I started seeing her when I needed some help and I would not be this amazing ball of sass and hotness you see here if I had not gone. You could try to see her, or I'm sure she'd give you a referral to another therapist."

"I'll think about it." I knew Cassie's therapist had helped her tremendously, I just didn't know if I was ready for something like it.

As the waitress came to leave our check and clear our plates, I realized my stomach was all twisted up in knots. What if Nick did not want to be with me when I left for school? There were so many unanswered questions. There was only one thing I did know for sure... I was in too deep to walk away without a broken heart.

Chapter 32
Nick

I pinched the bridge of my nose and tried to take a few deep breaths. I was completely overwhelmed and I didn't like the way it felt. I had submitted proposals for three new projects and all three of them were big. One was for a new, multi-year, multi-million dollar subdivision project; the other was for a new, smaller residential area that was made up of large upscale houses; and the last one was a commercial property, which would be a whole new venture for Blaine Construction, a totally new challenge.

True to his word, Bax helped me do the interviews for an assistant. There were a bunch of applications but none of the candidates really clicked. Out of necessity more than anything, I made an offer to a woman named Janet. She was very experienced, but had a rather blunt demeanor. Janet had been working for me for a few weeks, and there was no way I could have gotten all three proposals done and in on time if it hadn't been for her managing all the day-to-day matters, so that was good. It was helpful to have the mundane tasks off of my plate and taken care of by someone else, but there was still a lot of work to do. There always was.

If I was being honest with myself, part of the reason I was feeling so overwhelmed was because of Jenna. I hadn't been attracted to anyone for a long time, but there was the crazy and intense pull I'd felt for her since the very first moment I laid eyes on her. Looking back on it, I was completely fooling myself that night at the bluff when we kissed for the first time, thinking I could just end it when she left without any problems. Even then, I knew I was falling for her, I just wasn't willing to acknowledge it.

Problem was, she was leaving and I was not a part of her plan after that. She'd had her plans already set before we even met. I wanted to be with her, but I wasn't going to be a big asshole and try and make her change her plans or goals in any way, especially just to include myself in them. I was proud of her and thought it was incredible she was going to law school, and fucking that up for her was just not an option. Especially when she hadn't given me any indication that she wanted to continue what was going on between us when she left for school. Besides, how would that even work, for either of us?

I also wasn't ready to tell her how I really felt, for a couple of reasons. First of all, there was the whole issue of fucking with her plans; but the second reason was because, well, talking about feelings was not really something I did. In fact, just the idea of it scared the hell out of me. I had never told a woman I loved her because... well, because I hadn't ever really experienced anything I would call love. Like, yes. Lust, yes. Compatibility, yes. But never love. The scary thing was with Jenna... well, it could be happening. Only thing was, it couldn't. The expiration date on our time together sounded like such a good idea in the beginning, but after being with her, it sounded like the worst fucking thing imaginable.

I was sitting at my desk, pretending to look over some expense reports, but really I was thinking about Jenna. I had to knock that shit off and get my head back in the game or else Blaine Construction was going to start suffering. So far, I had managed to somehow keep everything together and still see

Jenna, but the stress of it all was starting to wear on me. The irony was, the only time I didn't feel completely stressed out was when I was with Jenna.

My cell phone started ringing and I looked down at the unfamiliar number. I had no idea who it was, but went ahead and answered. "Good Afternoon, Blaine Construction. This is Nick speaking."

"Nick! Glad I caught you! This is Clive. Clive Henderson. I'm one of the investors for the Rickson Estates development."

Rickson Estates was one of the jobs Blaine Construction was bidding on. It was the smaller development that was going to be primarily very expensive, upscale housing. The property had been purchased by a group of investors and they were looking for someone to come in and build all of the houses at once. The timeline was tight, but they wanted everything done so when people moved into the housing, there was no ongoing construction in the neighborhood. It was *that* upscale.

"Clive, nice to hear from you. What can I do for you today, sir?" I put on my most professional voice.

"Well, myself and the other investors were looking over all of the proposals submitted by different construction companies. We all came to the agreement that if we are going to work with someone, we want it to be more than just numbers on a sheet of paper. Call us old-fashioned, but we want to meet the people behind the bids and know who it is we are actually working with," he said. He was matter of fact but not intimidating, clearly an astute businessman.

"That certainly sounds reasonable. I'd be more than happy to meet with you and the other investors, when would you like to schedule this meeting?" I asked in my most professional voice, hoping I sounded calm and confident. I wanted that job for Blaine Construction. It was worth a great deal of money, and more than that, I wanted the Blaine Construction name forever attached to Rickson Estates. It was the first type of development like that in the area, and I had a feeling it wasn't going to be the last. Building Rickson Estates would put Blaine Construction in a position to be the leader and the model of future developments in the area – there was a lot riding on this deal, that was for sure.

"Well, we were on our way up to the property to take a look around and thought it would be a perfect time to meet. Do you think you could meet us there in an hour?" Clive inquired.

I looked down at my watch. It was already mid-afternoon and the property was about forty-five minutes away from my office, which meant forty-five minutes there and forty-five minutes back. Hopefully, it wouldn't take too long up at the property to do a little meet and greet with the investors.

"I can do that," I said confidently. "I'll see you there in an hour."

"I am pleased to hear that, Nick and I know the other investors will be as well. See you in about an hour." Clive hung up the phone.

I let out a big sigh. Heading up to the property was about the last thing I wanted to do, but if that was what it took to land the project, then I was going to do it. I started rolling down the sleeves on my button-up shirt to cover my tattoos and grabbed the blazer I kept stashed on the back door of my office.

I walked out of my office and into the reception area at the front of the building. Janet was sitting at her desk doing... I'm not really sure what she was doing, but she didn't look too busy which was concerning given the amount of stuff going on at the moment. "Janet, I'm going to go up and meet a couple of investors at the Rickson Estates property. Sounds like it is just a little meet and greet, but if I am not back by five o'clock, go ahead and lock up, please."

"It is at least an hour and a half of drive time there and back, boss. You're definitely not going to be back by five." Janet chomped on the big wad of gum she had in her mouth. I had asked her to stop with the gum several times already, but she really didn't seem to give a fuck what I said. I had a feeling Janet wasn't going to work out as my assistant long term – great, another project.

"Well, hopefully, I can just meet quickly with a couple of the investors, turn around, and come right back."

Janet raised her eyebrow at me. "Whatever you say, boss." She held out the keyring to a company truck with an annoyed expression on her face.

Yeah. Janet was not going to work at Blaine Construction much longer. "Thanks," I said, trying to arrange a smile on my face, as I took the keys and headed out the front door.

The drive was pleasant and took almost exactly forty-five minutes. When I rounded the corner to the plot of land that had been purchased for the building site, my stomach sank. There were at least half a dozen pickup trucks parked there and at least twice that many people out milling around.

"Fuck," I muttered to myself as I pulled up. "This is not going to be quick at all."

I parked next to the other trucks and got out as a man with a big white beard and a cowboy hat waved at me from where he was leaning against another truck. I walked over to him and he extended his hand for a handshake. "You must be Nick. I'm Clive. When I put the word out you were going to meet us here, everyone wanted to come." He chuckled as we shook hands. "With all of us here a few questions and concerns have come up. Why don't you come on over and I can introduce you to everyone and you can answer some questions we have for you."

Fuck, fuck, fuck, I thought to myself. It was not at all what I thought it would be, but Blaine Construction really needed to land the project. I put on my most professional smile as I looked Clive directly in the eye and said, "Sounds great. How about you lead the way and I will follow you?" I gestured for him to lead the way, making sure my head was in the game for the investor meet and greet.

Chapter 33
Jenna

"Hey! Are you the first one here? Where's Nick?" Cassie asked as she slid into the booth next to me. A group of us from work were meeting up for dinner at a local restaurant before going to see the new summer blockbuster together. Since I was the first one, I went ahead and got a table for all of us. Depending on how the night played out, we'd also talked about going out for drinks afterward. We didn't have a whole lot of time left to hang out as a group before I left and we wanted to make the most of it.

"He texted me a little while ago that he had to work late. He said to go ahead and order food and that he would be here as soon as he could." The message he sent was vague and had just come in a few minutes before Cassie arrived. I was hoping he would get there in time to grab something to eat before the movie.

"How are things with the two of you?" Cassie asked as she reached for a menu.

"Good, we just haven't seen each other for a few days. He's been really busy with some new development proposals and I worked a bunch of night shifts in a row."

"Have you two talked about what you are going to do when you leave for law school?" I had really been hoping Cassie would not bring that up. It was on my mind a lot but with Nick so busy, there wasn't a good time to talk about it with him and I was so nervous about it already.

I avoided eye contact with her as I mumbled, "No. Not really."

"Jenna! Seriously? What the hell? Don't you start class in a few weeks? Wait, you are still going, right?" Cassie eyed me suspiciously.

I sighed. "Yes, I am still going. The school actually called this morning to confirm I would be there and gave me some updated information."

"Why haven't you talked to Nick? You have had weeks to do this. Wait, does he even know you are leaving?"

"I feel terrible and have been worrying about it non-stop. Things are going so well that I don't want to do anything to ruin it. Then, when I finally worked up the nerve to have the conversation, he got busy at work and I had a few extra shifts. Now, we haven't seen each other for a few days." I nervously played with the napkin in my lap. "I'm turning into a mess about it. He knows about law school. I was upfront about it when we first met and I have brought it up, casually, a few times. I just don't know what's happening when I leave."

Cassie drummed her fingers on the table. "Isn't he going to find it totally suspicious when all of the sudden your apartment is packed up and you are gone?"

"Who is suspicious? Are we talking about Nick? I don't see him here." Mike slid into the booth next to Cassie and she turned to give him a look like he needed to stop talking.

"Good grief, Mike! What is it with you and butting into other people's conversations? So rude!" Kimmy exclaimed as she sat down next to me. She was followed by Steven.

"Where is Nick? He is still coming, right? Would be a bummer for him to miss the movie since we've been planning this for weeks," Steven said as he reached for a menu.

"He'll be here soon, there's nothing to worry about. He just got held up at work." Cassie looked right at me as she was speaking. That girl knew me too well. My mind had instantly wandered back to all of the times we had something planned and my ex Brett suddenly couldn't make it. With Brett, it turned out that his 'I have to work late' or 'I'm suddenly not feeling well' and 'this thing came up last minute' were really code for 'I am banging a whole bunch of other women behind your back.' He was the worst.

My insecurities started to run wild. Nick wouldn't do that... would he? No! No, he would not. "He was just held up at work and will be here as soon as he can," I told everyone, trying to quash the thoughts threatening to take over.

I could feel myself starting to panic and an all too familiar and unwelcome tightening in my chest. "I need to use the restroom. I'll be right back." Kimmy moved out of the booth so I could slide out and I quickly dashed away from the table.

When I got to the restroom, I stood by the sink and took a few deep breaths before splashing water on my face. I had my eyes closed when I heard a soft voice call out, "Jen, are you in here?"

"Yes, over here," I said between deep breaths.

I opened my eyes and saw Cassie standing next to me, her face etched in concern. "Oh, honey," she said softly, "Was it a panic attack?"

I closed my eyes again. "Yes. I could feel it start to happen and I just had to get out of there. I think I'm feeling better already getting some air."

Cassie started to rub my back as I leaned over the sink. "It's been months since something like this happened. You know Nick is not Brett, right? Is that what started it?"

"I don't know. I just started thinking about all the times Brett said he was working late and—" my voice was starting to get high pitched when Cassie interrupted me.

"I am going to stop you right there. Nick is not Brett. Nick cares about you. I can tell by the way he looks at you and the way that he treats you. He kissed you on a freaking Jumbotron in front of a whole stadium of people for goodness sakes. Brett is a no-good, low-life, piece of shit who needs to rot at the bottom of the ocean."

I took a deep breath as I turned to look at Cassie. "I had one when Nick took me on the picnic."

Cassie looked surprised for a moment. "A panic attack? Why didn't you tell me? How did Nick react?"

"I was embarrassed. I hadn't had one since the break-up, once Brett was out of my life. Nick actually helped and was really great."

"See! Totally different from Brett the bastard! What do you say we get back out there and have some dinner before we hit the movie?" Cassie gave me an encouraging smile. "I'm sure Nick will be here soon." She knew just what to say to comfort and reassure me.

I nodded my head. "You're right. I am totally overreacting. I'm sure he'll be here soon." I tried to return Cassie's smile even though my mind was still racing. I really wanted to believe Nick was just held up at work. He knew that tonight was important to me so he would be there... right? Yes, I told myself as we walked out of the bathroom. Nick cares about me and he would be there. He had not given me any reason not to trust him... but then again, in the whole grand scheme of things, we had not known each other very long. After that night at the club, everything just happened so fast between us. No. I was not going to let my mind wander round and round. I needed to stop jumping to conclusions and just wait for Nick to show up.

Cassie and I went back to the table and ordered our food with the rest of the group. I couldn't help but check my cell phone multiple times throughout dinner. No new messages. It wasn't like Nick to not respond at all.

When the waiter cleared our plates and brought our checks, Steven looked over at me as I was once again checking my phone. "Have you heard from Nick?" he asked. "Since all we have left is to pay, does he want to just meet us at the theater?"

"Good question." I scrunched up my face as I saw there were still no new messages. I quickly typed one out to Nick. *"Hey - hope everything is OK. We just finished dinner and are headed to the movie. It starts in about 30 minutes. See you at the theater?"*

I pushed send and stared at my phone. No response. Not even the little bubbles showing he was typing something. I sighed and put my phone in my purse. My heart was starting to feel heavy.

"Ready to go?" Cassie asked.

I looked up from my phone. "Yeah. Don't want to miss the movie." I gave Cassie a weak smile and she put her arm around me as we walked out of the restaurant.

"Don't jump to any conclusions. Has Nick given you any reason not to trust him?" She said to me quietly as we walked.

"No," I answered honestly as I glanced down at my phone again. Still no new message from Nick.

"Let's go see what everyone is saying is the best movie of the summer," Cassie said in an overly cheerful voice. I appreciated that she was trying to distract me.

When we got to the theater, I quickly sent another message to Nick. *"We are at the theater and the movie is about to start. We are going to go in, but I went ahead and bought you a ticket. It's waiting at the ticket counter for you. See you soon?"*

I quickly shoved my phone in my purse as the lights dimmed for the movie. I wasn't quite sure how to feel. I didn't want to believe Nick had just blown me off, but part of me couldn't help but have a really terrible feeling about it all. If he didn't want to come out for a night, there was no way he would want to make things work once I left for law school. It had only been a few days since we last saw each other and it felt like I was already 'out of sight out of mind', if that were the case, then I clearly was not as important to Nick as I thought. I tried to focus on the opening credits and forget about Nick. Though, I knew there was no way I would ever be able to forget about Nick.

I should have known it was all too good to be true.

Chapter 34
Jenna

The five of us were standing outside the theater after the movie. The night air was cool and I rubbed my arms as I pulled out my phone to see if there was a message from Nick. Nothing. I could feel the hot sting of tears starting to prick behind my eyelids. I tried to blink them away. I was not going to cry.

I typed out a quick message to Nick. *"You missed a great movie. Really worried about you. Just send me something to let me know you are OK."* I hit send and quickly shoved my phone into my purse.

Cassie came over to stand next to me. "I am so sorry, babe. I don't know what to say."

I gave her a weak smile. "Me neither."

"I knew there was a reason to be worried about him!" Mike jumped in.

Cassie immediately spun around to him, her tone laced with anger. "Oh! You did not just say that! Please tell me that you——"

"Seriously, Mike! Shut up! That is not helpful" Kimmy snapped at Mike, interrupting Cassie.

Even Steven weighed in, "Yeah, dude. That was a shit thing to say. We don't know what happened. Give the guy a break and don't be an ass to Jenna."

Mike looked at me sheepishly with flushed cheeks. "I'm sorry, Jenna. I just never wanted to see you get hurt by him."

I knew Mike was just trying to be protective of me and I appreciated that. I waved my hand in his general direction. "It's fine, Mike. Listen, I know when we planned this we talked about going out to drinks after the movie, but would you guys mind if I rain-checked? I think I'd like to just head home."

"Of course! We'll see you at work tomorrow!" Kimmy said as she gave me a big hug and then motioned for Steven and Mike to follow her. "Come on guys! Steven, you have the keys. We are going to give Mike some sensitivity training on the way home."

"I am sensitive! I have four sisters! I just was trying to look out for Jenna!" Mike protested.

Kimmy rolled her eyes and started to walk towards Steven's car. "Yet you still say stupid, insensitive shit!" she turned and shouted over her shoulder. I couldn't help but laugh. I felt so grateful for my friends.

Cassie walked up to Mike and stuck her pointer finger into his chest. "Just so we are on the same page, I don't date people that upset my best friend, so get your shit together."

"Wait? We're dating?" Mike's face broke into a huge grin. "Did you hear that everyone? We're dating! Cassie and I are dating! Best. Day. Ever!" He shouted.

Cassie put her hand on her hip. "Not if you are going to act like a giant, insensitive Neanderthal. You need to go now before I change my mind about you, Mr. Mike, and cut you off from all of this redheaded goodness." Cassie moved her hand from her hip and waved it down the length of her body.

Kimmy let out a low whistle from where she was standing a few feet away, by Steven's car. "Wow! That was harsh!" She said, laughing a little.

Mike was still grinning ear to ear. Cassie rolled her eyes and shrugged her shoulders. "Meh. He'll get over it. Or not. Anyway, I can't deal with him right now. I have other, more pressing things going on."

"Good night!" Kimmy waved at us before she climbed into Steven's car.

"Night!" Steven had rolled down the window and was shouting his goodbyes from the driver's seat.

Mike was still standing next to us. "Good night," he said to me, then he turned to Cassie. "I will see you tomorrow, Cassie," he said with a huge smile plastered across his face. At least someone had come out of tonight with good news. Cassie shooed Mike away with her hand which only made him chuckle a little through his giant smile. Mike turned back and looked at her again giving her another smile and a wave before he got into Steven's car. When Cassie thought I wasn't looking, she gave Mike a small wave and blew him a kiss.

The idea of them together still seemed just this side of totally crazy.

"Well, sister, it looks like it's just you and me. Let's get out of here," Cassie gave me a wink.

"Cass? Can I stay at your place tonight? I don't want to be alone." I didn't feel like I was in a good headspace and the idea of going back to my quiet apartment alone didn't sit right.

Cassie wrapped her arm around me as we started walking towards our cars. "Of course! Lucky for you, I have a bottle of red wine that has just been begging to be opened. Sound like a plan?"

I leaned into Cassie, relieved to have her there with me. "Yes, that sounds like a very good plan," I sighed.

When I got into my car, I pulled my phone out and looked at it again. Still no response to the messages I had sent Nick. The last message from him was at the start of the evening when he told me he had to work late. I typed out one last quick message before turning my phone off and shoving it deep into the bottom of my purse.

"Good night, Nick."

***

"Good morning sleepy head." I slowly blinked my eyes open as I looked around the room and remembered I was at Cassie's house. "I know I'm not nearly the same morning eye candy as he-who-shall-not-be-named-right-now, but I come with coffee." Cassie climbed up on the bed and handed me a large, steaming mug. "How did you sleep?"

I inhaled the delicious coffee scent and took a large drink of it before I shrugged my shoulders and said, "Meh. I've had better."

Cassie clasped her hands together, "Oh! You just lobbed me a giant softball! So many inappropriate comments I could make, but, I can tell from your eyes you were crying last night, so I'll hold myself together and let this opportunity pass. It just seems like you might not be in the mood for inappropriate jokes."

"Thanks, Cass. You really know how to read a room." I took another sip of coffee and let it warm me from the inside out as I pulled my knees up to my chest.

"Talent, darling. It's called talent." Cassie pretended to take a small bow while still sitting on the bed. "All joking aside, how are you doing this morning?"

"I didn't sleep well and I don't know what to think about anything. Other than that, I am just great," my voice was thick with sarcasm.

"Don't jump to any conclusions just yet. Have you heard from him at all?"

"No. I turned my phone off last night and stuffed it in the bottom of my purse to keep myself from obsessively checking it."

"That doesn't do you a whole lot of good. What if he's been trying to call you?"

"What if he hasn't?" I was quick to respond.

"Guess we won't know unless you get your phone and turn it on," Cassie challenged back.

I sighed and drank some more coffee before I got off the bed and grabbed my purse. I pulled out my phone and powered it back on. I chewed on my bottom lip as I nervously waited for it to load.

Nothing. No messages or calls from Nick.

I felt a fresh wave of tears start to stream down my cheeks. My heart felt like it was shattering into a million little pieces. I turned to Cassie, "Nothing. No text, no voicemail. Nothing. If something happened last night, why hasn't he tried to contact me this morning?"

Cassie looked at me sympathetically. "I don't know, sweetie. I was holding out for some type of explanation other than him ghosting you. He just doesn't seem like the type. What are you going to do?"

"Well, considering what time it is, I think I'll run home, shower, and go to work. My shift starts at noon today."

Cassie climbed down off the bed and came over to where I was sitting on the floor and hugged me. "I am so sorry, Jen. Check in with me any time today. I have an open house later this afternoon but will keep my phone on me. Unlike other people that we shall not speak of, I know how to use a phone and can respond to messages," she said rubbing my shoulders.

I hugged Cassie back. I was so grateful for her in so many ways. "Thank you. You really are the best. Thank you again for letting me stay here last night."

Cassie laughed as she stood up. "Girl! You know you are welcome to my guest room anytime. Unless I am about to get my groove on then I am going to have to ask you to sleep downstairs on the sofa since the guest room is right across the hall from my bedroom and that would be weird." Cassie shimmied her hips a little as she walked towards the door.

I couldn't help but laugh, even though I felt like crying. "You are so weird."

"Ahhhhhhhhhh ... I think you mean weirdly perfect. Have a good day sweetie. I need to get ready for work, just let yourself out whenever you are ready to go." Cassie blew an air kiss at me as she walked out of the bedroom door.

***

As I walked up the stairs to my apartment building I checked my phone again. Still nothing. I sighed as I resigned myself to the fact I wasn't going to hear from Nick. I just needed to get ready for work and try to make it through the day.

When I turned down the walkway to my apartment, I saw something in front of my door. "That's strange," I muttered out loud. I always had packages delivered to the main office of the complex so I had no idea what it could be. As I got closer, I realized the thing in front of my door was a bouquet of flowers. I picked them up and saw it was a dozen red roses. There was one of Nick's business cards tucked into the flowers and on the back, it simply said, "I am so sorry."

The flowers looked to be a tad bit wilted, like maybe they had been sitting in front of my door for a while. I went inside and put them in some water. I stared at the flowers in the vase. "Why would he put these here, and then not contact me? None of this makes any sense." I chuckled. "I'm talking to myself again. I have officially gone all kinds of crazy."

I toyed with the idea of sending another message to Nick or trying to call him but, ultimately, decided not to. Maybe after my shift. I was still so confused about everything and felt emotionally raw from last night. I just needed some time to sort out what I was going to do.

I got in the shower and as I stood under the warm water, trying to wash the night away, all I could think about was Nick. It was going to be a really long day.

Chapter 35
Nick

Dammit! I looked at the clock on the dashboard of my truck and realized that not only had I missed dinner, but by the time I got back to town, I would miss the movie as well. There had been talk of going out for drinks after the movie, but I had no idea where they were going. Jenna and I hadn't seen each other for the last few days due to our work schedules, and although we spoke on the phone, I didn't really get a whole lot of details about the events planned for the evening.

"Fuck!" I shouted as I slammed the palm of my hand on the steering wheel. I had completely screwed everything up. I knew the night was a big deal for Jenna since she was getting ready to leave soon and I really wanted to be there for her. What was supposed to be a quick meet and greet at the Rickson Estates property turned into the biggest, and longest clusterfuck. The investors had wanted to talk in extensive detail about the project and do a walk around of the site. It literally took hours. Turns out, some of the investors were considering pulling their funding and needed some reassurance about the project, something Clive had failed to mention on the phone call earlier in the day.

I wanted to text or call Jenna, but it wasn't until we were way out into the middle of the property that I realized I didn't have my phone. As a result, I was distracted for the rest of the meeting because all I could think about was Jenna. One of the investors actually called me out on it and made a snotty comment about *"if I couldn't give my full attention to the meeting, how could they be sure I would give my full attention to their building project."* I think I recovered well from the question, but I couldn't stop thinking about how Jenna had no idea what was going on. I had only sent her a really vague message earlier that I was working late and would catch up to them. At the time I sent it, I thought I was only going to be a little late, not miss the whole fucking night. I finally found my phone back by where everyone was parked, smashed to pieces. It must have fallen out of my pocket when I got out of my truck and someone ran over it as everyone was leaving. Fantastic, what a great end to a shitshow of an evening.

It was late and the whole situation was fucked up. I couldn't help but remind myself that it was one of the many reasons why I had not dated since starting Blaine Construction. It was a no-win situation. I had been distracted by the investors on Jenna's night and I wasn't able to give the meeting my full attention because I was worried about contacting Jenna. I hoped, by some miracle, I had not totally fucked up Blaine Construction getting the project. I also knew I'd completely let Jenna down by not meeting up with her and her friends like I said I would. Basically, I had fucked up on both fronts. I didn't want to potentially lose a big project for Blaine Construction and I didn't want to lose Jenna either, but I had no idea how I was supposed to be involved with both things at once. Something was going to have to give.

As I drove into town, I kept mulling the question over and over in my mind. Jenna was going to be leaving in a few weeks. I didn't want to lose her, but could I risk everything else to be with her? I thought of all the years of long nights and working seven days a week that had gone into getting

Blaine Construction off the ground. Not to mention all of the people who depended on me for employment and all the different contracts I had going for different projects. I needed to focus on Blaine Construction, but as soon as I had that thought, Jenna's face popped up in my mind and suddenly all the other stuff didn't seem to matter. Fuck! I had no idea how to make all of it work.

I decided since I couldn't call her, I would show up at her apartment and see if I could talk to her. I just needed to explain what happened. I stopped at a 24-hour grocery store and picked up a dozen red roses for her. I remembered from our picnic in the park those were her favorite. While I knew flowers were not going to fix it, I also knew I had to do something to show her she was important to me and how sorry I was about the shitshow I had created.

When I got to her apartment complex, I looked around and saw her car wasn't there. I went up and knocked on her door just to be sure she hadn't gotten a ride home from one of her friends. It was a little after midnight at that point, and I was sure they were still out getting drinks. I would just wait for her. I had to get everything straightened out, and the more time that passed, the worse it was going to be.

I sat down in my truck in the parking lot and waited. The longer I sat there, the more my head started to spin with ideas of where she was, and who she could be with. What if she thought I had just blown her off? What if she went out for a few drinks and then had gone home with someone else? That thought made me feel physically ill. Sometime around 2 AM, it became painfully clear she was not coming home. She obviously had to be somewhere with someone else. I dug around in my truck and found a business card. I scribbled a quick "I'm so sorry" message on the back of the card and stuck it in the flowers. I then took the flowers up and put them on her doorstep. Jenna had to come home eventually, and at least she would know I had been here. It was all I could do.

My heart was heavy as I walked back to the truck and drove home. In one night, I had probably lost two important things. Thing was, I had known all along I couldn't have both, but I had been so wrapped up in being with Jenna I hadn't been focused on what I needed to be doing. As a result, I had completely fucked everything up. I only hoped I could somehow fix this mess.

***

The next morning, when I went to get my phone situation fixed, I drove out of my way to go by Jenna's apartment. Her car still was not in the parking lot. I parked and ran up to her apartment only to see the roses still sitting out in front of her door.

She hadn't come home the previous night and still wasn't back that morning. I felt like I couldn't breathe. As I walked back to my motorcycle, all I could think about was that I had ruined everything with her. I felt an ache in my chest unlike anything I had ever felt before.

***

As soon as I got a new phone, I drove directly to Pete's. I was pretty sure Jenna was working and I was desperate to see her. When I walked into the restaurant, the first person I saw was Mike standing behind the counter. Based on the look he was giving me, it was not going to go well.

I walked up to the counter, "Hey Mike. I was hoping that I could please see Jenna."

Mike folded his arms across his chest and continued to glare at me. "No."

"Please. Just tell her I am here. I need to see her." I tried to keep my voice even, what was with this guy!

"I don't think so, man. You had a chance to see and talk to her last night. If she wants to talk to you, she knows how to get a hold of you."

I started to feel the panic and frustration that had been resting just below my surface bubble up. "You don't understand! I screwed up last night and part of the problem was my phone!"

Mike raised an eyebrow at me. "Hummmmmmmmmm... I see." The tone of Mike's voice made it very clear he thought I was full of shit.

I ran my hand through my hair as I closed my eyes and tried to take some deep breaths. I was trying really hard to keep myself from totally losing it right there in the restaurant. "Listen," I took another deep breath, "I really need to talk to Jenna. Will you please let her know I am here? If she doesn't want to see me I'll go." Even as I said that last part out loud, I prayed it wasn't the case. I didn't know if my heart could take it if she said she wouldn't see me.

Mike continued to look at me with great skepticism. "I will tell her you stopped by. That's the best I can do. After last night, consider yourself lucky I'm willing to do that for you. Now, I think it's time for you to leave."

Part of me didn't want to know but I had to ask. After having my thoughts spiral out of control all night, I hadn't been able to rein them in. "Will you... will you at least tell me if she's okay? She didn't go home to her apartment last night. Did she go home by herself?" I had to pause and take a deep breath. I closed my eyes as I almost whispered the next part. "Or did she go home with someone else? Did you see who she left with?" I tried to brace myself for whatever answer Mike would give me.

"Dude. Listen to me. Whatever happened with you was not cool. I don't know what your deal is, but Jenna is not like that. She was upset last night so she stayed at Cassie's house." Mike was looking at me like I had totally lost my mind. Part of me wondered if I had. It wasn't like me, at all, to get so worked up. It was just the thought of Jenna with someone else, true or not, cut me so deeply I didn't feel like myself.

I let out a huge rush of air and grabbed the counter. "She was with Cassie? Thank god! Are you sure?" I was so relieved it felt like I was breathing for the first time since the previous night.

"Yes. Now I have already told you more than I should. It's time for you to go." Mike's voice was firm and with an edge to it I had never heard from him before. Honestly, I hadn't known he was capable of that sort of thing. Mike had always seemed to be completely calm and laid back.

I put both hands up and took a step back. "Fine. I'm going. Please just let her know I was here and that my phone situation is fixed."

199

I turned and walked out the front door, not wanting to create any more problems than I already had. I took my new phone out of my pocket and looked at it for what felt like the millionth time that morning. Nothing from Jenna. It dawned on me she must have felt the same way the night before. It was a really fucking awful feeling. I swung my leg over my bike and sent her one more message trying to apologize. As the engine on my motorcycle roared to life, I hoped it wasn't too late to fix things with her.

Chapter 36
Jenna

I was in the kitchen at work waiting for my next delivery when I heard some raised voices coming from the front register. I immediately recognized the voices belonged to Mike and Nick. I remained frozen in place as I listened to their conversation.

When Nick finally left the restaurant, Mike came back into the kitchen where I was standing with tears running down my cheeks. "I am going to assume you heard most, if not all of that," Mike said as he grabbed me into a big hug.

I buried my face in his chest. "Yes, thank you for being an overprotective, big-brother type. You can be such an ass and such an amazing person all at the same time."

Mike chucked. "I guess that makes me the whole package." I laughed into Mike's chest. "Call him, Jenna. Hear him out and then make a decision about what you are going to do. Every story has two sides. Don't just go with only half the information," he said encouragingly.

"When did you get so wise?" I pulled away from Mike and started wiping my tears with the back of my hand.

"I think it was around the time I met this fiery redhead." Mike's face was beaming.

I looked at him for a moment. "You really like her don't you?"

"She is everything I have ever wanted, a whole lot of things I never knew I needed, and now I can't imagine living without her."

"Wow, Mike. That is really sweet." I was happy for Cassie. After everything she had been through, she really deserved to have someone good in her life. Mike was one of the good ones.

"She doesn't know it yet, but she's it for me. She is my forever." Judging by the look on Mike's face, I had no doubt that when Mike said she was his forever, it was absolutely true.

"You guys have talked about marriage?" I couldn't keep the surprise out of my voice. As long as I had known Cassie, getting married was never on her radar.

Mike chuckled. "Nope. Like I said, she doesn't know it yet. I have known since the first time I saw her. Don't worry, she'll figure it out."

Now it was my turn to chuckle. "Good luck with that. I don't know if Cassie will ever be tamed."

"Now... back to you and Nick. Go call him, Jenna." Mike waved his hand towards the break room.

"Alright," I agreed. "I'll call him on break."

***

A few hours later, I finally took my break. I went into the back, grabbed my purse, and pulled out my phone. I was surprised to see there were half a dozen missed calls and several text messages. I scrolled through the missed call log. They were all from Nick and started at about the same time as my shift. My phone had been in my purse in the back the whole time. I clicked on the text messages and started to scroll through them. They were all from Nick.

"I am so sorry. I screwed up. Please call me, I need to see you."

"I'm worried about you. I know this looks bad. I screwed up, but I don't know where you are. Let me know you are OK."

"I went to your apartment last night and waited to see you. You didn't come home. You weren't there this morning when I came by. Please tell me you're OK and I did not screw this whole thing up."

"I am so sorry. I know I fucked up. I am sorry. Tell me how to fix it."

"Please contact me. My phone is working now. Jenna, I am so sorry about last night. Give me a chance to explain."

I sighed as I read through all of the messages twice. I tapped out a quick message, unsure of exactly what to say. "Hi. I just got all of your messages and heard you came by Pete's."

Nick's response was almost immediate. "You have no idea how glad I am to hear from you. I am so sorry. Please give me a chance to explain. Can I see you?"

I chewed on my lip for a moment as I remembered what Mike said about getting Nick's side of the story. "My shift is over at 9 tonight. Are you free after?"

"Yes. Whatever time and place you pick, I will be there. Just tell me when and where."

"I'll come by your place when I get off work." I set my phone down and rubbed my eyes. I was starting to get a headache.

"Perfect. I will see you then. Thank you for meeting with me. I am so sorry about last night."

I read the last message from Nick and realized I had no idea what to think. The only thing I knew for sure was that Nick and I had a whole lot to talk about. Not just about last night, but about the fact I was leaving in a few weeks for law school. There was just so much hanging out there in the universe I started to feel all jittery. I decided to send a message to Cassie. *"Long story, but I am going to go see Nick tonight after work."*

I immediately saw the bubbles pop up that showed Cassie was writing a message back. *"WTF? That is a serious turn of events. I am sensing a juicy story. TELL ME!"*

"My break is almost over, but I promise to give you the full story after tonight."

"Boooooooooooooo! Too long to wait!" Cassie added a bunch of sad face emojis in her text.

I quickly responded. *"Mike can fill you in on part of it."*

"I don't want sloppy seconds for this story. You either lived it or I don't want to hear it."

I laughed out loud as I read Cassie's message. I knew she would make me feel better. I quickly typed out a message back to her. *"Mike did live part of it. He is a pretty good guy."*

All of Cassie's previous responses had come through quickly, but this time a few minutes passed with no response. I was ready to put my phone back in my purse when it dinged with a new message. *"I am even more intrigued. Mike is OK. Most of the time. Maybe even a little more than OK. Now get back to work!"*

I smiled at Cassie's Mike message. I realized she really liked him and it made me happy.

I slipped my phone back into my purse. I just had to make it to the end of my shift and go hash things out with Nick. Easy peasy, right?

Chapter 37
Jenna

I pulled up to Nick's house a little after nine o'clock. I hadn't even bothered to change out of my work uniform and I smelled like pizza.

I sat in the car for a few minutes before I walked to the front door. I was about halfway up the sidewalk when Nick swung the door open. "Jenna! I am so glad you're here! Part of me was worried you weren't coming tonight."

"I said I would be here. When I say I am going to be somewhere. I am going to be there." Nick winced. "I'm sorry! I didn't mean it like that!" Already I was sticking my foot in my mouth. Things were off to a great start. How was it that I always seemed to come up with the exact wrong thing to say?

"No, I deserve it," Nick said. We stood there awkwardly before he finally stepped out of the doorway. "Would you like to come in?"

"Yes. Should we go into the living room?" I tried to force a smile as I spoke, but it felt like I failed miserably. It felt more like a toothy grimace.

"Yes, that would be good," Nick replied stiffly, with an equally uncomfortable smile. It was clear we were both nervous. Our greeting seemed weirdly formal and without any trace of our usual playfulness. We walked into the living room. I sat on the sofa and Nick stood awkwardly in the middle of the room. Everything just felt really weird. I shifted nervously on the sofa while Nick just stood there. I knew I could be a really awkward person at times, but it was way too awkward, even for me.

"Jenna, I am..."

"Nick, about last night..." We both started speaking at the same time.

Nick ran his hand through his hair. "God! I am so fucking nervous right now. All day I have been going over what I wanted to tell you, but now that you're here, my mind is totally fucking blank. I also didn't sleep much last night and in the past twenty-four hours I have experienced just about every damn emotion a human can have— which is way too fucking many, by the way." Nick paced back and forth as he spoke, finally sitting down in the oversized chair directly across from me.

"I didn't sleep much either last night, so at least we are on a level playing field there." I gave Nick a small smile, attempting to lighten the mood a little.

When Nick looked up at me, I could see he had dark circles under his eyes. "Can I go first? Let me tell you about what happened and if you want to leave, I will understand."

"Okay," I answered softly, unsure of anything else I could say.

"So, I want to start by saying how sorry I am, Jenna. This was entirely my fault and I hate that I made you upset. I can tell by your eyes that you've been crying and it breaks my heart that I'm the one who did that to you." Nick paused for a second as his voice cracked. He took a deep breath and continued. "I really did plan on meeting up with you and your friends for dinner and the movie. I knew how important it was to you and that it had been planned for weeks. I wanted to be there with you."

I nodded my head as Nick paused again. He closed his eyes for a second before continuing on. It was clear this was difficult for him. "I got a call in the afternoon from an investor in one of the new building projects Blaine Construction has submitted a bid on. It sounded like he just wanted to meet face-to-face at the property. There is a whole lot riding on this deal, including the employment of a whole lot of people. The guy who called is one of the primary investors and I expected it to be a quick meet and greet. When I got to the property, there were way more people than what I had anticipated."

"Is that when you texted me you were going to be running late?" I asked.

"I sent that before I got to the property and saw all the people. I swear I thought I would get out there, take a quick look at the property, and set up another meeting for today or tomorrow. It turned out some of the investors that were there waiting for me were considering pulling their funding and they wanted a way more extensive look at the property than I had expected. They also had way more questions than I had anticipated, especially for a meet and greet. We were at the property for hours."

I was confused, "Why didn't you just send me another message or call me and let me know what was going on?" My tone was a little harsher than I had intended, but it seemed like such a simple thing, especially since he had contacted me earlier in the evening.

Nick nodded. "I was going to do that exact thing, but when I went to grab my phone from my pocket, it was gone. We were way out in the middle of the property and there wasn't much I could do. I thought maybe I left it in my truck, but at that point, we were really far from where the cars were parked and I had a group of investors following me around the build site, asking questions about the proposal."

"So why didn't you send me a message when you got back to the truck?" I was starting to feel a little annoyed by the whole situation. I'd been so upset and a simple text message could have spared me a rollercoaster of emotions.

"Also a great idea, however, when we finally got back to where all the cars were parked, my phone wasn't in the truck. I started to get a little panicked at that point, because I had already missed dinner, and I was pretty sure the movie had already started. I felt like a colossal asshole." Nick looked at me with a very sorrowful expression etched across his face.

I shook my head. "Nick, that doesn't explain why I didn't hear from you until this afternoon."

"Well, I finally found my phone. It was laying on the ground by where the investor had parked his truck. It must have fallen out when I went to say 'hi' to him and shake his hand. It must have been really close to the truck too because it was totally smashed."

"Smashed? Like it had been run over?" I asked in surprise. Suddenly, things were starting to become clearer to me.

Nick nodded his head. "That is what it looked like. It was an accident. It was fairly dark by the time we were leaving so there was no way he could have seen it."

"Oh," I said quietly. I was starting to feel like a jerk for not having a little more faith in Nick and knowing he would not intentionally blow me off. However, I had also not forgotten the conversation I overheard at Pete's where Nick made some incorrect assumptions about why I didn't go back to my apartment last night.

Nick suddenly cleared his throat. "The smashed phone is on the dining room table if you don't believe any of this."

Did I believe him? I thought for a moment before I answered. Finally, I made my decision; "I don't need to see it. I believe you," I said simply.

A look of relief washed over Nick's face. He let out a big breath before he jumped back into his explanation. "Last night I knew how badly I screwed up and how late it was when we finally left the site. I also realized I didn't actually know your phone number since it was just programmed into my phone. I stopped and grabbed the flowers and thought I would meet you at your apartment so I could explain and apologize."

"I didn't go home last night..." I just trailed off and didn't finish the thought.

Chapter 38
Jenna

There was an awkward silence that hung between us. Suddenly, Nick blurted out, "Roses. I remembered that red roses were your favorite from our picnic. I sat outside of your apartment and waited for you last night. The longer I sat there, the worse I felt and the more I started to get these crazy ideas stuck in my head."

"Like, what kind of crazy ideas?" I was almost afraid to ask, though his chat with Mike earlier had clued me in a little.

Nick hesitated and then let out a big sigh. "I knew that I screwed up and I was afraid you would think I had just blown you off. When you didn't come home... well, I started to convince myself that, maybe, you were so upset you went home with someone else."

"Like sleeping with someone else?" I stared straight at him with a questioning look on my face. I was shocked he would think that and wanted to clear it up immediately.

"I know it sounds stupid now, but the thought that I had somehow ruined things with you really started to mess with my head. I waited outside of your apartment until around two in the morning and then left. I was pretty upset and needed to clear my head so I came back here to get my bike. I rode around for the rest of the night. I swung by your apartment this morning on the way to get my phone situation fixed and when the flowers were still outside and your car wasn't there, it just fueled all of my crazy thoughts." Nick looked embarrassed and wouldn't meet my eyes as he spoke.

"Nick, I need you to look at me because I need you to know something." Nick looked up and directly into my eyes. I needed him to understand how serious I was about what I had to say. "Nick, I have been the person who has been cheated on in a relationship, and I would never, ever do that to anyone. Especially someone I care about."

"It's a relief to hear you say that out loud, even though, deep down I knew it. My mind just got out of control and I wasn't thinking rationally. I want you to know, for what it's worth, I am not and never have been a cheater. I would never do that to anyone I am with, and I expect the same in return." Nick continued to look directly at me and gave me a small smile.

"I'm glad to hear that." I really was. Especially considering everything that had gone on with Brett.

An awkward silence crept back in and once again Nick was the one to break it. "I spent the morning getting a new phone. Luckily, they were able to transfer everything from my broken phone to my new one, it just took forever. As soon as I had a new phone and your number again, I tried to contact you. When you weren't responding to my messages and calls, I panicked. That's when I went to Pete's to try to see you and talk to you, but Mike was *not* having it."

I smiled thinking of how Mike had been so protective earlier. "Yeah... I know about that. Listen, Nick, I am going to be totally honest. I did not know what to think last night. I didn't want to think you'd just blow me off, but then I started making assumptions based on experiences from a past relationship. I know that wasn't right or fair to you... I know you're not him and I am sorry for equating you two. But those scars run deep. I was really hurt by him and last night reminded me of it all more than I care to admit."

"You have nothing to apologize for," Nick said quickly. "I think anyone in your shoes would have thought I just blew everything off. It is actually a crazy series of events."

I felt the butterflies in my stomach start to flutter as I realized Nick obviously cared for me. I decided it was time to just get it all out there... I was saying yes to total honesty. "I think part of the reason I was so upset is because I was really scared. I was scared that somehow it was the end of us and that you weren't going to be in my life anymore."

I started to tear up once the words were out. I had no idea how I could have any tears left after the last twenty-four hours. If nothing else, I was probably severely dehydrated. Stupid leaky eyes and overwhelming emotions.

Nick immediately rushed from his chair to me on the sofa. He grabbed me in his strong arms and scooped me up into a tight embrace. I melted into him and buried my face in his shoulder. He kissed me on top of the head and started rubbing my back. We stayed like that for a while. I finally broke the moment and lifted my face up to look into his eyes. Those endlessly deep brown eyes that made me feel safe and cared for.

"Jenna," Nick's voice was husky as he reached his hand forward and stroked my chin gently with his thumb. "I don't know what this is between us. It started with mutual attraction and having some fun, but it seems to have grown into something else. Please tell me I'm not alone in feeling this way." The look on Nick's face and in his eyes pleaded for an answer.

I knew I had to continue with complete honesty. "You're not alone, Nick. I feel it too. All I know is I don't want this to end. That scares me because I'm going to be leaving for law school soon."

Nick shifted his position away from me and a different look flashed across his face for an instant. It was there and gone so quickly I couldn't pinpoint exactly what it was. There was a slight change in the tone of his voice as he responded. "That is a whole other conversation that we need to have. I knew it was coming, I guess I was just trying to pretend it wasn't there"

"Me too," I whispered. "I know we need to talk about it, but can it be tomorrow? I'm so exhausted, I don't think I can handle it now."

"I wholeheartedly agree with you for the exact same reason. I want you to know, Jenna, I am so very sorry for the past twenty-four hours. I never want to do anything to hurt you like that again." Nick leaned forward and brought his lips to mine kissing me softly. It was a kiss filled with apology and sincerity.

"Oh! I almost forgot!" Nick exclaimed when the kiss broke. "I've memorized your number. Just in case I ever have a phone mishap again."

I couldn't help but laugh. "Good thinking. Smart and sexy." I wiggled my eyebrows at him.

Nick suddenly turned serious again. "I know it has been crazy, but would you stay here with me tonight? We're both exhausted, but I can't imagine sleeping without you in my arms. Plus, we can have that other conversation in the morning."

I smiled at Nick and wrapped my arms around his neck. "Yes, Nick. I am saying yes to staying with you tonight... however, I have one condition."

"Name it."

"I need a shower. I came right from work and I smell like pizza."

There was a sudden, mischievous glint in Nick's eyes. "Well, I think that I can accommodate that. In fact, I think I can do one better."

"Oh really? What's that?"

"I was a little distracted today and I am actually still wearing my clothes from yesterday. Perhaps I should join you in that shower. You know, to save water." Nick winked at me and I felt my cheeks flush as a smile crept over my face.

"It only makes sense," I nodded my head. I was relieved as all the weirdness and tension that filled the room dissipated and we settled back into the easy, playful version of us.

"Well, then it's settled." Nick scooped me up and threw me over his shoulder in a fireman's carry. I started laughing and shrieking. Nick playfully swatted me on the butt. "Come on you dirty girl. Let's get you all cleaned up."

Chapter 39
Nick

I woke up the next morning and my heart skipped a beat when I saw Jenna sleeping in my bed. She was curled up on her side facing me and she looked so peaceful as she slept with a little half-smile on her face. I figured what we did in the shower, and then again after, had something to do with putting that smile on her face. Her long brown hair was splayed out on the pillow and I was suddenly hit by an overwhelming feeling... I wanted her with me all the time. I really didn't want her to leave. It felt like as long as we were together, somehow, we could figure out all of the other stuff. As messed up as the whole situation had been with the investors, when I thought I may never see her again, I realized none of it mattered as much without her. Somehow, this little brunette bombshell had done the impossible and found her way into my heart.

I laid on my side and just watched her sleep. Wanting her to stay was so fucking selfish of me, I couldn't ask her to do it. She'd had her plans to move and go to law school before I came along, and no matter how I felt about her, I wouldn't stand in the way of her achieving her goals. I wasn't included in her original plan, and there was no reason to think that I would also be going forward. But the fact remained that what had started out as something casual had now turned into something else completely — at least for me. The irony was, I had finally found someone I wanted to be with and she had already planned to leave before we'd begun.

The time we had left together was limited... and then I was going to have to let her go. I was not going to be the one to stand in her way and hold her back. My chest started to feel tight and I had to get up and move. Fuck! I'd experienced more feelings and emotions in the short time I had been with Jenna than I had in the entire rest of my life combined. How the fuck did people handle having all these feelings, all the damn time?

I slowly and quietly climbed out of bed, so I wouldn't wake Jenna. I threw on a pair of sweatpants and went down to the kitchen to start some breakfast.

The coffee was ready and the bacon was sizzling in the pan when I heard Jenna's bare feet pattering down the hall. I looked over as she walked into the kitchen wearing one of my t-shirts. Her hair was all wild and a sleepy expression covered her face. She looked so perfect that it made my breath catch for a moment. When I was finally able to compose myself I turned to her and smiled. "Good morning, beautiful. Did you sleep well?"

Jenna smiled at me and let out a sleepy moan. "Mmmmmmmmmmm. I did. Better than I have in a while. How long have you been up?" She asked, looking around the kitchen, blinking in the bright daylight.

"Just long enough to get the coffee going and start on some bacon and eggs. Hope you're hungry," I said, smiling. God, she was cute first thing in the morning.

"Starving! Can I pour you a cup of coffee?" Jenna walked over to the cabinet where I kept the mugs. When she reached up to grab one, the t-shirt that she was wearing rode up just enough to show she wasn't wearing anything under it. Fuck me.

217

I came up behind her and wrapped my arms around her waist. "You look so amazing in my t-shirt with your hair all wild. In fact, you look so amazing, I may just have to give you all my other shirts." I'm sure she could feel how sexy I found her in my shirt by what I pressed up against her backside.

Jenna put her hands over mine. "I would be totally okay with that."

"Oh yeah?" I whispered in her ear as I started kissing my way around her neck and down her shoulder. I just couldn't keep my hands - or my mouth - off her.

"Mmmmmmmm," she moaned, rolling her head to the side to give me better access to her neck. "I would. Because that means you would be shirtless all the time. I would be very supportive of that."

I couldn't help but chuckle into her neck as Jenna let out a little shiver. She spun around in my arms and rose up on her tiptoes before placing a soft kiss on my lips. I looked down at her tenderly. "I am glad you are here this morning," I said in a voice barely above a whisper.

"Me too," she said right before delivering another kiss.

I could hear the bacon in the pan sizzling. "I better get back to the bacon before it burns."

"Right, and I'm on coffee duty." Jenna spun back around and started filling up the mugs.

"Do you want to eat on the balcony this morning?" I asked as I stirred the scrambled eggs and flipped the bacon. Jenna nodded and sipped her coffee. "If you want to take the coffees out there, I'll meet you with the food," I said, glancing up from the food in the pan.

Jenna came over to the stove and gave me a quick kiss on the cheek. "Sure. See you in a few minutes." I couldn't help but watch the delicious swish of her hips as she walked away. I quickly put the food on a couple of plates and headed out to the balcony. I wasn't looking forward to the conversation we were about to have, but I knew what I needed to do. Just because I knew it needed to happen, I didn't have to like it.

We ate on the balcony in comfortable silence. It was only after we finished eating that the silence seemed to shift into awkwardness. We knew we had to talk, but neither of us wanted to take the plunge and start. I had no problem having tough conversations and taking people on at work, but this; this was different. She was different and I didn't want to make what felt like an already tenuous situation worse.

I was trying to think of a good start when Jenna spoke up. "I'm leaving in a few weeks for school and we haven't really talked about...us...and what that will look like. I think we need to do that now, especially in light of what just happened."

I nodded my head in agreement. "You're right. I knew this was coming... you told me the night we left the club together. I guess I was just too busy enjoying the moment to think about what comes next."

Jenna shifted in her seat. "I guess it would be helpful to start with what we are? How do you define us?"

What a loaded fucking question.

Chapter 40
Nick

How would I define us?

I wanted to say I had never felt the way I did with her with anyone else before. That I hadn't ever imagined someone like her in my life, but ever since I had been with her, I didn't want to imagine what life would be like when she left. I wanted to say the other night when I thought I lost her, I had never been more scared or more heartbroken. I wanted to tell her the thought of her with anyone else unleashed a wild feeling of jealousy that made me feel crazy. I also wanted to tell her how proud I was of her pursuing her dreams and that as much as it hurt me, I wasn't going to stand in the way. I understood that she'd had a plan before we'd even met.

Instead of saying all of those things, I rubbed my hand down my face and took a deep breath before leaning back in my chair. I gave Jenna the vaguest answer that I could think of. "I would say we are two compatible people that enjoy being with each other."

Jenna sat staring off at something in the distance for a while before she turned to me. "If that is the case, then where do you see this going?"

I thought for a moment. "Well, I can't move with you. Blaine Construction is a part of this community and I have too many people depending on me for employment. I have worked really hard the past few years to get it up and running. It's not something I can leave or leave in someone else's hands."

"I'm not asking you to move with me," Jenna said, so quickly it took me by surprise. "I'll be honest and say the thought had crossed my mind, but I understand you are committed to Blaine Construction and this town, which means you need to stay here."

I closed my eyes and took a deep breath. "I'm not asking you to stay. I understand your dream has been to go to law school and it was a plan that was in place before we even met. I could never stand in the way of that." I felt myself starting to choke up a little as the words came out of my mouth.

"So where does that put us? You can't leave, I can't stay and there's going to be at least a four-hour drive between us for the next three years." Jenna said, sounding defeated – or did I imagine the sadness in her voice? I was having a hard time reading her.

There was a long, awkward pause as we both let the reality of our situation soak in. We were at the part where I should end things and tell her to go and follow her dreams unencumbered, but I just couldn't. I was not enough of an asshole to keep her from leaving, but I was just selfish enough, I couldn't completely let her go. I knew there was an expiration date on what we were doing, but I no longer wanted it to end.

"Listen," I said slowly as I tried to piece together in my mind how to make everything work. "We have been having a great time together, which is why I think neither one of us wanted to bring this up earlier. However, we are both at a place in our own lives where we have other commitments."

"This is true..." Jenna turned to look at me. The expression on her face was hopeful.

I sighed. "Honestly, I have never been much of a relationship guy and I have never really seen myself settling down..." The look on Jenna's face went from hopeful to disappointed. I immediately wished I could take my words back. In part because of the look on her face, and in part because as soon as I said them, I realized that while they may have been true once, things had changed and they no longer were. As I was sitting there and trying to cling on to... whatever it was we had. I realized I could see myself with Jenna in the future; in a big house, filled with kids, dogs, all of the family shit I never wanted before but suddenly now wanted with all my body and soul... and I wanted it with Jenna.

Holy shit! Was I in love with Jenna Morgan? Is this what being in love with someone felt like?

The thought froze me in place for a moment. It wasn't supposed to be like that, I wasn't supposed to fall in love with her.

"Nick, what is going on?" I suddenly snapped back to attention. "I asked you a question, Nick, and I need you to please answer it."

"I'm sorry, what was the question?" I had been so stuck in my head I had zoned out completely and hadn't even been listening to her.

Jenna sighed. "What are we doing, Nick? What is the end game?"

"Why don't we just keep things as they are, only we'll be living in two separate places?" I blurted out.

Jenna looked confused. "What do you mean by that?"

Fuck. What did I mean by that? I just opened my mouth and started talking. "What if we just kept things as they are, but we just see each other less? You're going to be busy with law school and I'm going to be busy with the new projects Blaine Construction has going, so... so we just see each other when we can." Damn, it actually didn't sound too bad for something I just made up on the fly.

"So, let me get this straight. You don't want this to be a relationship, but you want to keep in contact and see each other when we can?" Jenna did not sound at all convinced it was a good idea.

"I know it sounds... different. I don't want you totally out of my life, Jenna, but I also realize we can't physically be in the same location. We are both going to have crazy schedules and seeing each other when we can is a no-pressure way of making things work."

Jenna scrunched her face up. "This all seems very loose and undefined..." she started to say.

"That's the beauty of it," I jumped in and smiled at her trying to convince her that it would work. She could go to law school and pursue her dreams and I could still be a part of her life.

"What you're talking about seems more like a friendship than anything else." Jenna said, letting out a heavy sigh.

"It's more like two people who are pursuing different things but enjoy being together when they can." There was an edge of panic in my voice. She looked and sounded like she was going to say no, which left the only other option being us just completely ending things.

That was not an option as far as I was concerned.

"Alright," Jenna said hesitantly. "I will say yes. We can try this out and see how it goes."

I leaned back in my chair as I felt flooded with relief. "Do we still have some time until you leave?" I asked.

Jenna nodded her head. "I leave in just under two weeks. Although, right now, I really need to get home to shower and change for work. I put my notice in at Pete's Pizza, but I still have a few more shifts scheduled." Jenna looked away from me and stared down and her hands folded in her lap. "I honestly need some time to process everything as well. There has been a whole lot to take in."

"Yes, of course. Let me walk you out to your car." Something seemed really off with Jenna. I didn't want her to leave like that, but I also understood she had to get to work.

As we walked out to her car, the energy between us felt different. It was strained which was a completely new feeling between Jenna and me. When we got to her car, I couldn't take it anymore. I grabbed her in a hug and clung to her like my fucking life depended on it. She grabbed on to me as well and we just stood there holding on. The hug felt different too and I started to worry she was already slipping away. I cleared my throat and my voice came out all ragged. "Well, I guess you need to get going. Will I see you again soon?"

"Yeah, that sounds good," was all she said before she quickly got into her car.

I stood in the driveway and watched her pull away. My heart felt heavy and my eyes glistened with unshed tears. My shoulders slumped forward and I pinched the bridge of my nose while closing my eyes to keep the tears from falling.

For a moment I wondered if I was doing the right thing. I was in completely uncharted territory with new feelings and I had no fucking clue what the hell to do about it.

Chapter 41
Jenna

The week seemed to fly by. I had just finished my last day at Pete's Pizza, and we were going out for an informal goodbye party. I was at Cassie's house getting ready, or more accurately, I was at Cassie's house and she was getting me ready.

"Is Nick going to meet up with us tonight?" Cassie asked as she flipped through a rack of dresses in her closet.

"I think so... I hope so. Actually, I don't really know." I was laying on Cassie's bed looking up at the ceiling, trying not to think about Nick and how confused I was about everything that had happened over the past week.

Cassie stopped flipping through the hangers and poked her head out of her closet. "Ummmmmm...what kind of answer is that? Is everything okay with you two? You've been super vague about Nick ever since the night he stood you up, which was not really a stand up. Did you two kiss and make up?"

I sighed and rubbed my temples. "I honestly don't know what is going on. We talked about the whole broken phone thing and I thought we were past it. But, the next day we had a talk about what happens when I move and it honestly just left me more confused than before we spoke about it."

I felt the bed move as Cassie came and laid down next to me. "Holy shit. You guys finally did it. I was wondering if it was ever going to happen. How did it go?"

"It was confusing. Basically, he is not leaving, I am not staying, but he wants to keep everything the same, we'd just be seeing each other less."

Cassie rolled over on her side to face me. "Uhhhhhh...what the fuck does that even mean?" She said looking at me quizzically.

"He told me he's not a 'relationship type' of guy and he doesn't see himself settling down." Saying the words out loud stung just as much as when Nick said them the first time.

"Well, that is mighty interesting. What you guys have been doing together is a fucking relationship, no matter what Nick says. You spend a whole lot of time together, you talk on the phone and text regularly, and you have been doing other consenting adult activities..." Cassie paused to wiggle her hips and her eyebrows at me, causing me to laugh. "You are both not seeing other people and you both seem to genuinely care about each other. Sounds an awful lot like a relationship to me."

I sighed and propped my head up with my arm. "I know. That was all true up until this past week. Having our conversation seemed to shift things with us. We haven't stayed the night with each other since then. Actually, I've only seen him twice this past week. Once was when we went to lunch together, but it was cut short by a work emergency he had to leave for. The other was when he stopped at Pete's to grab a slice and a soda while I was working."

"Do you think he's doing that on purpose, or do you think he is really busy with work?" Cassie asked the question I had asked myself all week.

"I don't know, and that's the hard part! Did we ruin everything by trying to define what we're doing? Maybe we just had different ideas about what this was. On one hand, I wanted some type of commitment and for Nick to fight for us. On the other hand, I know that practically speaking, we're both pursuing our career goals and we are both at a place in our lives where being in a relationship may just not be feasible. I may need to accept that I want more from Nick than he can give."

Cassie sat up and crossed her legs under her. "So, I am going to tell you this as your absolute best friend who cares deeply about you. The communication between Nick and you is shit! You have to figure out how to effectively communicate with each other if you are going to make things work. This is especially true for you and Nick if you're going to be living in different cities, hours apart."

I groaned and buried my face in the pillow. "I know. I just don't know how. I am afraid I'll say the wrong thing and then it really will be the end."

"Jenna. I can tell by the way Nick looks at you that he likes you a whole lot. Mike said Nick was really upset when he came to Pete's looking for you after the night of no communication. Nick would not have been upset if he didn't care about you. The guy took you on a picnic and kissed you on the freaking Jumbotron in front of a whole stadium of people." Cassie was trying to cheer me up, but all of that added up to the Nick before our conversation about the future.

"True..." I really wanted to believe Nick cared as much for me as I did for him but there was a part of me that was holding back. I was too afraid of having my heart broken to fully turn it over to Nick. Having Brett break up with me was bad enough. What I felt for Nick was so much stronger than what I had ever felt for that loser.

Cassie either didn't notice, or didn't care, that I had zoned out because she just kept on going, listing all the ways Nick had shown me he cared. "He bought you your favorite flowers when he screwed up and sat outside your apartment waiting for you. He ordered pizza every night for a week to try and see you again before he even knew your name. Guys that don't care don't do those types of things."

"Then why can't he tell me he cares about me?" The frustration I felt was clear in my tone.

"Have you told him how you really feel?"

"Not really... okay, no." I realized I had been a hypocrite for being irritated at Nick. He hadn't told me how he felt, but I was doing the exact same thing.

Cassie threw her hands up in the air. "See? Shit communication!"

I sighed. I knew she was right. My conversation with Cassie was just adding to the massive jumble of confusion I already felt when it came to Nick. Meeting Nick was totally unexpected and the events of late had my head spinning.

"You have got to tell him how you feel," Cassie said earnestly.

"What if I don't know how I feel?"

"I think you do, Jenna. You're just scared to put it out there. You're too focused on the negative that you assume will happen and not the positive that should happen."

I threw a pillow at Cassie. "I hate it that you are so right about things all the time."

Cassie laughed as she effortlessly caught the pillow. "Get used to it babe, because I am pretty much right all of the time. The sooner you accept that, the better it will be for all of us. Now, let's get you out of this," Cassie wrinkled her nose as she waved her hand over the jeans and t-shirt I was wearing, "and into something more fitting for a going away party."

"Do I have a choice?" I joked.

"Nope. It's part of being my bestie that I get to dress you up like a real-life Barbie doll. Now get a move on because I'm going to be doing your hair and make-up, too. You have to look extra hot to tell panty-melter Nick how you feel about him tonight."

"Tonight?" I suddenly got nervous. Could I really do it tonight?

Chapter 42
Nick

I had been a mess ever since the conversation Jenna and I had about her leaving. She was all I could think about, and the more I thought about her, the more I realized I was absolutely in love with her.

I, Nick Blaine, a self-proclaimed bachelor for life, was in love with Jenna Morgan.

Problem was, I couldn't tell her. I had never told a woman I loved her before and the thought of it completely scared the shit out of me. I wasn't sure the words would actually come out of my mouth even if I wanted them to. There was also the fact she was leaving for law school and I wasn't going to do anything to fuck that up for her.

I had to put some distance between us... which I tried to convince myself was the right thing to do. I thought it would somehow make everything easier when she left if things had cooled down between us a bit. Good idea in theory, but in reality, I was a miserable mess without her. The fact I was so miserable without her just reaffirmed how much I was in love with her, and the vicious cycle in my mind would start all over.

"You are an absolute fucking miserable prick to be around, Blaine. I'm regretting bringing burgers to your office for lunch. I could be doing something way more fun. Like having a root canal. Or trimming my Granny's toenails. Or scrubbing the bird shit off my car with a toothbrush... should I go on with my list of significantly more fun things I could be doing instead of sitting here with a sad sack like you?" Bax popped a fry in his mouth as he gave me a disapproving look from the other side of my desk.

I looked down at the burger he'd bought for me. It was usually one of my favorite lunches, but I just didn't have an appetite. Not since Jenna and I had spoken about our future. I tossed the burger down on my desk. "Sorry, man. I just have a lot on my mind."

"Let me guess, it has to do with a petite, brunette, pizza-delivery-driver-soon-to-be law student? Am I close?" Bax had a smug expression on his face as he popped another fry in his mouth.

I rubbed my hands down my face and realized I hadn't shaved for a couple of days. Fuck, what was I going to be like when she really left? I looked up at Bax and knew there was no point in trying to lie to him. "Yeah," was all I said.

"Isn't she still here?" Bax pointed to my burger. "Are you going to eat that? Because if not, I will. Can't let a masterpiece like that go to waste."

"Have at it." I handed him the burger. "And yes. She is still here," I said, sighing.

"Then why so glum, chum?"

"Has anyone ever told you, you can be really fucking annoying?" I snapped at Bax and he started laughing.

"Pretty sure that you have told me a few times during the duration of our friendship. But seriously, why are you acting like such an ass if she is still here?" Bax took a big bite of my burger.

"I just...I just can't be around her right now. I need to put some distance between us." I leaned my head back in my chair and closed my eyes.

"If that is the case, why don't you just end it? If you don't want to be with her, just move on."

Bax had no idea how I really felt about Jenna, but his statement still pissed me off. My eyes flew open and I sat up quickly in my chair. "I never said I didn't want to be with her. I said I can't be around her. Big fucking difference, Bax. Watch what you say when you talk about her!" I shouted much louder than I had intended.

"Jesus, Nick. What the hell?" Bax shouted back at me. Slowly, a look of realization started to move across his face. "Oh fuck, Nick! Are you in love with her?" His look slowly changed to one of shock. I didn't say anything. "You are! You are fucking head-over-heels in love with her!" Bax leaned back in his chair. "Holy shit, man!" He suddenly started laughing. "I told you so! I fucking told you so!" He said pointing at me as his whole body rocked with laughter.

"Shut up, Bax," I snapped like a school boy, unable to come up with anything better to say.

"Fill me in on how you, Nick Blaine, the man who hates feelings, is committed to bachelor life and has repeatedly said... he has 'no time for relationships or the drama that comes with them,'" Bax was obnoxiously making air quotes, "finds himself in love. Inquiring minds want to know."

I realized I had been acting like a giant asshole to Bax and tried to rein myself in a little. "I don't know. It just happened. We were talking about her leaving and it just hit me that I didn't want her to go and that I was in love with her." I shrugged my shoulders at him. I was happy to be in love with Jenna but I felt defeated, not jubilant or buoyed up by the feeling, given our circumstances.

"So what did she say when you told her?"

"I... I didn't." As I said the words out loud I realized how ridiculous they sounded.

"Sorry? I must be losing my hearing. It sounded like you just said you didn't tell her." Bax looked at me like I had lost my fucking mind, which really wasn't too far from the truth.

"I didn't," I repeated.

"Why the hell not?" Bax said in exasperation.

"It's complicated." I said stubbornly.

"You are stupid, Nick, if you think I am going to be satisfied with that answer."

I sighed. "Jenna had this plan to go to law school before we even met. It's been one of her goals for a long time. I am not going to do anything to fuck up any part of that for her. Her plan has never included me. I don't know how I would even fit into it. I can't leave, she can't stay; we are just going to keep things like they are but see each other less." I shrugged my shoulders. "Only that is already proving to be more difficult than I thought, which is why I need the distance."

Bax had a look of utter surprise on his face, his mouth was even hanging open a little bit. "Are you being serious?"

The question confused me. "Yes," I said blinking at him, was I missing something?

"Nick Blaine, for someone who runs what is on the cusp of becoming a multi-million dollar construction company, you have got to be one of the dumbest fucking people I have ever met," he said, a smirk spreading across his face as he slowly shook his head at me across the desk.

"Fuck you, Bax."

"Ok, maybe you're not totally dumb. Maybe you're just emotionally stunted from all those years of repressing your feelings about... well, about everything." Bax held up a hand to keep me from talking. "First of all, I get that you think you are being all noble by not wanting to mess with her plans, but Nick, they are her plans. Shouldn't she be the one that gets to decide what to do with them? If you tell her that you love her and she decides to do something different, that is her choice. Not yours. Secondly, have you talked to her about how you could fit into her plan for going to law school? People do relationships long-distance all the time and make it work. She is only going to be four hours away. So you stop working so fucking much and go see her on the weekends. You are both smart people and can figure it out. I don't even know what this bullshit is about 'being together but seeing each other less.' What, do you want to just be friends with benefits with her? Is that what you want?" He was ticking off his points on his fingers as he made them, I hated that he could be right about a lot of them.

"No... fuck. I don't know Bax. This is a lot." What he said made sense - maybe I had been going about it all wrong? I rubbed my hands over my face. I was even more confused about things with Jenna than I had been before talking to Bax, and I'd been pretty damn confused, let me tell you.

"You guys really talked about it and this was the best you came up with? Not telling her how you feel and some weird not-really-a-relationship plan?" Bax tossed the burger wrappers and fry containers into the garbage. "When are you going to see her again?"

234

"Tonight. She's having a going away party with her friends from work at High Five." I ran my hand through my hair.

"Well, don't fuck this one up by missing it and getting your phone run over. You can't recover from that twice." Bax laughed at his own joke.

"Bad timing, Bax," I mumbled.

"No time is ever a bad time to bring up that little golden nugget," he said, grinning at the idiocy of the whole saga. It was clear I was never going to live that night down as far as Bax was concerned. "Back to the topic at hand: you have got to tell her how you feel tonight and let her make her own choices for what's next."

"What if I can't say it? Bax, this is big. I'm already screwing it all up. What if this makes it even worse?" I couldn't seem to adequately express how scared I was to say those three words out loud to her.

"What if it doesn't? For some unknown reason despite your many, many flaws, Jenna seems to really care about you. Has she told you how she feels about you?"

"No..."

"Well then, it appears you two are a match made in poor communication heaven," he joked.

I glared at Bax. "If you're so wise to all the ways of relationships why are you still single?" I challenged trying to get a point against him, though he'd trounced me on every level the entire afternoon.

He just laughed as he turned to walk out the door, "Ain't no woman around who's been able to tame the wild stallion, also known as Baxter Douglas."

"You are so stupid," I said to Bax as I rolled my eyes, suppressing a grin and trying really hard not to laugh.

"Tonight, Nick!" Bax shouted as he walked out the door. "Tell her tonight!"

"Tonight?" I muttered to myself as I suddenly got nervous. Could I really do it?

Chapter 43
Jenna

Cassie and I arrived at High Five and grabbed a table in the back. We were the first ones there and the place was already starting to get busy.

"First round of drinks is on me. What do you want?" I asked Cassie as we settled into our seats.

Cassie rolled her eyes at me. "You should not be buying drinks at your own going away party! However, if you absolutely insist, I would say surprise me, but don't pick wrong," she said with a wink.

I laughed. That was Cassie's standard answer whenever someone asked her what she wanted for food or drink. The secret was, Cassie was the most un-picky person I had ever met when it came to food and drinks so there was rarely ever a 'wrong' answer.

I walked up to the bar and ordered our drinks. While I was waiting, I noticed a guy sitting at the table to my right looking at me. He looked to be about my age, blond, clean-cut and wearing jeans with a button-down. I could feel his eyes on me and when I glanced over again he smiled at me, so I smiled back. Thankfully our drinks were ready. I quickly grabbed them and hustled back to the table. Something about the whole situation made me uneasy.

When I got back to our table, I saw everyone had arrived, including Nick. My eyes were immediately drawn to his and I could tell something was not quite right with him. "Hi, Jenna," he said softly.

"Hi, I'm glad you could make it tonight." I smiled at him but the whole interaction felt weird.

"Me too," Nick said with a half-smile. He sat down across the table from me looking nervous and uncomfortable. I was a little upset he did not make any move to come over and sit next to me. As soon as he sat down, he started talking to Steven.

Kimmy was sitting next to me and squeezed my arm. "I can't believe you're leaving in under a week! This is all so crazy! I am going to miss you tons, but I'm super-duper excited for you! Please tell me you will at least stop in at the shop when you're back in town."

I peeled my eyes away from Nick and looked at Kimmy. "I will for sure! I am going to miss all of you as well. Your friendship means so much to me and I'm so glad I had the opportunity to meet all of you."

"Things won't be the same at Pete's without you," Steven said with a smile, tipping back his chair and crossing his arms over his chest.

"Things everywhere won't be the same, without you," Nick said, as he stared directly at me. The tension in the air was so thick I felt like could physically feel it. Nick and I sat staring at each other. A storm of emotions passed across his face, but they moved so quickly I couldn't decipher them. What the hell was going on?

I think everyone else felt the tension radiating off both Nick and me, as the whole table went completely silent.

"So, Jenna... how's the packing going?" Mike finally asked, breaking the silence.

I slowly moved my gaze away from Nick and over to Mike. He was sitting next to Cassie with his arm across the back of her chair. A pang of jealousy rose in my chest. Why wasn't Nick doing that to me? The pang quickly sparked into anger. Why was he even there if he was going to act like he didn't want anything to do with me? Wait, why was he acting like he didn't want anything to do with me? Did it have something to do with our conversation about the move? Or was he really done with us being together?

My tone was completely flat as I answered Mike. "Ummmmm, it really hasn't been moving along at all. I don't need to be out of my apartment until the last day of this month and I can't move into my new place near the law school until the first of next. Cassie is going to help me get packed up over the next few days."

"I love me some packing and moving," Cassie started to say, "who am I kidding? I hate it so much the only person I will do it for is Jenna. Even then, I made her swear to keep me well supplied in wine and snacks the entire time." Cassie was looking back and forth between Nick and me as she spoke.

Nick shifted around in his chair and refused to look in my direction. There was something behind me he kept looking at that seemed to be distracting him. I finally reached my limit, he was acting stupid and I needed to get away from the table. "I'm going to go get another drink. Anyone else want anything? No? Okay. I'll be right back." I jumped up and made a beeline for the bar.

I had not even placed my drink order when I felt someone walk up behind me and stand very close. "Any chance you'd let me buy that drink for you?"

I turned around and saw it was the blond guy who had been smiling at me when I was at the bar earlier. "Ummmmm..." I stammered.

The guy put both of his hands up and gave me a big smile that showed off his amazingly white teeth. "No strings attached. I just think you are incredibly beautiful and wanted a reason to come talk to you."

I wasn't quite sure what to do. I never went out much in college, and when I did, Brett was there so guys didn't come up and hit on me. At least I think that's what Mr. Blond Guy was doing. Maybe he could tell I was having a weird night and was just trying to be nice? I couldn't think of anything to say, so I just decided to be polite. "Oh, thank you. Yes, that would be very nice of you to buy me a drink."

The guy seemed to like that answer because he moved closer to me and leaned up against the bar just a few inches from where I was standing. "No, thank you. The fact you said 'yes' to the drink means I get to stand here a little longer and talk to you some more." Again, he flashed his perfect teeth in a big smile.

An awkward giggle slipped out of my mouth and I blushed. Okay, I was pretty certain he was hitting on me and I really had no idea how to respond. The guy didn't seem to care because he just kept talking. "So, I'm going to be honest and say I was watching you from across the room, trying to figure out how I was going to talk to you tonight. It looks like you're here with a group of friends, but not anyone in particular..."

"She's here with me!" The guy was cut off by a deep voice I immediately recognized, but the tone was one I had never heard before. It was so sharp and harsh it put me on edge.

"Nick?" I looked up at him as he rushed up to the bar and put his arm around my waist. His normally warm and caring brown eyes flamed with anger as he stared the guy down. Nick was practically growling as he stood there; his arm possessively wrapped around me, his nostrils flaring.

This version of Nick was almost scary. I had never seen him like that before and wasn't quite sure what was going on.

The guy who had been talking to me didn't even seem phased by the fact that Nick was several inches taller than him and was clearly pissed off. He turned to me and pointed at Nick. "Do you even know this guy?"

"Yes, but-" I started, before being cut off.

"I clearly fucking said she was with me so you had better back the fuck off. I've been watching you checking her out all night and I don't fucking appreciate it." Nick's voice was low and every word seemed to have extra emphasis on it.

The guy stood up a little straighter, but Nick still towered over him. He looked at Nick with all his bravado and said, "Oh yeah? Maybe you better calm yourself down there cowboy, because you sure as hell weren't acting like she was with you until this very moment."

What was happening? A crowd started to gather around us. This kind of stuff only happened in movies, not in real life. And definitely not to me. Nick's grip on me tightened as he pulled me closer to him. I just stood there, my body completely tense and frozen in place.

The guy turned and looked at me with a big, cocky smirk on his face. "Baby, I can guarantee you, if I had a woman as beautiful as you here with me tonight, every other guy in this whole damn place would know you were with me. I'm man enough to treat a woman right."

Everything seemed to shift into slow motion. The next thing I knew, Nick's fist was flying into the guy's face and blood was spurting from the guy's nose. There was yelling and chaos as the employees ran over to intercede. Nick put both of his hands up and started walking away. No one paid him any attention, they were all focused on the other guy who was now bleeding all over the floor.

I was standing there with my mouth open trying to wrap my mind around what had just happened when I felt someone grab my arm. "Jenna! Holy shit! Are you okay?" I slowly turned my head and saw Cassie holding on to my arm. "Nick flew up from the table and booked it over here. I thought he was going to come over and talk to you, but then I saw the crowd start to gather and - oh fuck! Did Nick punch that guy in the face?" Cassie was going about a million miles an hour as she took in the scene in front of her.

I couldn't really comprehend what it was Cassie was saying. "I need to go find him," I said to no one in particular, I felt as though I were in a daze.

"Do you think that's a good idea? He literally just punched some random dude in the face!" Cassie's voice was filled with worry as she maintained her grip on my arm.

I turned to her. "I'll be fine. I know he won't do anything to me. I've never seen him like this. I don't really know how this all happened." I struggled to snap out of the feeling of being in slow motion, despite the people rushing around me attending to the guy Nick had punched. I know my voice sounded flat and monotone, but I just couldn't seem to pull myself back together. All I could think about was finding Nick.

Cassie paused for a few moments before she let out a big sigh. "Be safe. If you don't come back in or call me in thirty minutes, I'm coming out after you." I gave Cassie a quick hug. "Thanks, Cass." I walked across the club and out the front doors. I had no idea what I was going to find or if Nick was even still around, but I knew I had to go find him.

Chapter 44
Nick

That was not how it was supposed to go. I looked down at my hand as it started to swell; shit. 'This was not how it was supposed to go' was the fucking understatement of my lifetime. As soon as I saw Jenna, I'd felt super weird and awkward. I didn't know what to say or how to act, how do you act when you are trying to tell someone you are madly in love with them? I had no idea, but I'd guess punching some stupid fucker in the face was not on the list of acceptable behavior.

I'd been watching that asshole checking her out all night and I didn't like it one bit. He was sitting behind her but across the room. She couldn't see him, but I could from where I was sitting. I asked Steven about him. He had no idea who the guy was but had also noticed the creep leering at Jenna. I instantly hated the guy and wanted him to stay the fuck away from her. I had never been jealous or protective of anyone before, but when it came to Jenna... well, things with her were different.

When she went to get drinks and I saw the guy slither over to talk to her and then he was standing so close to her, well, I will admit, I lost my shit completely. I jumped up so fast I knocked my chair over and booked it across the room. He could say whatever he wanted to me, but the way he was talking to Jenna sent me right over the fucking edge. I hadn't punched anyone like that in years. I grew up with Bax and his loud mouth and as a result, we'd been in a few scrapes over the years, but nothing that personal. I felt like such a fucking idiot for losing my shit in front of Jenna.

I was outside sitting on my bike looking at my hand, wondering if I could somehow fix things when Jenna walked up.

"Hey," she said softly. I couldn't look up at her. I was too embarrassed and just couldn't face her. I had completely ruined another night for her. I didn't deserve to be with her. Maybe I was right staying away from relationships if that is what I turned into?

"Nick, look at me," she said a little more forcefully. I couldn't make myself look up at her. I knew I couldn't handle it if she looked at me with disappointment in her eyes. "Okay. Fine. You want to act like a little kid and give me the silent treatment? Go on ahead. Have a nice night." There was definite anger in her voice and I could hear her turn and start to walk away.

"Wait! I'm sorry. Please don't go! Don't leave like this!" I shouted after her. Perhaps it was the panic and desperation in my voice that made her stop in her tracks so suddenly. She stood there for a few moments before she turned and started walking back towards me.

"Nick, what the hell was that back there?" she demanded. I didn't know quite how to answer. "No!" Jenna shouted. "You don't get to do this! You don't get to barely talk to me or barely see me for almost a week and then come here tonight and act like... like a jerk!" Her voice cracked and I could see her eyes start to glisten with tears which made me feel like an even bigger prick.

I had to say something to defend myself and try to salvage things. "I watched him check you out all night. He was sitting at a table behind you but he was directly in my line of sight.

He was a fucking creep, Jenna. I didn't want him hitting on you."

Jenna crossed her arms and glared at me. "You don't get to ignore me all night until another guy comes up and starts to talk to me. And you sure as heck don't get to freak out and go all Hulk on him!"

"I couldn't stand seeing him with you!" I answered quickly. Fuck, I had really screwed the whole thing up. I couldn't even look her in the eye. I hated seeing her so upset and it felt like nothing I said was going to make it any better.

"You are the one that does not want a relationship!" I could hear Jenna was crying as she shouted at me. I kept my eyes on the ground. I deserved her anger, but I couldn't stand to see her crying because of me. "Dammit, Nick! Look at me! What the hell is going on? Answer me!" Jenna said between sobs.

I couldn't stand it anymore. I jumped off my bike and in just a few strides was standing right in front of her. I held on to her upper arms - just touching her helped ground me. I wanted to wrap her in my arms, and hold her, and kiss her, and tell her about everything, but then, I remembered all the reasons I couldn't and knew there were even more reasons after what I'd just done. A powerful jolt of sadness ran through me and I could feel my own tears start to fill my eyes.

Dammit! I needed to get out of there before I fucked everything up even more. I let go of Jenna's arms and backed a few steps away from her. "It wasn't supposed to be like this," I whispered.

"What, Nick? What wasn't supposed to be like this?"

"Everything. Every fucking thing was not supposed to be like this." I wasn't supposed to fall in love with her. I wasn't supposed to be so upset about her leaving. I wasn't supposed to punch some fucking idiot in the bar over her. I wasn't supposed to be hurting her and making her cry. I wasn't supposed to be fucking everything up so royally.

"Nick, what are you talking about?" Jenna took a step towards me just as I took one towards her.

I put my hand on her cheek. She was so perfect and so beautiful. I wiped her tears away with my thumb; each tear pulled at my heart, knowing I was the reason she was crying. She didn't need me and all my issues in her life... not when she was getting ready to fulfill her dream. I leaned down and pressed a light kiss to her lips. "I should go," I whispered as I pulled away from her. I was so confused by everything I was feeling. Fuck, I was confused about the fact I was having so many feelings period. Everything that happened tonight only added to the confusion and I couldn't understand anything, especially where things stood with us.

"Wait, what?" Jenna asked with a look of surprise on her face. If I waited any longer I wasn't sure I could leave her. I had to go. I quickly walked past her and over to my bike. I looked at her for a few moments trying to memorize everything about her before I left.

I drove not thinking about anything but the road in front of me. I couldn't think about what was behind me... it was too much.

I didn't even realize where I was going until I pulled my motorcycle into one of the parking spots and killed the engine. I was at the bluff overlooking the city where I took Jenna the night we ran into each other at The Star and I first learned her name. I couldn't help but smile at the memory of her refusing to tell me her name, instead telling me to call her Pizza Girl. I wondered if, on some level, I had been in love with her from the very beginning and just had no idea at the time what it was. I was never supposed to fall in love with her, so how did it all happen? We were just supposed to be together for a short period of time, have some fun, and then go our separate ways.

The more I thought about it, the more I realized that even if falling in love was not what was supposed to happen, the only thing that could help quiet my head was being with Jenna.

I needed her like I needed my next breath.

I had to go back. I had to see her. I had to apologize to her. There was no doubt I was confused and scared shitless about the depth of my feelings for her, but I had no right to do what I had done to her. I needed at least one more night with her. What would very likely be our last night together.

I quickly fired up my bike and turned it around to head back to High Five. I only hoped that, once again, I was not too late to try and fix it... at least for tonight.

Chapter 45
Jenna

I stood on the sidewalk in complete shock as I watched Nick drive off on his motorcycle. I slowly made my way back inside as I tried to make sense of what had happened. I couldn't believe he just left. He rode away and didn't even look back.

When I got to the table, Cassie jumped up and launched herself at me wrapping me in a hug. "Thank god you're back! You literally had two minutes and thirty-six seconds until I was coming out to get you. What in the fucking hell happened tonight?"

I looked at Cassie with a blank expression. "I don't know what happened. Nick was acting weird here at the table and then he punched a guy for talking to me. Outside, he wouldn't talk to me. When he finally did, he made virtually no sense. He mostly said he was sorry and that things should not have happened this way."

"What about you? Are you okay?" Cassie asked as we sat back down at the table with the rest of our group.

"Yes... no... I don't know. I am so confused. I feel like ever since we actually had the conversation about leaving for law school, everything has been all messed up."

Steven was sitting across from me and leaned forward as he started talking. "For what it's worth, the whole time Nick was sitting over here next to me, he was pissed that guy was checking you out. When he saw that guy come up to talk to you, Nick totally lost it."

That made me even more confused about what was going on. "Why?" I asked Steven. "Why wouldn't he even acknowledge me tonight, and then turn around and act like a crazy person when someone else did?"

Steven shrugged his shoulders. "Well, I am not an expert by any means, but I think the guy really likes you and was incredibly jealous.

I shook my head. There was no way that could be right. "He made it very clear he does not want a relationship," I told Steven.

"Does he want you out of his life? When you leave are things over?" Steven asked.

I let out a big sigh. "Not exactly. We talked about trying to keep in contact and see each other when we can."

"That is your guy's great plan?" Mike asked. "He is a successful business owner and you are going to law school... you two aren't idiots, but that, I must say, is a stupid plan."

Cassie turned to Mike. "Their communication is shit."

Mike nodded. "I can see that."

"Oh, come on, Mike! Like you know the first thing about relationships and communication," Steven argued back.

Mike leaned forward in his seat, "Hey! I'm in a relationship and..."

Cassie quickly cut Mike off, "Don't make me reconsider that decision." Mike leaned back but continued to glare at Steven.

What was with everyone's short fuse? Kimmy clapped her hands to get everyone's attention. "You guys are insane! Get back to Jenna and Nick. I need to see how this ends! Their drama is better than a soap opera!"

"Uhhhhh... thanks, Kimmy?"

Kimmy gave me a big smile. "No problem! Now, just to recap. Nick says 'no relationship' but is acting like a jealous crazy-person when it comes to Jenna. Jenna is confused by the mixed signals, but neither one of them is any good at communicating or expressing their feelings. Okay, now keep going!" Kimmy bounced up and down in her seat with excitement.

"Okay, thanks for that recap, Kimmy," was all I could think to say. The whole situation was so weird. I was not the kind of person that led a life other people were interested in hearing about. Well, I had not been that kind of person before Nick. Why did he just leave the way he did? Did it mean things were over between us? The thought sent a chill through me.

"No problem!" Kimmy responded cheerfully. She was enjoying everything way too much.

Mike cleared his throat. "Have you considered that he may be totally into you but doesn't know what to do about it?"

"I don't know what to think about any of this," I responded honestly.

"How do you feel about him?" Cassie asked.

I stopped to think a moment before answering. "I like him. A lot. I was not expecting to meet someone like him, and especially not now. The timing is awful, but it hurts that he doesn't want to commit to us and see where it goes."

"Have you told him that?" Cassie asked, although I had a sneaking suspicion she knew exactly what the answer was.

"What if he likes you too, but doesn't want to stand in the way of the plans you already had before you met him?" Mike chimed in. "I mean, you had everything pretty mapped out for law school before Nick was even in the picture."

Oh boy. That actually made a lot of sense. "I hadn't considered that... but what if he doesn't feel the same way and is just too nice to end things? Or what if he wants to have his cake and eat it too? Have me around when it works for him, but no real commitment?" My head was spinning with all the uncertainty.

Cassie looked at me and smiled gently. "Nick is the only one who can answer that, honey. You need to ask him."

"Ahhhhhhhh!" I rubbed my temples. "All of this is too much! I don't know about the rest of you, but I have had about all the excitement I can take for one night. Thank you for coming out and for all the advice, but I'm ready to head home." I just needed to get out of there. I could feel a headache coming on and I was so overwhelmed and confused, nothing seemed to make any sense.

Kimmy reached for her purse and stood up. "Me too. There is no possible way this night can get any better. Best to end on a high note."

"Yeah, it's about time to head out." Steven stood up as well.

I hugged everyone and thanked them again. As we walked out the front door together, we talked about making plans to try and get together again before I left. I was so wrapped up in the conversation it startled me when Kimmy started shrieking and pointing. "Holy shit! I did not think it was possible, but this night just keeps getting better! Jenna look!"

I slowly turned my head to see where she was pointing. My mouth immediately went dry and my heart rate exploded. I blinked my eyes twice just to be sure I was actually seeing things correctly.

There across the street from the front door of High Five was Nick Blaine leaning up against his motorcycle, legs crossed in front of him looking hotter than sin. We locked eyes and it felt like a whole conversation passed between us without speaking a single word. I could see he was just as confused and scared as I was.

As if there was some type of magnetic pull drawing us together, we started walking towards each other and met in the middle of the street. "Hi," Nick said softly.

"You came back," I whispered. I still could not believe he was actually there.

Nick ran his hand through his hair, looking incredibly nervous. He turned his gaze towards my face and I was drawn into his deep brown eyes. "I am really sorry about tonight Jenna... especially the way I left. I was totally out of line."

"Oh," I answered not really knowing what else to say. I knew we needed to talk, but in the middle of the road outside of High Five was not the place for that conversation. Instead, I looked down and saw his hand, which was starting to bruise and looked swollen. "How's your hand? Is it hurt?" I asked, suddenly concerned he had injured himself.

"It'll be fine." Nick looked away from me for a minute and ran his hand through his hair again. He took a deep breath before he turned his head back to me and continued. "Look, Jenna, I don't know what is going to happen tomorrow or the day after that or at any time in the future. What I do know is that tonight, right at this moment, I need you. I need to be with you."

"Oh, Nick..." I whispered. My heart was racing.

"I realize I have absolutely no right to ask you this, especially with the way I acted, but will you do that? Will you be with me tonight?" The look on his face was so vulnerable, his eyes so hopeful.

Part of me knew it was a bad idea and that I was just setting myself up for more confusion and heartbreak. The other part of me did not care one bit and knew that in some strange way, I needed him just as much as he seemed to need me.

There was really only one clear answer. "Yes, Nick. I am saying yes. I want to be with you tonight." Nick grabbed me and pulled me up against his rock-hard chest before he crashed his lips into mine. The kiss was filled with so much passion and longing. Everything around us seemed to melt away until it was just Nick and me clinging to each other in the middle of the street.

When Nick and I finally pulled apart we were both breathless.

"Uhhhhhh guys, I hate to break up this party for two, but you're in the middle of the street and blocking traffic!" Mike shouted at us from the sidewalk.

"Shhhhhh! Don't interrupt them! This is amazing! I feel like I need a bowl of popcorn!" Kimmy bounced up and down on the balls of her feet.

I leaned into Nick. "Give me just a minute."

"Okay." Nick cupped my cheek in his hand and I rested my palms on his chest. I gave him a quick peck on the lips before I turned and ran over to Cassie.

"I'm going with Nick tonight."

"I can see that," Cassie replied. "Do you know what you are doing? Are you going to be okay?" Her voice was filled with genuine concern.

I answered her as honestly as I could, "Yes, I know what I'm doing and no, I don't know if I'm going to be okay."

Cassie shrugged her shoulders. "Fair enough. Be careful and don't do anything I wouldn't do."

Mike stepped forward, "How about just be careful and if he acts like an ass again, call us and we will come get you."

Cassie laughed, "That works too."

"Alright, thank you," I quickly told them both as I turned and ran back across the street to Nick. He handed me a helmet and I hopped on the back of his bike.

Somehow it all felt so familiar but so different at the same time. I knew we were at a turning point. I just hoped it wasn't going to be a turn in the wrong direction.

Chapter 46
Jenna

"What the hell do you mean you woke up the next morning alone?" Cassie was in the kitchen waving a wooden spoon around as she was talking. We were at my apartment packing up the last things as I prepared to leave the next day. My law school classes started on Monday.

I sighed. "Exactly that. I woke up in his bed, but he was already gone. He left a note."

"Oh. A note. That totally makes everything all better." Cassie said sarcastically as she started waving the spoon around again and using it like a pointer for added emphasis. "Who the hell does that? No one sneaks out of their own fucking house and leaves a note. Please tell me you burned his place down on your way out."

"No, I didn't burn the place down." I couldn't help but smile a little. I appreciated that Cassie totally had my back.

"Well, what did this amazing piece of great literary work say? Do you need me to go burn his fucking condo down?"

"It basically said 'thank you for a memorable night' and that 'he got a call there was a problem at one of the job sites so he had to go, but didn't want to wake me.' No need to commit arson."

"That's it?" It was obvious from the tone of Cassie's voice she was not impressed.

"It also said to 'go ahead and help myself to anything in the fridge' and 'he would call me.'"

256

"Did he?" Cassie threw the wooden spoon in a box and started wrapping my dishes in bubble wrap.

"Yes," I said, wrapping up a drinking glass and gently placing it in the moving box.

"How was that?"

I paused and reached up to grab another drinking glass. "Strained," I replied as I started wrapping the second glass. "It's like when we are together, it's all fireworks and amazing. When we're apart, we both seem to shut down and retreat back into our shells and start putting up walls again."

"Have you guys talked any more about where things stand between you?"

I looked down at the glass in my hand. "No. Any time it comes up we both shut down and it feels like neither of us really says everything we want to."

Cassie stopped what she was doing and focused her full attention on me. "Okay, you have identified the issue so, how do you fix it?"

"Good question."

"So, you woke up to a stupid-ass note and no Nick. How was everything before that?" Cassie resumed wrapping dishes and packing them in one of the many boxes.

I grabbed a coffee mug and tried to focus. It was hard to pack when my mind and heart were all jumbled up with thoughts of Nick. "It was amazing. We got back to his place and he actually lifted me off his bike and carried me to his bedroom, bridal style."

"That is like something straight out of a movie... or a really hot romance novel!" Cassie said with a wide-eyed dreamy expression.

"I know! He was so sweet and tender all night... I thought he was trying to apologize and make up for what happened that night, but now part of me wonders if it was him trying to say goodbye." I could feel my heart sink at the thought of that being our last night together. It had been a beautiful night, but I wasn't ready for Nick and I to be over.

"Well, now you've had a few days to obsessively worry and over-analyze everything which I am sure has helped tremendously." Cassie's voice was, again, laced with sarcasm.

I chuckled. "You know me so well."

Cassie started to tape up the box of dishes and wrote 'Food Room' on it in marker. She had labeled all of my boxes with silly phrases. "I take it there was very little talking going on during your night with Nick."

I smirked. "Not unless you count moaning, grunting, or yelling out each other's names."

"Now that's my girl!" Cassie held her hand up for a high five, and I smacked it with my palm. "Are you going to see him tomorrow before you leave?"

I had completely stopped packing and was leaning against the counter talking to Cassie. "I don't know. I hope so. When we talked on the phone, he asked what my plans were for the next few days, so I let him know. We've exchanged a few texts since then but nothing more."

"So, what are you going to do?" Cassie asked as she started taping together another box.

"I don't know. It feels like he's pushing me away and I just keep bobbing along. I miss what we had before all of this stuff about me leaving became an issue. I don't know if we ignored that fact for too long or if it was always there. Cass... I just miss him." I started to tear up.

Cassie stopped what she was doing and turned to me. "Oh, girl. You are in so damn deep with him," she said, shaking her head slowly.

The tears started to slide down my cheeks. "Cassie, I think I'm in love with him, but I am afraid he doesn't feel the same way, and if I tell him it will drive him away for good. The idea of him being gone for good hurts worse than this stupid 'friend plan' or whatever it is we're going to try."

I started sobbing. Cassie came over and wrapped me in a big hug. "I think that is the most honest thing you have said about your feelings for Nick. But Jen, I am the wrong person to be telling. You need to tell him, not me."

"What if this is the end, Cassie? I don't think I can handle that."

Cassie pulled back and held me at arm's length. "You know I am never leaving you, right? You never gave up on me when, in all reality, you probably should have. That means you're stuck with my hot ass forever."

I couldn't help but laugh through my tears. Cassie and I had a whole lot of history together and after the past year, she was the only person left in my life I could count on. "While we're on the subject of things that you should tell Nick, have you told him about some of the stuff you went through in the past year?"

I sniffed and wiped some tears away with the sleeve of my sweatshirt. "Not in a lot of detail, no. Just little bits here and there."

"You should tell him. It might give him a better idea of where you are coming from."

I paused for a moment to consider what Cassie said. "I don't want him to think I'm crazy..."

Cassie held her palm up, signaling me to stop, as she interrupted. "If he hears any of your past and thinks you are crazy, then he was not even good enough to be with you in the first place. Again, you have got to *talk to him*. You can't just keep trying to portray this half picture as the full meal deal."

I buried my face in my hands. "Why are relationships so complicated?"

"Because it involves two people stripping everything back until there is nothing hidden and then accepting the other person for all they are. The good and the bad."

"Is that how things are between you and Mike?"

Cassie shifted around and looked uncomfortable for a moment, which made me raise an eyebrow at her. "We're working on it," she finally said.

"Does he know what happened with you in college?" I asked.

"Some of it. It was not an easy conversation to have, but it is a part of me and my past and has made me who I am today. I'm still working on myself and Mike knows that." Cassie picked up a roll of bubble wrap and started packing again. She looked at me with a soft smile. "Sometimes it's a lot easier to give someone advice about what they should do with their problems than it is to follow that advice in your own life." I wasn't quite sure what she meant by that and Cassie didn't elaborate any further so I let the subject drop.

Cassie and I fell into a comfortable rhythm as we continued packing. A few hours later, we were taping up the last box when I heard the familiar rumble of a Harley turn into the parking lot of my apartment. I felt a smile break out on my face and I could not contain my excitement. "He's here!"

Cassie stood up and dusted herself off. "Well, that's my cue to leave. Think about what we talked about earlier, okay?"

"I will. Are you and Mike still coming by in the morning?"

"Yes. I'll text you first. I don't think I could recover from the trauma of accidentally walking in on you and Nick going at it in the middle of the living room that early in the morning."

I blushed. "Cassie! Too much!"

Cassie laughed. "My point exactly. Seeing that would be way too much!" I started laughing and smacked her on the arm. Cassie stopped laughing and paused. "Hey, not to change the subject, but shouldn't he be up here knocking on your door by now?"

I tipped my head to the side to see if I could hear him walking up the stairs but heard nothing. "He should. That is weird. I'll walk down to the parking lot with you. Maybe he's making a call or something before coming up.

Cassie and I walked down to the parking lot. Nick was sitting on his motorcycle at the edge of the lot. Cassie gave me a little shove forward. "Go talk to him. Tell him how you feel. You've got this."

I turned and gave Cassie a hug. "I'll see you tomorrow," I told her before I turned and started walking across the parking lot towards Nick.

I was going to tell him how I felt and go from there. I could do it, right?

The closer I got to him the more nervous I felt. I took a deep breath. I could do it... right?

Chapter 47
Nick

What the fuck was I doing? I came to see Jenna. She was leaving the next morning, and, yet, I found myself completely unable to get off my bike and walk up the stairs. I had done it dozens of times before, but suddenly it was like my feet were stuck in concrete. I just needed to see her one last time before she left... but I didn't want that day to be the last time I saw her.

The past few days had been a bit of a shit show. After the night of the broken phone incident, Blaine Construction did get the contract to build Rickson Estates. It was a huge project, and already a giant pain in my ass. The investors were a very needy group of people. The last night Jenna had been at my place, one of the investors called early in the morning with an 'emergency' at the site that needed to be taken care of 'right away.' I left Jenna a note, but when I got to the site, the 'emergency' turned out to be something that could have easily waited until Monday. I had been really irritated having to leave Jenna for that, and she was gone by the time I got back home.

It also looked like Blaine Construction was going to be awarded the contract for the other big project I'd bid on, a multi-year, multi-million dollar subdivision. I should have been thrilled to have landed both contracts; it solidified Blaine Construction as the top construction company in the area. Instead, I was frantic, making sure to hire enough people for the projects to run smoothly and had been working non-stop.

It completely took away from any time I could have spent with Jenna before she left. The nagging voice in my head that kept telling me: *'this is why you don't get involved in relationships'* grew louder and louder every day.

Jenna walked out of her apartment with Cassie and my heart skipped a beat seeing how beautiful she was. She was wearing cut-off jean shorts and an oversize sweatshirt, with her hair in a messy bun on her head. She looked so fucking perfect. I assumed, based on how she was dressed, she had been packing all day. She really was leaving. I physically felt a sharp pain in my chest at the thought.

Jenna walked across the parking lot towards me. "Hey! I'm glad to see you. Do you want to come up? We could order some take-out for dinner?"

I couldn't even look at her, because if I did I was going to want to kiss her. If I kissed her, I wasn't going to be able to let her go. I looked at the ground and tried to keep my expression as neutral as possible. "I don't think I can do that tonight. I'm sorry. I... I just needed to see you before you leave."

"Oh. Okay." Her voice was barely above a whisper. I glanced up at her and saw the flicker of disappointment cross her face before she quickly erased it. Fuck, I hated disappointing her... it felt like I was constantly screwing everything up when it came to her. The voice in my head chimed in; *'this is why you don't get involved in relationships.'* Jenna just looked at me for a moment. "We don't have to get food." She paused for a few beats. "Do you want to just come up and talk?"

I ran my hand through my hair. With the way the past few weeks had gone, it was a wonder I hadn't rubbed a fucking bald spot on my head. This was not going how I had hoped. Jenna stood close to me and I reached out to tuck a stray piece of hair behind her ear. "Not tonight. I just wanted to come by and make sure you were all packed and ready for tomorrow. I also just wanted to see you one last time before you go." I could barely choke the words out. I felt like, if I just kept repeating over and over that she was leaving, it would somehow make things easier.

My hand lingered by the side of her face. I just wanted to touch her. She leaned into my palm and at that moment I almost told her not to go. I wanted so badly to tell her to stay so we could give this thing between us a chance and maybe, in time, she could fall in love with me the same way I had fallen in love with her. I pulled my hand away and reminded myself I was not going to be the asshole who swooped in and stood in the way of her achieving her goals. I loved her too much for that and I wanted her to be happy.

Jenna looked startled when I pulled my hand away from her. "Nick, why are you talking like this? This is a 'see you later' situation, not a goodbye. We agreed to keep in touch and see each other when we can. Remember?"

I gave her as much of a smile as I could... it was a completely half-assed effort. "You're going to be busy with your first few weeks of school and getting settled into your new place. This is an exciting new chapter for you and one you've been planning for a long time. I'm really proud of you following your dream. Don't let anything hold you back from achieving it," I told her.

265

"Why don't you plan on coming to see me in two weeks?" Jenna's voice was shaky. "You can see my new apartment, I can show you around the school... let me share this with you, Nick. It's a long drive, but we can spend the weekend together. After that weekend we can pick another one and I'll come back here. We can make this work."

I couldn't stand it any longer. I climbed off my bike and pulled her into a big hug. I wrapped my arms all the way around her and rested my chin on the top of her head. It was amazing how perfectly we fit together... like I was made to hold her in my arms. Jenna turned her head and rested her cheek on my chest. I was sure she could hear the frenzied beating of my heart since it felt like it was about to explode out of my chest.

I kissed the top of her head again. "I never planned on meeting anyone like you, Jenna. You came whirling into my life during a time I thought I had everything figured out about what I was doing and where I was going. I am so happy I got to share this time with you."

Jenna pulled her head back away from me. "Nick, I need to tell you something. I..."

It was then that I noticed her tears. "Hey, are you crying?" I blurted out. I tipped her head up so she was looking at me. My heart shattered a little at the look on her face and the tears in her eyes. I had done that to her. Again. I didn't fucking deserve her. "Dammit! All I seem to do and say lately is stupid shit that makes you cry. I am so sorry, Jenna. Please don't cry. It breaks my heart to see you this way and it breaks it even more knowing I'm the one who did it to you."

Jenna seemed to be searching my face for something. I leaned down and kissed her gently on the lips before burying my face in her neck. I could smell her strawberry shampoo and it reminded me of the night we ran into each other at the club. My resolve almost cracked again, and once again I almost told her to just stay. But I wasn't going to take law school away from her. Instead, I whispered, "I should go."

Jenna grabbed the front of my shirt. "Please don't leave," she whispered back.

"Jenna..."

"Yes?" She said quickly.

"I am so sorry. It was never supposed to be like this." I was never supposed to fall in love with her. I was not going to get in her way.

"Tell me what you are talking about, Nick." Jenna reached up and took her face in my hands. I closed my eyes and leaned my forehead against hers. I couldn't tell her. I wanted to, but the words just wouldn't come.

I kept my forehead pressed against hers. "Will you call me and let me know you made it there safely tomorrow?" I asked with my eyes still closed as I tried to soak in the feeling of just being with her.

"Yes. Will I see you again before I leave?"

"I don't know if I can do that, Jenna." I had already almost fucked everything up by asking her to stay. I didn't think I could keep myself in check around her much longer.

"Will I see you in two weeks? Please, Nick. Please come and see me."

"Okay," I told her. Two weeks would be enough time to get my shit together and figure out what I was going to do.

"Promise?" Jenna whispered.

"Yes," I whispered back.

We stood there in the parking lot with our foreheads pressed together, tears running down both our faces. "I have to go," I told Jenna as I pulled away and got back on my bike. If I didn't leave, I knew I would not be able to let her go. I turned the Harley on and started to pull forward. I stopped before pulling out into the street and looked back at her again. I gave her a little half-smile and a wave and she waved back.

Two weeks. Two weeks until I would see her again. Two weeks to figure out how I was going to put my life back in order without her. Two weeks to fucking figure it all out. Two weeks to get my shit together.

Two weeks to miss her. Two weeks without feeling her in my arms. Two weeks without seeing her smile. Two weeks spent wishing I'd told her I loved her. Instead, once again, I drove away and left the woman I loved.

Fuck, it was going to be a long two weeks.

Chapter 48
Jenna

"Hey, early bird! To what do I owe the pleasure of this wake-up call?" Cassie said after she answered the phone on the fourth ring.

"I'm sorry! I didn't realize you were still in bed!" I looked at the time on my phone. "Wait, it's after ten in the morning! What are you doing still in bed?"

"It was a late night," Cassie said with a giggle.

"Who is it? Is that Jenna? Good morning, Jenna!" I heard Mike shout from the background.

"Shhhh..." Cassie was still giggling. "I'm on the phone. Go back to laying there looking all adorable and sleepy."

"Cassie! Is Mike there with you? Good grief! Why did you answer the phone?" I could feel myself starting to blush and I wasn't even with them.

"Because I have barely had a chance to talk to you since you left two weeks ago and I miss you. Forgive me for the enthusiasm I had when I saw your name flash up on the phone."

"I miss you too! It's been crazy here. I'm in class all day and studying by myself or in a study group every night. I haven't had time for much else."

"I get it. Doesn't mean I have to like it though. I'm still super proud of you for becoming an ultra-hot, badass lawyer lady."

"Thank you, Cass. I miss you tons." I really did. Being away from Cassie had been tough. "Hey Cass, I am going to do a total topic switch on you... have you seen Nick lately?" I chewed on my lower lip, nervous about what her response was going to be.

"I saw him briefly at a work event earlier this week. It was a celebration for the groundbreaking on the Rickson Estates project. Why?"

I sighed. "It's just...I haven't heard from him for few days and he's supposed to be here today to spend the weekend with me. I wanted to figure out for sure what time he is coming so I can finalize some plans for us."

"Have you talked to him much since you left?"

"It's been sporadic, we've been talking and texting a bit. I've left some messages for him and sent him some texts, but haven't heard back from him in a few days. I'm starting to get worried. How did he seem when you saw him? Is he doing okay?"

Cassie didn't respond right away which made me nervous. "Honest answer? No, honey. He didn't seem okay. He looked... well, he looked pretty fucking rough. Like he hadn't slept for days. He didn't stay long and seemed really distracted while he was there. I tried to go and talk to him, but it kind of felt like he gave me the slip."

That made me even more worried about him. "Oh no! Do you think he's sick?"

"I think he's lovesick," Mike shouted. "He's been in the shop a few times to grab a pizza and always asks about you, Jenna. I think the guy really misses you."

I could hear Cassie rustling around in her bed. "Stop listening to my phone call and shouting from the damn peanut gallery!"

"It's hard not to hear when you're laying right next to me." I couldn't see him but I knew Mike was smiling and rolling his eyes.

"Hey! Guys! Focus! No pillow talk while I'm on the phone to hear it!" I didn't trust them to keep things G-rated while they were in bed together and there was no way I wanted to hear any of that, thank you very much. "If he misses me so much, why isn't he returning my calls? I'm super excited to see him this weekend and all I want to do is talk to him."

"I have an idea about that," Mike shouted.

"Here, I'm handing the phone to Mike so he'll stop shouting and you can hear him. You know, since he has totally interjected himself into our phone conversation." Knowing Cassie the way I did, I was certain she stuck her tongue out at Mike as she handed him the phone.

"Again, I am right here and it is impossible not to hear the two of you talking." I could hear Mike sigh as Cassie handed him the phone.

Now it was Cassie's turn to shout from the background, "I'm going to go make some coffee while you two chat!"

"Okay, Jenna, you need to look at this from his point of view," Mike sounded very serious as he started in on the conversation.

"How do I do that?"

"Luckily, I am here to be your guide," Mike said with a chuckle. "Picture this: you unexpectedly meet someone you are totally into. Everything is going great, only it turns out your 'someone' had this big life change all planned out and put into motion before you'd even met."

Even though Mike couldn't see me I nodded my head. "Okay. With you so far."

"This raises several interesting questions. Do you try to stop the life change from happening for the other person, or do you just accept that it is going to happen? Where do you fit into another person's life change if you were not a factor when the decision to make the change happened? Is there even a place for you in this life change?"

It felt like a lightbulb was starting to flick on in my head. "Oh my goodness, Mike! I never even considered any of this!"

"Well, kind of hard to do when you two crazy kids lack so much in the communication department on the tough stuff."

I decided to ignore his jab. I was too invested in the idea of finding out more about where Nick was coming from. "So let me get this right, you're saying he might really have feelings for me? He might just be acting this way because he doesn't want to stand in the way of me going to law school, and he may not feel like he fits into this new part of my life?"

"We have a winner!" Mike's voice sounded all goofy like he was announcing the winner on a game show.

I chewed on my lip as I thought more about it. "I don't know, Mike. What if he's just realized he isn't into me and doesn't want this?"

Mike sighed like the answer was so obvious. "If that was the case then why would he be asking about you? Or take any of your calls? Or respond to any of your texts?"

It all made so much sense. "Thank you for this, Mike! I feel a new sense of hope. I am going to make this work! This weekend when he's here we really are going to sit down and talk to figure things out." I was feeling better than I had for the past several days.

"I am back! What did I miss?" Cassie shouted in from the background. I could hear the phone rustling as Mike handed it back to her.

"Your boyfriend is a pretty good guy, Cass."

"Yeah," her voice grew soft, "I came to that conclusion a while ago. I think I'll keep him around. For now." I heard the rustling of blankets as Cassie started laughing and shrieking.

I instantly felt uncomfortable. "Well, okay guys! Sounds like you have moved on to other activities! I'm going to hang up now!"

"Bye, Jenna!" Cassie shouted, still laughing.

"Bye!" Mike shouted as I quickly hung up.

For the first time in weeks, I felt like I had a clear idea of what I wanted and, at least, some better insight into why Nick had been acting so vague and aloof. We were going to work it out and things were going to come together. I needed to tell Nick I loved him and show him he was still an important part of my life. To let him know I wanted us to work despite being physically apart.

I just had to wait for him to arrive so we could get everything sorted out.

Chapter 49
Jenna

Morning turned into the afternoon which turned into evening. I hadn't heard from Nick and the more time passed, the more worried I got. I tried to call him a few times, but each time it went straight to voicemail. I decided to try one more time and was surprised when he answered.

"Helllllllllllo. Is this Jenna?" Nick's words sounded slow and slurred. I immediately had a bad feeling.

"Hi, Nick. This is Jenna. I haven't heard from you all day and I was starting to get worried. Are you... are you okay?"

"Mmmmmmmm... I'm all good now."

I hesitated before responding. I had to ask him, even though I knew the answer. "Nick, are you drunk?"

"Been having a few drinks, yes." He was having trouble getting his words out.

"Where are you, Nick?" My pulse was racing and I started to feel an overwhelming sense of dread in the pit of my stomach.

"At my... at my house, Jenna."

"What's going on, Nick? You're supposed to be here visiting me for the weekend. Why are you home and why are you drunk?" The silence on the other end of the phone lasted so long I worried he had passed out. "Nick! Nick! Are you there?"

"I can't come. I'm sorry, Jenna. I just can't do it."

"You can't do it or won't do it?" I choked on the words in my throat. What the hell was going on? I was on the verge of tears but I tried to hold them back and keep calm.

"Can't do it. Just can't do it, Jenna Morgan. This is too hard." Nick slurred his words as he continued to drink between statements.

I couldn't help it anymore. The tears started to escape down my cheeks. "Were you even planning on coming or were you just going to blow me off?" The tears rolling down my face as a mixture of anger, hurt, and disappointment washed over me.

"I wanted to. All I want to do for you Jenna is the right thing. This is so hard... the right thing. I can't keep fucking up. You deserve better, Jenna."

"What are you talking about?" I asked through my tears.

"This! You! Me!" Nick shouted into the phone in a frustrated sounding growl. I heard glass shatter in the background.

"Nick! Are you okay? What just happened? It sounded like something broke!" I was worried he hurt himself.

"I threw the bottle at the wall. It broke. I am not okay. I just threw a bottle at the wall."

"Nick, you're scaring me. Do I need to call someone to come help you? Did you cut yourself?"

"No cuts," Nick said in his slurred speech. "No one can help me with my hurt. It just keeps getting bigger. I miss you too much."

I was so confused about what he was saying and what was happening. "Nick, I am not sure what you are talking about. Tell me what is going on. Help me understand how I can help you."

"It wasn't supposed to be like this."

"What wasn't supposed to be like this?" My heart raced and I was pacing back and forth in my living room. I was starting to feel frantic and desperate. I hated that there was a distance between us... physically and emotionally. I hated that we hadn't been really open with each other, the way we should have been before I left. It felt as if everything had just grown into a bigger, more complicated mess and I had no idea how to fix it.

"Jenna, this is just not working and it is time to move on," Nick said.

I gasped, then choked out a small gurgling noise as the words rang in my head.

The same words Brett sneered at me when he broke up with me on graduation day.

The same worlds Cynthia used when she fired me from my dream job.

Now the words Nick was telling me.

I couldn't breathe. Everything felt like it was closing in around me. I started to gasp for air as I sunk to the floor.

'This is just not working and it is time to move on.' I knew what it really meant. *I* was not working and it was time to move on from *me*.

I dropped the phone as I started sobbing. My heart felt like someone had ripped it out of my chest and stomped on it. I gasped for air as my chest tightened and waves of nausea washed over me.

Somewhere in the far off distance, I could hear Nick still on the phone. "Jenna! Jenna! It wasn't supposed to be like this! I'm sorry Jenna. Goodbye. Goodbye, Jenna. I am sorry. I am so damn sorry."

The phone went silent. The only sounds in my apartment were the sobs consuming my body and my heart shattering.

I took a few minutes and tried to take some deep breaths before picking up my phone. I knew what I had to do. I dialed the number with shaking fingers. "Hello? This is Jenna. I need you right now. I need you now more than I have ever needed anyone before."

Chapter 50
Nick

The phone ringing sounded like a jackhammer smashing into my head. I didn't even open my eyes as I felt around for it. "Hello?" I said in a thick and groggy voice once I found it and answered the call.

"Nick. It sounds like I woke you up, did I?" I couldn't quite focus on what the person on the other end of the phone was saying. It was way too early, and I was way too fucking hungover, to fully comprehend what was going on.

"Yes, you woke me up," I snapped. "Why are you calling?"

"Well, it is noon on Monday so get your ass out of bed and meet me at Pete's Pizza in twenty minutes," the voice on the phone snapped back at me. It was only then it finally sunk in that Cassie was the one calling me... only, I had no idea why.

Her words slowly continued to sink into my pounding head. "Wait, it's noon on Monday?"

Cassie snorted. "Actually meet me in thirty minutes, and be sure to take a shower before you leave. I don't want to deal with you smelling like a whole fucking weekend of stale booze and regret."

"Mmmmmmmmm hummmmmmm," I moaned into the phone. I just wanted to hang up and go back to bed. Or actually, get into bed since I had passed out on the sofa.

"Nick Blaine, I am serious!" Cassie shouted so loudly it caused my eyes to fly open. I immediately shut them. The light pouring into my condo was way too bright. Cassie continued talking, "This is not optional! I am setting the stopwatch on

278

my phone and if you are not sitting across from me at Pete's in thirty minutes, I am coming after you."

I groaned... fuck, my head hurt. "Why?"

"Why will I be coming after you? Because I will be incredibly angry, Nick. In case you have not figured it out yet, I can be really fucking scary when I am angry." I had no doubt at all about that. Cassie could be scary sometimes even when she wasn't angry.

"No, why do you want me to meet you?" I slowly tried opening my eyes again.

"Why do you think, you idiot?" Cassie snapped at me. Clearly, it had been the wrong thing to ask. "Who is the one person we have in common? I am hanging up now and starting the timer. Get going!"

I rolled off the sofa and fell onto the floor. Fuck, I felt like shit. I knocked over a couple of empty bottles of whisky as I stood up. Damn, for a moment, I couldn't remember why I thought a weekend of drinking my weight in whisky was a good idea, and then it all came flooding back to me. Everything I had been trying to forget. I rubbed my eyes trying to get the image of Jenna out of my head. Fuck.

I stumbled to the shower and turned on the water. As much as I didn't want to, I knew I needed to go meet with Cassie.

***

With two minutes to spare, I walked through the front door of Pete's. The bell clanging made me cringe. Despite the shower and downing a couple of bottles of Gatorade on the way, I still felt like shit. In more ways than one.

279

"She's at a table in the back waiting for you." Mike greeted me with a very clipped tone as he glared at me from behind the counter.

"Thanks, man," I mumbled back.

"Listen, I know Cassie can take care of herself, but if you act like a jerk or even show her an ounce of disrespect, I will be back there in a heartbeat. I don't mess around when it comes to her." The way Mike looked at me as he said it left no doubt in my mind how serious he was.

I put both hands up. "I'm not looking for trouble."

"Well, for a guy that's not looking for trouble, you sure have caused a lot of it lately," Mike snarled. He nodded his head to the right. "Go on back. I have customers to attend to."

I walked into the back part of the restaurant and saw Cassie sitting at the furthest table. "Nick, sit down and take your sunglasses off. I am sure you are hungover as hell, but you don't get to try and hide. Not for this conversation." Her voice was pure ice and, I am not going to lie, that, coupled with the look on her face, scared the crap out of me.

"Yes, ma'am," I replied.

"Good answer." Cassie waited for me to pull out the chair across from her and sit down. She slowly and deliberately leaned forward which, somehow, just made her more intimidating. Cassie was the kind of loose cannon you didn't fuck with and it was clear she didn't have any goodwill towards me. "Now listen to me. I spent the four-hour car ride back here this morning thinking of all the ways that I was going to end you and dispose of your body for what you did to my girl, Jenna."

I hung my head in shame. "I would deserve it. I have really fucked all of this up and destroyed everything good we had," I mumbled.

"I am glad we can agree on something. It wasn't until I hit the city limits that I realized things may not be entirely your fault. Don't get me wrong, you totally acted like a giant fucking jackass, but there are probably some things you may not fully understand about Jenna."

My completely hungover brain caught up to the fact she had made a four-hour car ride and had seen Jenna. "Wait? You were with Jenna? How is she?" I lifted my head up as my heart seemed to skip a beat just hearing her name.

Cassie looked at me with complete disgust. "Not good, Nick. She's pretty broken. She called me Friday night after your poor drunken excuse of a phone call. She needed me, so I drove there that night and stayed all weekend with her."

My head dropped again. I didn't think it was possible to feel much worse, but Cassie's description of Jenna sent me to a new low. "I am sorry. It wasn't supposed to be like this," I mumbled.

"Jenna said you keep saying that, only she has no idea what it actually means. Care to fill me in?" Cassie raised an eyebrow at me as she drummed her red manicured fingernails on the table. I couldn't bring myself to respond. "Right." Cassie finally said, clearly growing annoyed at my silence. "Moving on. I don't make it a habit to talk about other people's stuff behind their backs, but I am trying to do this for the greater good. See, I think you both love each other, but for whatever reason, can't tell each other and won't be fully honest. It's pretty clear you are both miserable apart, so I am hoping you take this information and use it to fix this giant clusterfuck of a mess you've made."

I looked up at Cassie. "I'm listening," I said slowly. For the first time since our phone call on Friday I had a small glimmer of hope that, maybe, there would be some way I could salvage it all...

Chapter 51
Nick

"As long as I have known Jenna, she has had a life plan she has been working towards. The basics of it were to get married, so she could have her perfect suburban life with her perfect husband and her perfect children. She would go to law school and be a successful lawyer, making her and her husband this hugely successful power couple. In all honesty, I don't think that dream was fully Jenna's but was more the dream her parents had for her. Going to law school is the only part I can confidently say really was hers. She wanted to be a lawyer so she could help people long before I met her."

"I knew going to law school was one of her dreams," I said. "There was no way I was going to interfere with that." Cassie had to know that, right?

Cassie raised her eyebrow at me again. "Okay, good. Now you are contributing to the conversation and we are actually getting somewhere. When we went to college, Jenna met Brett. I always thought he was a giant waste of space, but he fit perfectly into the role of the potential husband in Jenna's life plan. Her parents were crazy about him and he comes from a well-off, very influential family. I think pleasing her parents was why she stayed with him so long. Lord knows he did not have any other redeeming qualities."

Brett... the name didn't sound familiar. "Wait... is this the guy she dated all through college?" I asked as the pieces slowly started coming together.

Cassie made a face like she had just sucked on a lemon. "Unfortunately, yes. He was straight-up, fucking awful. Over time, the confident, fun-loving friend I had known for years started to change. Brett cheated on her multiple times. He strung her along with promises of a white-picket fence and everything she ever wanted coming true as long as she stayed with him. Her confidence eroded and she started making her life all about him. A huge part of that was the pressure from her parents to keep the loser and be a perfect little robot on Brett's arm."

I could feel my anger start to flare. "I had a hunch he was no good, but nothing like this. Why would he do that to her?" I unconsciously started to clench and unclench my fists. I felt that surge of protectiveness flare through me... the one I had only ever felt for Jenna.

"Simmer down there, Blaine. You look like you are about to lose your shit and I can't have you punching anyone else in the face." Cassie nodded her head towards my fists on the table. "Why did he do it?" Cassie continued "Jenna is the whole package; smart, beautiful, kind, and driven. She looked really good hanging dutifully from his arm in public while he acted like a philandering asshole in private."

Since Cassie had commented about punching someone, I felt the need to clarify and apologize. "About that night at the club..." I started. Cassie quickly waved her hand at me and I stopped.

"I am providing information now, not you. You will get your turn. So where were we... okay, so Jenna's parents are garbage people who kept pressuring Jenna to be this made-up, perfect version of herself while Brett ran around town dipping his dong in a vast assortment of women, none of which were his girlfriend. Unfortunately, I was not a good friend to her during that time, so poor Jenna was on her own trying to please everyone and maintain all of these unrealistic expectations."

"I can't imagine you ever not being a good friend to Jenna." Cassie might have been a little off her rocker, but she was incredibly loyal and protective of Jenna. Jenna had mentioned she and Cassie had been friends since the fifth grade and had stuck with each other through a whole lot of shit.

"Well, I wasn't," Cassie said quickly with a hint of sorrow in her voice. "During the first few years of college, I got really wound up in the party scene. Like really wound up. There were many times my poor decision-making got me into trouble. I would call Jenna and she would always come to get me or bail my ass out. When she lets you into her life, she is the most loyal and fierce friend you could ever want to have. The only times she ever stood up to Brett were times when it involved something with me and whatever mess I found myself in."

Cassie paused and looked out the window for a moment. "There were some other things that happened and well... long story short, Jenna was the one who saved me and eventually helped me to move past the bad stuff." Cassie was quiet for a few moments before she continued. "By that point, I was failing college, so Jenna helped me out of the mess I had created by tutoring me in all the classes I was failing... which was literally all of them. I was ready to just drop out. I wouldn't have graduated from college if it wasn't for Jenna." Cassie turned away from the window and looked back at me.

"I owe her my life in more ways than one, and there is nothing I won't do for her. She never gave up on me, even when she really probably should have, which is why I will always be there for her."

I hadn't known Cassie for very long, but I could recognize a serious conversation where she disclosed information about herself was rare. "I don't even know what to say..." I had no idea about most of what she was telling me. If I was lucky enough to fix things with Jenna, it was clear we had a whole lot to talk about.

"Well, it's a good thing I'm the one doing the talking." Just like that, Cassie seemed to snap back into the present moment. "All of the pressure Jenna was under eventually wore her down. She started having crazy, anxiety-induced panic attacks in addition to totally losing her confidence and her own identity. She became a shell of what she was before that fucking asshat came into her life and it was really awful to watch. I tried many, many times to get her to ditch the dead weight that was Brett, but she would never do it." Cassie paused for a moment and looked down at the table. It was clear this was difficult for her to talk about.

"Fast forward to graduation." Cassie looked up again and leaned her elbows on the table. "After the graduation ceremony, Jenna went out to this fancy dinner with her parents, Brett, and Brett's parents. She thought he was going to propose to her that night at dinner with their families. In her mind, her life plan was right on track... she had graduated as one of the top in our class and had been accepted to law school. The engagement was the missing piece of her perfect plan and the piece her parents had been harping on her about for years. Only, instead of proposing, when the check came, Brett dumped her - in front of both of their parents. She was mortified. To make matters worse, her parents were convinced that, somehow, the break up was all her fault, and after causing a very public scene, they essentially broke up with her, too. In the end, everyone walked out and left her at the restaurant by herself."

"Jesus, this is horrible! I had no idea, and you're right, they are all total fucking garbage people! Jenna is the most amazing person I have ever met and she doesn't deserve to be treated like that!" I was beyond angry at all of the people Cassie was talking about. Jenna was so good and kind, then it suddenly hit me. I had done the same thing with the way I handled things and treated her. I looked up at Cassie and it was like she could read my mind. "Shit! I did the same fucking thing to her... fuck, Cassie... am I... am I now on the list of awful people who treat her terribly?" I felt sick at the thought. I loved her so much but nothing about what I had done, and the way I had treated her lately, would show that.

Cassie just stared me down. "Not yet, which is why I'm here. Hang on for a little more story and then we'll get to you. So when bastard Brett and her gross family all left her, Jenna was a mess. She still has not had any communication with her parents since that night. Jenna had to put off law school for a year because she was not in any place, emotional or otherwise, to start. It took her months until she was able to heal enough to start her job at this law firm where she really wanted to work."

Fuck. I knew what happened next. My heart ached for Jenna and everything that she had been through. "Is that the place she got fired from right before starting at Pete's?"

"Yes." Cassie looked a little surprised that I knew that part but quickly recovered. "Losing that job was also a huge blow to her and why we started the 'saying yes' plan. After the first blow dealt by Brett, she was so closed off to everything and convinced she was the problem. The second blow of being fired just reaffirmed that in her mind. She needed to get out there and essentially get herself back. I suspect Brett's family had something to do with her getting fired from the law firm since they are major clients there. Just in case you hadn't figured it out yet, they are garbage people too."

Cassie stopped for a moment. I did not know how any of the series of events Jenna had endured could possibly get any worse. Cassie took a deep breath and looked right at me. "So one last piece of the story and then I have some questions for you I expect you to answer honestly."

"Okay" I said quickly, wanting to get it over. I had no idea what could possibly be next or how it could get any worse but I had a feeling, based on Cassie's expression, it was about to.

Chapter 52
Nick

Cassie stared at me for what felt like forever before she finally started speaking again. "I take the fact you look like you are either going to start crying or punch something as a good thing. If you didn't care a great deal for her you wouldn't care about any of the stuff I've been telling you."

"I do. I do care about her so much. So much it terrifies me." I couldn't believe I said it out loud and to Cassie, of all people. Although it wasn't that surprising given I had nothing to lose at that point. It felt like I had already lost everything when I lost Jenna.

"I thought so, which is going to make this next part rough to hear, but you need to know it. The reason Brett gave her for ending their relationship was 'this is just not working and it is time to move on.' That is also the exact same reason they gave her at the law firm when they fired her. It was also..."

"What I said to her on the phone on Friday," I whispered. My blood ran cold, I could feel all the color start to drain out of my face as the realization of what I had done to her sank in. "Fucking hell! I had no idea!" I started to shout as the panic filled every pore of my body. "She must really hate me now! Dammit! Out of all the stupid things I could have—"

"Hey! Calm down," Cassie interrupted me. "You didn't know. Hell, it sounded like you were plenty drunk on the phone with her. I wasn't even sure you would remember telling her."

I felt like I was going to completely lose my shit right there in front of Cassie. I didn't know what else to do; I felt worse than I had ever felt before in my life. I tipped my head back and looked at the ceiling so Cassie would not see I was trying my damndest not to cry. My heart absolutely broke to think of all the hurt Jenna had gone through, and that I had contributed to it. "Unfortunately, I wasn't drunk enough to forget what I said to her. I spent all weekend trying to drink that away, and block out the awful feelings and emptiness I feel without her around." I couldn't believe I was telling Cassie everything but I was fucking desperate to fix things with Jenna. If having an incredibly uncomfortable conversation with Cassie was a step in the right direction, I had to be all in.

"Well, Nick, I am going to tell you, getting blackout drunk is a terrible coping mechanism and never turns out well. Now, tell me the truth about your feelings for Jenna." I tipped my head back down and looked at Cassie who was sitting on the other side of the table with her arms crossed. The look on her face was just daring me to not answer her question.

I sighed as I dropped my elbows to my knees and rested my head in my hands. It was going to be easier if I didn't have to look at Cassie while I spoke. "It was never supposed to be like this. I was never supposed to fall in love with her. This was supposed to be just a fun time until she left. I wanted to tell her so many times but just couldn't do it. At first, it was just a mutual attraction, but it grew into so much more. It was easy to ignore the fact she was leaving until it was actually happening. I didn't want to stand in the way of her going to law school or be a distraction when she got there."

"That explains your stupid not-really-a-plan-but-trying-to-make-it-a-plan for when she left." Cassie did not sound impressed.

"Selfishly, I wanted her to stay, but I would never actually force her to make that choice. Believe it or not, I am not a big enough asshole to actually do that to her. Unfortunately, when the time came for her to leave, I couldn't just walk away from her either." I finally lifted my head and looked at Cassie, who was staring intently at me. "I don't want to be without her. Ever. I tried to cool things down before she left, but I just couldn't. I knew she had to leave, but I couldn't see how I was going to fit into things when she did. That night when the guy was hitting on her at the bar, I was so angry and jealous I was literally seeing red. After what I did, I felt awful for acting that way in front of Jenna and that she had to see that. I tried to walk away then, but I just couldn't."

I had to stop and regroup. It was the most in-depth admission of feelings I had ever made to anyone, including Bax, who I'd known for years and years. Cassie sat there in silence, as if she was waiting for me to continue.

I took a deep breath and forged on. "Knowing she was leaving has just been too much to bear. The night before she left, I wanted to come over and act like everything was going to be okay, but I was so broken inside. I couldn't even get off my bike to go into her apartment. She was just standing there all beautiful and perfect. When she started crying, I knew it was because of me, which tore me up even more. I didn't know how to fix it other than to remove the thing that was hurting her so much... me." I stopped and closed my eyes... I could picture her perfectly; standing there as I foolishly drove away from her. It felt like there was a giant gaping hole in my heart the size of Jenna.

Cassie's voice snapped me back to attention. "So, tell me about this weekend," she said as her arms remained crossed and her gaze was steady.

I ran my hand through my hair and down my face. "I'm sure you know we have talked some over the past two weeks. Every time I'd talk to her it broke me a little more, knowing I couldn't be with her and that we're in this messed up situation. It just got harder and harder every time I spoke to her. I regretted not telling her how I feel about her, regardless of how she feels about me. At least that way she'd know. I was ready to go visit her last Friday. Then I started thinking about how hard it was to talk to her, and how hard it would be to see her, hold her, and then have to leave her again."

Cassie uncrossed her arms and leaned forward. "So you started hitting the booze?" I felt like a little kid being scolded.

"Yeah. Pretty soon I was drunk and hating myself even more. I started to believe Jenna was better off without me. I felt so awful ending things with her I pretty much drank the whole weekend away."

"So why didn't you ever tell her how you felt?" Cassie leaned back in her seat and shot me a look full of skepticism.

I shifted around in my seat. "I am not a relationship guy..." I started to say.

Cassie angrily interrupted me. "That is a total fucking bullshit excuse and you know it! Try again!" she yelled at me.

I felt backed into a corner. "Honestly? I was scared! I am scared about how much I care about her!" I yelled back. Cassie smiled. She looked over my shoulder and waved. I turned around to see Mike glaring at me from a few tables over. I lowered my voice. "I was so scared she didn't feel the same, and I was scared it wasn't going to be enough to make this work, once she left. I have never felt this way about another person before! I don't know what to do about it!"

"The communication between the two of you is absolute shit. If you are going to make this work, you both need to figure that piece of the puzzle out."

"How do I fix this?" I pleaded to Cassie. "I have messed this whole thing up so fucking much. Is it too late? Does she really hate me now?" I was desperate to get Jenna back, if she'd have me and it wasn't too late.

"Before you charge in trying to be the white knight, I need to tell you something: you need to make a decision about what you want with Jenna and stick to it. No half-in, half-out shit. One of her greatest fears is not being enough, so if you are in, you are all in." Cassie's expression was stone-cold serious.

I didn't even hesitate. "If she'll have me, and I have not totally ruined this, I am all in. That's not even a question in my mind."

Cassie gave a small nod of approval. "How you fix this is all on you. I can't tell you how to do it. I can tell you to be good to her and remember that if you're not, I have already planned how to end you." I had absolutely no doubt Cassie was serious.

"All I want to do is the right thing for her. I love her, Cassie. I have never felt this way about anyone else and I can't imagine that ever changing." Much to my surprise, it felt really good to actually admit and say out loud.

Cassie gave me a big smile. "Then go get your girl."

293

"Thank you for this. I will be forever grateful." I meant it. I didn't even want to think about what would have happened if Cassie hadn't called me that morning.

"Well, was I right?" Mike walked over to the table and went to stand behind Cassie, putting his hand on her shoulder.

Cassie reached up and put her hand on his. "You were pretty spot on, babe. Nick, just so you know, Mike had your back during this. He seemed to understand where you were coming from better than anyone else."

I reached my hand out to shake Mike's. Much to my surprise, he met it with a firm shake back. "Thanks, man. I'm glad that at least one of us had an idea about what was going on since clearly I did not... actually, can I ask for your help with one last thing?" An idea was starting to form in my mind. One I hoped would work.

Chapter 53
Jenna

I knew when I called Cassie on Friday night and told her I needed her, she would be there. She had proven, time and time again, she was the one person I could count on. When she left early Monday morning, she said it was because she had to get back for some 'time-sensitive business.' I was bummed she had to leave, but really grateful she came when she did.

I was sitting on my sofa in pretty much the exact same spot I had been sitting all day. My heart was still in pieces about Nick and how things had ended. It was so quiet in my apartment that, when my phone dinged with an incoming message, it actually startled me. I reached over to the coffee table and grabbed it looking to see who the message was from.

I should have known it would be from Cassie checking in on me. "*Hey, babe! How are you doing?*"

I typed out a message back to her. "*Same as last time you asked.*"

I was about to toss my phone back on the table but Cassie's response was almost immediate. "*You need some new material. All day, every time I check in on you, it's the same damn thing.*"

"*Still heartbroken, still sitting on the sofa, still wearing my pajamas. Nothing has changed.*"

"*Hang in there sweetie. You are my favorite.*"

I couldn't help but smile as I typed back; "*I love you too.*"

I tossed my phone back on the coffee table. I might as well have gone to bed. It was Monday and I had skipped all of my classes. I didn't study all weekend and knew I would have a bunch of catching up to do. I needed to get some rest and hit it all the next day.

I was about to head to my room when the doorbell rang. I didn't know anyone who would be visiting me on a Monday night. Someone must've had the wrong apartment. I went over and opened the door... and gasped in surprise when I saw who was on the other side.

"Hi, Jenna," Nick said softly.

It took me a minute to recover from the shock of seeing him. When I finally found my voice I narrowed my eyes and crossed my arms. "Nick. What are you doing here?"

"I... I came to see you. I have some things I need to tell you," he said quickly.

"I think you were pretty clear on Friday when we talked on the phone," I said, the anger in my voice springing from the hurt I felt as the words he had said on Friday replayed in my mind.

"Jenna I am so sorry. I was a jerk... an absolute asshole and you didn't deserve to be treated like that. Ending things with you is not what I want. It is the exact opposite, in fact." The look on Nick's face was so earnest, I was certain he was telling the truth, but what he was saying left me even more confused. It was the exact opposite of what he had said on Friday night.

"Then why did you do it?" I snapped, more out of confusion than anger. I couldn't keep playing games... not when my heart had already been shattered.

Nick sighed and shifted around. "Can I please come in and we can talk?" he pleaded.

"Nick, I don't know if that's a good idea..." my gaze shifted down, away from his face. It was only then I realized he was holding a pizza box. When I looked at it a little closer, I saw it was a Pete's Pizza box. "What is that?" I asked, nodding my head toward the box.

"Well, I kind of figured coming here and asking you to hear me out might be a long shot after everything I've done lately, so I brought something to help convince you," Nick gave me a small nervous smile. I was surprised to see how uncomfortable he appeared. Then again, he was randomly standing on my doorstep with a pizza box. As soon as I had the thought, I realized how strange the whole situation was, especially when coupled with everything that had happened since we agreed to the whole 'non-relationship' plan.

"A cold pizza? That's going to convince me to hear you out? If it really is from Pete's, it has been in your truck for at least four hours." I still was not sure why he was standing on my doorstep with a cold pizza.

I could see Nick deflate a little. "Jenna, this is how we began, with a delivery from Pete's," he said in a quiet voice. He paused and seemed to gather back some of his confidence. "We have a whole lot of talking to do and a bunch of things to work out, but I want us to do those things together. I am hoping we can start over. With you and me together, in a real relationship."

The look on his face was one of absolute vulnerability and hopefulness. It tugged at my heart, but he deserved an honest answer. "I don't know, Nick. My... my heart is really broken and I am not sure I can do this...have a conversation, be around you... any part of this..." I waved my hand back and forth between us as the right words seemed to escape me.

Nick lowered his head and I thought he was going to turn around and leave. Suddenly he looked up and seemed to stand up a little straighter. He closed his eyes for a moment, took a deep breath, and began talking. "Jenna, I am scared out of my mind that you are going to shut the door and I am never going to see you again. I know I have screwed up. Multiple times. I am probably going to screw up again in the future but this right here... what I feel for you... this is worth fighting for. It just took me way too long to realize it."

"Oh, Nick." My hand flew up to cover my mouth as my eyes started to tear up. His words were not at all what I'd expected.

Nick seemed to sense my hesitation. "Jenna, all I am asking for is a chance to come in and talk. If we do that and you still want me to go, I respect you and I will respect your wishes and leave." The hopeful look was back on his face as he searched mine, looking for some hint of an answer. "May I please come in so we can talk, Jenna?"

I hesitated as I tried to decide on my answer. I knew this was another crossroad and I needed to pick the right path for me. As I was thinking, Nick opened the pizza box and tipped it slightly toward me. I peered into the box... there was a pizza inside and across the top of it, spelled out in olives was 'Say Yes!'

I looked at it for a minute and then started laughing uncontrollably. "A 'saying yes' pizza?" I asked between giggles.

Nick's face flushed and he gave me a sheepish smile. "We started with a pizza delivery and some help from the saying yes plan. I hope now you'll say yes to us working through this."

I stopped laughing and raised my eyebrow at Nick. "I assume, somehow, Mike helped you with this?"

"I did have some help from Mike. I also had a long conversation with Cassie today."

I was initially surprised to hear he had a conversation with Cassie, but as soon as I thought more about it, it made perfect sense. "So you must have been the 'time-sensitive business' she needed to attend to this morning," I muttered.

Nick looked confused for a fleeting moment and shook his head. "I am not sure what that means, but I hope you're not upset I spoke with her."

"Not at all. I trust Cassie." I leaned against the doorframe as I continued to weigh my options. "How about I say yes to your offer of coming in and talking," I said hesitantly. I quickly followed it with, "Just talking, nothing else. We'll see how the talking goes and go from there."

Chapter 54
Jenna

A look of relief washed over Nick's face. "I'll take it!" He said happily as I stepped aside so he could come into my apartment. He walked in and placed the pizza box on the counter. Nick turned and looked at me, then reached out like he was going to touch me. He quickly caught himself and pulled his hand back. His eyes got big as he realized his mistake. "I'm sorry! You look so beautiful and I'm so happy to see you... I just want to hold you and... well, I'm sorry."

I shook my head. "No touching. It will just make me too confused and I need to fully focus on this conversation. I'm going to be completely honest, Nick. I still don't know how this is going to go, but you're right, we do need to talk." The room filled with tension and awkwardness as we stood there staring at each other. It was clear we were both nervous and neither one of us wanted to make the first move or say anything. I gave Nick a half-smile, "Plus I'm wearing flannel pajamas and I haven't showered today. I'm kind of gross right now."

Nick scrunched his face up like he really didn't like what I said. "Stop that. You're beautiful no matter what you are wearing. Remember Jenna, you originally took my breath away in a Pete's Pizza uniform." His face softened into a smile.

I blushed as I thought of the black Pete's Pizza shirt and jeans I had been wearing when we first met. The uniform was only a small step up from the pajamas I had on. I gestured to the sofa. "Let's sit." I felt like tension in the room was lifting a little as we sat on opposite sides of the sofa. I pulled my knees up to my chest and Nick shifted around awkwardly until he finally settled on a position facing me.

"I spent the whole drive here rehearsing what I was going to say to you so I could be sure to get out what I needed to tell you. Now that I am actually here, everything I was going to say seems stupid and wrong so I am just going to go for it."

I nodded my head. "Okay," I whispered.

Nick took a deep breath. "I thought my life was exactly where I wanted it. Blaine Construction was ready to completely take off after years of hard work. It's been my sole focus for a long time and I thought that the success of Blaine Construction was everything I wanted."

Nick paused as he shifted nervously in his seat. He closed his eyes for a brief moment and drew in a deep breath before he continued. "In the most unexpected way at the most unexpected time, you came into my life and nothing has been the same since. I had no idea ordering a pizza that night would change everything. From the moment I laid eyes on you, I knew you were someone special. Ever since that first day, and every day after, I have not been able to get you out of my mind. I knew you were planning on moving and that going to law school was a dream of yours. I never wanted to stand in the way of any of it or interfere with you pursuing your dreams.

"I thought I could be with you for just a short time, but it became clear that wasn't possible. My insecurities made me feel like there wasn't going to be a place for me in your new chapter, since it had been planned out long before we'd even met. This is new territory for me. I have never had feelings so strong for anyone else and they scare me."

I was completely blown away by the honesty and sincerity in what Nick was saying. Everything was starting to make so much sense. I was starting to see how affected by everything he had been. "Oh, Nick. I never intended to make you feel that way..."

"I know," Nick said with a small smile. "Part of it is my own baggage which I brought right into the middle of us. When we were first together, it was easy to ignore that you were leaving and pretend it was just not going to happen. When we finally talked about it, everything became real and I panicked. I tried to distance myself from you thinking it would make things easier when you left. The only thing it actually did was make me crazy, thinking about losing you and not having you in my life. I want you in my life, Jenna. No matter what it looks like."

Tears started to fall down my face. Nick looked like he wanted to reach out and touch me again, but instead, he moved around in his seat and put his arm on the back of the sofa as he kept talking. "I realize now that instead of shutting myself off, I should have told you how I felt. I was being selfish and only thinking about my feelings, not how my actions were impacting you or how you felt. I am really and truly sorry for that, Jenna. If we start over... when we start over, we need to trust each other and have better communication. Talking about feelings is totally new territory for me... Jesus, having any feelings is new for me, but Jenna, I want to make this work. I want all these crazy fucked up feelings with you. Jenna... I just want... I just want you."

I drew in a shaky breath. "I agree about communication and trust...*if* we start over." I was sure to put emphasis on the word 'if' since I was still not sure what I wanted moving forward. "This was not entirely your fault, Nick. I was there too, and I was so afraid of doing something wrong or saying the wrong thing I didn't say anything at all. I also let some of my baggage cloud my perception of what was going on between us, which was wrong." I pulled my knees down and positioned myself so I was looking directly at Nick. I wanted him to know how much I really meant the next thing I was going to say. "I am sorry for my piece in all of this too, Nick."

A look of tenderness washed over Nick's face at my apology. He looked away from me for a brief moment and ran his hand through his hair before looking back. "I was never upset with you. I was more upset with myself. Especially when it came to things like losing my temper and punching the guy at the bar, or the way I shut down on the last night I saw you. I am also upset about the way I acted when we last spoke. I let all the wrong emotions control me. I convinced myself you were better off without me in your life and I needed to let you go so you could move on with following your dreams."

"You can't make decisions like that for me, Nick." I couldn't help but wonder how different things would have been if only we'd been able to have this conversation weeks ago. We both definitely had a role in how everything played out.

Nick slowly nodded his head. "I see that now. Telling you 'this is not working' is, and will always be, one of the biggest regrets in my life. I am so sorry for that and the way I hurt you. I hope you will give me the opportunity to spend every day from here on in trying to make it up to you and let me prove how much you mean to me. I got some good advice today about making a decision and sticking to it. If you will have me, Jenna, I am all in without any hesitation. I want to be with you and never leave your side."

Now I was the one that wanted to reach out and touch him. The look on Nick's face was filled with complete sincerity, while his eyes were wrought with vulnerability. He really had put himself all out there and he'd done it for me. He did it because he wanted to be with me. "Nick..." I paused not really sure how to start. "While we're being open with each other, I need you to know I bring a lot of baggage with me. You've already seen some of it and how it has impacted my life... how it has impacted us, during our time together."

Nick started to scoot a little closer to me on the sofa but stopped like he was frightened I was going to jump up and run away. When he seemed satisfied that I wasn't, he reached his hand out to me. I slowly put my hand in his and realized how small my hand felt wrapped in his... and how right just even this simple touch felt. "Sweet, Jenna," Nick started his voice raspy with emotion. "Cassie filled me in on some of it. I am not Brett and I am not your parents. I am not going to leave you because things didn't go as planned. I am here fighting for you. I want to be with you, Jenna. I want to wake up every morning to your beautiful smiling face and fall asleep with you every night in my arms. I want the good days and the bad. Nothing in my life makes sense anymore, Jenna, without you in it."

I had been staring down at my hand in Nick's while he spoke and when I looked up, his eyes were wet with tears. "It's not going to be easy, Jenna, but if we truly work together, we can do anything. Neither of us is perfect, but we are stronger and better together. I am miserable without you, Jenna."

We sat there on the sofa holding hands as tears silently fell from both of our eyes. I looked into Nick's eyes and asked him about the one thing I still did not fully understand. "Over the last few weeks, you have repeatedly been saying that 'it was not supposed to be like this.' What did you mean by that, Nick?"

Nick squeezed my hand before looking up at me. "It was not supposed to be like this. I was not supposed to fall in love with you, Jenna Morgan, but I did. I love you, Jenna. I love you so damn much."

Just like that, my heart burst with a wonderful, but foreign, feeling. The feeling of being loved completely and accepted unconditionally. Any walls I had remaining crumbled and my body was flooded with a comforting warm feeling all over.

I leaped across the sofa, closing the remaining distance between us and landed in his arms. I buried my face in his shoulder as I clung to him. This man had opened up and given me his heart in a way that no one ever had before. I knew at that moment my heart would be safe with him, that he would treasure and protect it the same way I would his.

I kissed Nick softly on the lips before bringing my face level with his and looking into deep dark eyes that were filled with nothing but love for me. "I love you too, Nick Blaine."

In an instant, Nick's lips were on mine. We became a tangled mess of frantic limbs and wildly roaming hands as we tried to soak up all of each other. Nick suddenly pulled away and as we breathlessly gazed upon each other, a grin slowly broke out on his face. "So, Jenna. What do you say about starting over and giving this relationship a real go?"

I couldn't stop a huge smile from breaking out on my own face. "Yes, Nick. I am saying yes."

Chapter 55

Jenna

Three Years Later

"I can't believe I couldn't be there for the actual graduation! All these years, and I fucking missed the big moment!" Cassie let out a big sigh and made an exaggerated pouty face.

"Honey, the doctor was not kidding when she said no traveling. Your due date was two days ago... you probably shouldn't even be here. You should be at home resting." I watched Cassie as she waddled across the floor and leaned up against the counter.

"Who knew when this guy slipped one past the goalie and knocked me up his timing would be so lousy? I mean, nine months ago he should have been thinking about what a big day today was going to be and planned accordingly." Cassie was waving her hand towards Mike as he came over and kissed her on the cheek before rubbing her massively pregnant belly.

"Pretty sure that nine months ago, Jenna graduating from law school was the furthest thing from my mind," Mike smirked as he raised an eyebrow at Cassie. "Remember, you were there too and I don't recall you thinking about Jenna's graduation either. You were a little distracted."

Cassie groaned and rolled her eyes. "Well, I am not missing your graduation party for anything, so this little nugget is just going to have to hold on a little longer. She's already two days late, so another afternoon shouldn't matter."

I laughed and rubbed Cassie's belly. "Awwwww... the little princess was just waiting for Auntie Jenna to move back and for Uncle Nick to finish setting up her room at our house."

Kimmy clasped her hands together in front of her. "This little baby is so loved already! I think it is so sweet you and Nick are making her own room for her at your house."

"Have you seen their new house?" Steven snickered. "I'm pretty sure we could all have a room there and there would still be plenty left over."

I laughed as Nick wrapped his arms around me from behind before leaning in and kissing my neck. "I'm just excited Nick and I are finally going to be able to live together. It's definitely time for us live in the same place and the same house!" I turned my head back and smiled at Nick.

"I'll second that! Cheers to Jenna finishing law school!" Nick said as he moved around to stand at my side.

Everyone raised a glass and let out a cheer. I looked around the room and felt my eyes mist up. I considered everyone in the room my family, and I was so happy they were all there to celebrate my graduation. It had been a long three years, but everyone stuck by me and supported me the entire time.

I snuggled up next to Nick who had his arm around me. I was so incredibly happy I thought I could burst. Nick and I had been together for three years and our relationship was stronger than ever. We had had some bumps over the years, but we remained steadily committed to each other and our relationship. We both grew and changed and blossomed

308

together. No matter what, every day we reaffirmed our love and commitment to each other.

"So, the sign on the door says 'Closed for Private Party.' I suggest we do just that and get this party started!" Cassie shouted as everyone raised their glass and cheered again. "Plus I could be shooting a baby out at any minute and I fully intend to enjoy a whole lot of cake before that happens! Let's get a move on!"

While I had been away at law school, Pete decided to retire and sell the pizza business. It turned out Cassie and Mike were the perfect buyers. Since the restaurant had been such a big part of us all coming together, it seemed only fitting to have my graduation party there.

While Nick, Steven, and Kimmy had been at my graduation that morning, Mike and Cassie transformed Pete's Pizza with streamers, balloons, and a big banner that said 'You Are A Badass, Jenna!' I had a sneaking suspicion Cassie had been in charge of the banner.

***

A few hours later, Cassie and I sat together in one of the back booths, each with a big slice of graduation cake in front of us.

"Are you enjoying your party?" Cassie asked as she licked a big glob of frosting off her fork.

I couldn't help but smile from ear to ear. "This has literally been one of the best days of my life! To be surrounded by everyone I love and that loves me, celebrating this huge accomplishment... I don't know how it could possibly get any better."

Cassie had a mischievous smile on her face. "Oh, I can think of a thing or two that might up the amazing factor of today." Cassie scraped the last little bits of cake and frosting off her plate before pointing her fork at the piece in front of me. "You going to eat that? If not slide that bad boy on over here."

I laughed and slid the cake over to her. "It's all yours."

"Come to momma you frosting-covered slice of heaven," Cassie said as she shoved a big bite of cake in her mouth and started talking around it. "You have to fully exploit the benefits of being pregnant because, as I have discovered, there are not many. Being able to eat whatever you want is one of the few pluses. I am pretty sure our baby girl is going to come out covered in a fine dusting of Cheeto powder and her hair will look like ice cream with sprinkles."

The truth was, even though the pregnancy had been a total surprise, both Mike and Cassie were over the moon about becoming parents. Kimmy was right when she said that baby girl was already tremendously loved by all of us.

I looked out at everyone in the restaurant as they ate pizza and cake while they talked and laughed with each other. "I just can't help but think back to the day we graduated from college and how different today's graduation was."

Cassie finished chewing the piece of cake in her mouth before she responded. "You mean because you are celebrating with good people rather than fucking worthless garbage people?"

"Well, there is that," I laughed. "The day we graduated from college I was under so much pressure, from myself and others, to be this really weird, unrealistic version of what I thought was a perfect life. That version of 'perfect' was really nothing like what I actually wanted. Looking back on it, I was so unhappy. Thank goodness Brett never actually proposed to me that day." I involuntarily shuddered at the thought.

Cassie smiled, "Yeah. All things considered, we've done pretty well for ourselves, babe."

"You and Mike are about to become parents, which is crazy!"

Cassie rolled her eyes. "Tell me about it!"

"You are both crazy for each other..."

"Well, sometimes we are both just straight-up crazy," Cassie laughed. "Somehow it just works though. I am really happy, Jenna. More than I ever thought I would be. Things were a shitshow for a while, but... Mike is... he is the piece of me I always felt was missing." Cassie was looking over my shoulder with a wistful smile on her face. I turned and saw she was looking at Mike as he brought out another pizza and laughed with Nick and Steven about something.

"You deserve it, Cassie. All of it. You also have two incredibly successful, booming businesses. Pete's Pizza has exploded since you and Mike bought it, and you totally downplay it, but I know from Nick that Cassie Charles Real Estate is well on its way to becoming one of the top agencies in the area."

Cassie blushed a little. "We're doing pretty well. It helps to have an in with the most sought-after construction company in the state. Blaine Construction has really made a name for itself."

I started beaming. "I'm so proud of Nick and all of his hard work! Blaine Construction has expanded so much and is such a huge part of the community. Nick has achieved exactly what he wanted to."

Cassie licked the frosting from her second piece of cake off her fork before tossing it down and patting her belly. "And you, my friend, are well on your way to being a super kick-ass lawyer. Just imagine how different things would have been if you hadn't said yes to the job at Pete's Pizza or to Nick and all of the other opportunities that have come your way."

"It is pretty wild how one word and an open mind changed everything."

Cassie mumbled something that I couldn't quite hear as she looked around the room. "What did you say, Cass?" I asked.

Cassie turned to me. "Can you help a giant pregnant lady up out of this booth? It's time for me to go and do something."

"Sure." I helped Cassie up and watched her waddle her adorably pregnant self to the other sitting area in the restaurant. I decided to follow her to see if she needed any help.

I was almost to the sitting area when Kimmy grabbed my arm and spun me around. "Hey! Jenna! Can you help me with something over here?" Kimmy started walking me in the opposite direction. Steven saw us and his eyes got big before he rushed over.

"Steven! I was just telling Jenna how much we needed help with that thing. That thing over there," Kimmy said in a weird voice.

Steven looked confused for a moment before suddenly he said, "Yes! The thing! The thing that is... in the kitchen! It is in the kitchen!"

"Yes! The kitchen! Let's go!" Kimmy started tugging on my arm again.

I looked back and forth between both of them. Something was not right. "You guys are acting weird. What's up?"

"Nothing! Why would you think something is up?" Steven said talking to me but looking at Kimmy.

"Yeah... why would we be up to something?" Kimmy asked nervously.

"Jenna! There you are!" Mike shouted as he quickly walked over to us. "Hey, Jenna can you please come with me for a minute?"

I eyed Mike suspiciously as I put my hands on my hips. "All of you are acting crazy... what is going on?"

Mike quickly glanced around. "Uhhhhhh... Cassie needs help with something in the other part of the restaurant."

"That's where I was originally going!" My friends were terrible actors and even worse liars. Something was definitely up.

Mike shrugged his shoulders. "She didn't need help then, but she needs it now?"

I cocked my head to the side. "That much has changed in two minutes?"

Mike rolled his eyes. "Just come with me." I sighed and followed Mike into the other part of the restaurant as I muttered under my breath about how crazy everyone was acting. Mike suddenly stopped just outside the entryway to the other sitting area. "Go on in," he urged me.

I slowly walked into the room. It was lit by dozens of candles. There were red roses everywhere, their red petals covering the floor. The intoxicating scent of the roses filled the room. I gasped as I looked around, the whole room was incredibly beautiful.

Nick stepped forward. I turned to him and smiled. "Nick this amazing! What's it for?"

"It's for you," he responded in his husky voice.

"Oh, Nick! I don't even know what to say! This is amazing!" I couldn't stop slowly spinning in a circle to take in the whole room.

Nick chuckled. "Well, hopefully, you'll know what to say in a minute."

I turned back to face him. "What are you talking about?"

Instead of answering Nick took my hand in his and got down on one knee.

Oh. My. God. It was really happening!

"Jenna, you are the most amazing woman I have ever met. Strong, brave, smart, incredibly sexy, beautiful both inside and out. You make me want to be a better man every day... a man that is worthy of your love."

Tears started to run down my face. I loved Nick so much. I loved him with every fiber of my being and I knew he loved me in the same way. "Three years ago when I was at your apartment hoping we could start our relationship over, I told you I was all in with no hesitations. Nothing has changed. Not even for a second. In fact, I want to be all-in with you forever."

Nick reached into his pocket and pulled out a small, blue box. He opened it and turned it towards me. I gasped. Inside was the most beautiful diamond ring I had ever seen. Even in the dimly lit room, the diamond sparkled brilliantly. Nick looked up at me. "Will you do me the honor of becoming my wife? Jenna, will you marry me?"

I didn't hesitate. There was no doubt in my mind what my answer was going to be. "Yes, Nick! Yes, I want nothing more than to marry you! I am saying yes, yes, yes! A thousand times yes!"

Nick jumped off the ground and grabbed me around the waist. He picked me up and spun me around as I laughed. I slid down his body and our lips immediately found each other.

Nick pulled back from the kiss. He took the ring out of the box and slid it onto my finger. "I love you so much," he whispered.

"I love you too," I whispered back right before our lips locked again in a passionate kiss that left us both breathless.

When we finally came up for air, Nick looked at me and smiled. "You know they're all out there trying to listen in and see what's happening, right?'

I laughed. "I would expect nothing less."

"Well, let's go and tell them you're going to be Mrs. Blaine," Nick said as he took my hand in his and intertwined our fingers.

"I sure do like the sound of that," I smiled as I leaned my head onto Nick's arm.

"Mr. and Mrs. Blaine?" he asked.

"Yes." I turned and stood on my tiptoes to kiss Nick lightly on the lips.

"Me too." Nick squeezed my hand as we walked out into the main part of the restaurant. Everyone was standing together, staring at us in anticipation.

"She said yes!" Nick shouted.

Everyone cheered and came over to hug and congratulate us. I couldn't stop smiling and my heart felt like it was going to burst with love. I had just said yes to my happily ever after.

Did you enjoy Saying Yes?

Leave 5 stars and a nice comment to share the love!

♠

Didn't like it?

Write to us to suggest the kind of novel you dream of reading!
https://cherry-publishing.com/en/contact/

Subscribe to our Newsletter and receive a free eBook!

You'll also receive the latest updates on all of our upcoming publications!

You can subscribe according to the country you're from:

You are from...

US:
https://mailchi.mp/b78947827e5e/get-your-free-ebook

UK:
https://mailchi.mp/cherry-publishing/get-your-free-uk-copy

Made in the USA
Middletown, DE
23 May 2021